THE
MURDER
QUESTION

BOOKS BY ALICE CASTLE

THE MURDER QUESTION

ALICE CASTLE

bookouture

Published by Bookouture in 2022

An imprint of Storyfire Ltd.
Carmelite House
50 Victoria Embankment
London EC4Y 0DZ

www.bookouture.com

ISBN: 978-1-80314-484-9
eBook ISBN: 978-1-80314-483-2

To Ella and Connie, with love

ONE

'We Found Love' was blasting out of the tinny speakers of Beth Haldane's Fiat 500. She leant forward in the driver's seat to switch to something else. Dulwich friends would no doubt find the song's line about a hopeless place hilariously appropriate, as Beth was off to visit her newlywed friend, Jen, in Camberwell. But Beth wasn't like that. The area, with its wide Georgian streets, herds of red buses sweeping towards central London and the optimistically named Butterfly Walk shopping centre was fine. Absolutely fine. Though, of course, it wasn't quite SE21. And she loathed the song anyway.

Just as she found the comfortingly stuffy tones of *Gardeners' Question Time* instead, the car in front of her shuffled forward a couple of feet and she had to follow suit, slamming her car into gear, lurching on a little, then yanking the handbrake again. Oh, the joys of the rush hour. Though why it was called that, when no one was able to rush at all, was one of life's mysteries, she thought, with a flick of her heavy ponytail. Maybe it was the whoosh of drivers' blood pressure ascending as the centipede of traffic wound its way down East Dulwich

Grove, past the no-nonsense gates of the College School and the redbrick behemoth that was the old Dulwich Hospital.

She was one of the lucky ones in this traffic jam, Beth knew. Her deadline was still a good hour away. She didn't need to fetch her ten-year-old son, Jake, from his class until 5 p.m. But something was definitely getting to her, even if it wasn't the gridlock. No mystery: it was guilt. She'd finally taken the plunge. She'd booked Jake in for tutoring to help with his assault on the citadels of privilege or, in layman's terms, the looming Wyatt's entrance exam.

Wyatt's was the most prestigious boys' school in the area and, some said, in the whole of the south of England. Part of her knew that he didn't need a single extra lesson, and they would then still have been able to afford the odd takeaway, but a slightly greater part of Beth's tiny frame had given in to nerves and the urgings of her frenemy, Belinda McKenzie. Belinda had been relentlessly having her three children tutored in every possible skill since they had first started to put one foot in front of the other, in ways which their mother had decided were variously too slow, too awkward or too fast. She was a great believer in the improvability of human nature, which Beth did sympathise with, and hurling money at problems, which was where Beth usually parted company with her.

But this time, Beth had somehow allowed fear and peer pressure to overrule common sense. To onlookers, her long fringe, sturdy build and diminutive stature might say adorable little Shetland pony but, inside, Jake's exams made her feel like an overbred dressage horse, nostrils flaring, quivering with nerves before going into the ring to do utterly impossible things with her hooves. Except that she couldn't go into the ring at all. It was down to her boy, and while she had total faith in him, she'd somehow have even more if they just went with this. So she had found herself filling a coveted spot when one of Belinda's protégées had had to drop out. Normally, a chat with her wonderfully sane best friend, Katie, would have set her straight, but as Katie had waded into tutoring ages ago, Beth felt she was probably being foolish resisting. And she didn't want to blight Jake's chances. If the exam went belly-up, she certainly wanted to believe she had done everything possible for her son.

So, poor Jake had already been dropped off at the tutor's house by Belinda in her enormous 4x4 battle bus, right after school, and now Beth was chugging along to be in position to fetch him and two of Belinda's lot after the lesson. She intended to stop for tea and gossip at Jen's house beforehand, but if the traffic got any worse, she'd only have time for a quick hello on the doorstep.

Beth looked across at the package beside her on the passenger seat. It was a small wedding present, which she'd had tucked away since the summer. She'd bought it online and it had arrived too late for the simple ceremony, held at the Horniman Museum on the South Circular, but she was hoping it would be just the thing. Hard to believe it was already three months since the service, just after all the kerfuffle at the Picture Gallery and before the long summer holiday. It was second time around for both Jen, who was keeping her previous surname Patterson, and her new husband, Ted Burns. They must have pots, pans and plates aplenty between them. But nothing like this, she thought, patting the gift fondly.

On the car radio, Bob Flowerdew and Pippa Greenwood were getting aerated about rhododendrons. Beth, only too happy to swap vicarious exam panic for a pleasant plant-based reverie, wondered if *GQT* was only allowed to hire presenters with horticultural names. The show was all-action, no-holds-barred garden porn for people like her with tiny dysfunctional plots but whopping imaginations. She was soon enjoying a lavish fantasy in which her own kicked-to-bits backyard became an oasis of beauty, and she was being begged to join the elite Dulwich Open Gardens mob. She was just cutting a ribbon on her miraculously transformed garden with her own mono-grammed secateurs when the car in front zipped forward. From that moment on, the traffic unsnarled as easily as though a signal had been given on high. Five minutes later, she was drawing up outside her friend's home.

Jen's little house wasn't part of the huge sweep of grand tea-caddy houses on Camberwell Grove itself, but clung to the edges of one of these fine terraces. It was a converted coach house, once home either to a pair of high-stepping carriage horses owned by one of the big houses round the corner, or the coachman himself. Beth thought the original builders would probably have allowed two horses a bit more space than this dinky cottage provided, though she was sure it would have been considered ample for servants. It was a two-storey building, done over in stucco to ape its grand neighbours but dwarfed by them. There were two pretty shrubs on either side of the bright blue front door. Despite her addiction to GQT, Beth had no idea what kind they actually were. All she knew was that, as far as she was concerned, Jen's was the prettiest house around.

Beth wasn't a fan of the inhuman scale of Georgian archi-tecture. She would have been lost even in the entrance halls of those big slabs of places up the road. Their massive first-floor drawing rooms – a major selling point, with their ceilings drip-ping intricate plasterwork – had all the charm of airport hangars for her. No, if she had to buy a place in Camberwell herself, Jen's house would be it.

Beth pressed the bell. She heard a slight scuffling from inside, and it was a minute before the door was flung open. Jen's cheeks were flushed, but a bright smile of welcome was pinned on her narrow, attractive face.

'Beth, lovely, it's you! Been ages...'

'Since the wedding, I think. It's been mad. I haven't seen you at the school gates.'

Jen's daughter, Jessica, was at the Village Primary with Jake, and usually the women did a fair bit of idle hanging out while the kids were busy with the important stuff inside.

'No... well, we're trying a new routine. Come in, come in,' said Jen, leading the way hurriedly to the kitchen. Like Beth's own, it was an extension to the house, invisible from the front and tacked on at the back in the 1960s when no one had cared much about planning permission or, apparently, architectural style. The room was a basic cube but had just been refitted, Jen's first action on moving in.

Beth cooed over the beautiful boulangerie-style floor tiles while Jen closed the door to the hall, put the kettle on and rooted in the pale grey cupboards for mugs and teabags. When they were settled at the table, Jen fussing over a scattering of Jess's clobber, Beth smiled expectantly. 'So? Married life? Bliss?' she said lightly.

Jen looked up briefly from the pile of books and comics, then concentrated on aligning edges, neatening the pile. 'Course! Fantastic. We had a great honeymoon – well, sort of honeymoon, as we had Jess with us, too – in Italy. Then back here, and just, well, settling in, you know?'

Beth didn't really. It had been so long since James, her husband, had died, she could barely remember that half-a-couple, 'we' not 'I' state of mind. She smiled a little wistfully.

'Anyway, what about you?' Jen changed the subject. 'Any further on the slavery thing?'

Everyone had been fascinated, and horrified, by the discoveries Beth had recently made in the dusty archives of Wyatt's School. What could have been a public relations disaster for the centuries-old school, though, had turned into a triumph – for Wyatt's, and for Beth. She'd promptly been put in charge of a rapidly created research institute, bringing the disreputable past of the founder, Thomas Wyatt, to light.

'I don't want to jinx it, but it's going really well,' said Beth, flushing a little with excitement as she outlined her plans for the institute. Jen was one of the few friends she could really discuss work with. Though now something of an IT guru, working behind-the-scenes wonders for local companies, not to mention manning the barricades of Belinda McKenzie's personal fire-walls, Jen had also been a journalist back in the day. Although they hadn't been close friends for that long, this meant she and Beth did have a huge amount in common – not least the fact that both had abandoned their first loves, career-wise, and diversified to make a living.

From the outside, it often seemed that the other mothers at the school lived charmed lives, gliding between their chariot-sized cars and multi-million-pound homes, with gaggles of perfect, Mini Boden-clad children in tow. Beth knew full well that appearances could be deceptive, and there was much beneath even the smoothest of surfaces. But women who worked, and enjoyed it, were in shockingly short supply where they lived, so Jen was special.

Jen hadn't always been single. There'd been a long and dreadful on-off phase when her faithless husband, Tim, had seemed to be oscillating between Jen and a younger version – a woman called Babs Pine. But eventually, after keeping the playground mummies scandalised for a while, there had been a divorce, and Jen had officially joined Beth in the very select local lone mummies club. Like Beth, she had little family support, as she was an only child whose elderly parents had died long before, and this strengthened their alliance even more.

'Are they letting you have a free hand? Really letting you delve into the context?' Jen wrinkled her lightly freckled nose. 'I'd imagine that, being Wyatt's, they'd quite like to airbrush some of what went on.'

Beth paused for a moment to think. Her first impressions of Wyatt's had not all been positive. She'd been intimidated by the centuries of prestige, and by the polish of the headmaster and his team. But beneath the daunting efficiency were warm hearts, which had welcomed her and rapidly adopted her as one of their own.

'I can honestly say that they're not like that. They've really faced up to the whole issue and want to be as transparent about it as possible. And, of course, as a bit of a side effect, that sort of candour does also come over rather well.' Beth smiled.

'Ah, that Dr Grover. Loved him that time on *Newsnight*. I must say, he is pretty dreamy.' Jen flicked the teabags out into the sink with a teaspoon, and they were exchanging a chuckle when the kitchen door flew open.

'Dreamy? Who's dreamy?' It was Ted, Jen's new husband, with a mock-angry expression on his face. A big cuddly bear of a man, with thick, tufty hair and a five o'clock shadow so heavy it had almost reached beard status, he towered over slender Jen and made Beth look like a My Little Pony doll.

Jen laughed and pushed him playfully away, sloshing milk into two mugs. 'Don't be silly. Want a tea?'

'Now that's more like it. Beth, how're you?'

'Great, really good, thanks. Didn't know you were here, Ted. Working from home today?'

Ted was in IT, too, though Beth was hazy about the details of his job. And about quite a lot of the nitty-gritty of the tech world, if she was honest.

'Can't a man hang around in his own house any more, without facing the third degree?' Ted lowered his eyebrows and gave Beth a stage glower, before breaking into his usual easy grin. 'Few things to sort out. I'm on a temporary secondment at the moment, gives me a bit of flexibility, you know? I'm just doing a bit of troubleshooting with a new package we're installing. It's running late, of course. Plus, it means I can keep an eye on the wife.'

Beth, who was all for flexible working and had a habit of stretching the concept as far as it could go, and back again, nodded intelligently and hoped he wasn't going to explain too much about the project.

'That must be great, the two of you working together,' she said. There was a loud clatter as Jen dropped the teaspoon into the stainless-steel sink.

'Oops.'

'Butterfingers,' Ted said fondly. 'So, who were you two talking about, before I so rudely interrupted?'

'Er, Beth was just saying Dr Grover's very attractive. I was disagreeing, wasn't I?' Jen said, with a meaningful look at her friend.

A little surprised, Beth stepped up. 'Yes, he's not, um, everyone's cup of tea.' This was a downright lie; there wasn't a mother in Dulwich who wouldn't consider trading in her current model for Dr Grover, given half a chance. Particularly the mums with boys, as Dr G held the key to admissions in his hands, as well as possessing brains, charm, charisma, and lots and *lots* of nice ties. He somehow made the simple act of wearing one look sexy. Eat your heart out, Christian Grey, who had to do so much more with his to get pulses racing. But that seemed to be unsayable, all of a sudden. Beth looked down into her cup. Oh well. Not long till she had to pick Jake up.

'So, where was it this summer? Algarve? Lake Garda? Montpellier?' Ted plonked himself at the table, briskly shoving Jess's comics right down to the other end. 'Not *that* much of a tan, so I'm thinking maybe Normandy?' he said, casting an eye over Beth's perpetually wan complexion.

Beth smiled. They'd lucked out this summer, and spent a week with Katie in an Airbnb villa. 'A week in Corfu. So beautiful. Have you been?'

Ted's face immediately darkened. Jen came round behind him and put a hand on his shoulder. 'Ted's ex has a house there,' she said quietly.

'Oh? I'm sorry,' said Beth. 'Well, how about your honey-moon? Italy, Jen was saying?'

Beth had hit on the right topic. Twenty minutes later, they were only halfway round the Uffizi, but Beth had to dash off to pick up Jake. At the door, she turned to Jen, while Ted loped back up the stairs to his laptop. 'Jess? Where's she? Do you want me to pick her up while I'm driving around?'

'Actually, she's got footie practice this afternoon. But another time would be great. She's at her dad's this week, so he's doing the honours,' Jen said, rolling her eyes and using that dry tone people seemed to reserve for their exes.

'All week? That's tough on you.'

Jen smiled wistfully. 'Yeah. I really miss her. But it's good for her to have some time with him. Great to see you, Beth.'

'Can I pop in next week? I'll probably see you at the school gates but that's always such a rush. This is a nice way to catch up – and it's lovely to have something to do while I'm in Camberwell,' Beth said, hoping she wasn't being too frank. The shopping centre wasn't exactly Bluewater. But Jen was brilliant, as always.

'Course, I'd love that. Same time, next week.'

As Beth unlocked the car, she suppressed a shiver. For the first time this year, she felt a real hint of autumnal chill in the air. Then she slid behind the wheel and turned the key in the ignition, consciously trying to switch her thoughts as well. It would be good to see how Jake had got on, then she'd whisk him home for a super-quick supper and cosy early bed. He'd be excited, she'd got his favourite *Spiderman* comic waiting for him as a treat.

Despite her efforts, there was still the hint of a frown linger-ing. And then, on the seat beside her, she spotted the wedding present, still in its pristine white and silver paper, the card wedged into the silver ribbon trim at a jaunty angle. Drat. She'd completely forgotten to hand it over. She glanced over at Jen's, but the door was firmly shut. Oh well, she needed to get going now anyway; couldn't keep the kids waiting. Jake wouldn't have minded too much, but Belinda McKenzie's boys each had a full half-hour practising their many musical instruments to slog through as soon as they got home, and who knew what other improving activities lined up by their tireless mama on their behalf.

Beth pulled away from the kerb. It was early September, but such a dark day that she had to flick her headlights on.

* * *

Jen closed the door as quietly as she could, and padded back to the kitchen, her feet in their cosy socks making barely a sound. She'd just shut the door when it crashed back on its hinges, whacking her in the shoulder. Ted stood in the doorway, staring at her. She wasn't sure whether to look him in the eye or not. Sometimes it was things like that which set him off. Eventually, as the silence stretched and she rubbed her arm, she decided to risk it. She darted a look upwards. Big mistake. At once, he was right up against her, pushing her backwards. When she felt the cold steel of the sink against her back, she realised she had no further to go. Now the metal was digging in, and her shoulder was throbbing too. She kept her eyes fixed on his sweater, which was about all she could see. What was it that had set him off this time? Better wait for him to speak.

'Nothing to say now? Different when your friend isn't here,' he sneered. 'Not so brave now, are you? So defiant? What have you got to say about me now, eh? Eh?'

'I don't know what you mean, Ted,' said Jen quietly, trying but failing to keep weariness and fear out of her voice. It was hard to sleep at night and, God knew, the days were hardly restful.

'You were talking about some man you fancied, weren't

you? I could tell. Don't pretend. You know that doesn't work. You know I can see inside your head. I can read your thoughts. You don't have any secrets any more. You're my *wife*,' he said, taking her by the arms and shaking her.

Jen took a deep breath and wondered how long it was going to go on for this time. It was getting harder and harder to know what might trigger him. A chance word, even a look. Any expression he didn't like. Any outfit slightly more daring than her usual uniform of jeans.

'Ted, please. We've got to stop this. This isn't right. Just let me go,' said Jen, trying to keep her voice low and as emotionless as possible. Displays of feeling, weeping or begging were like kerosene on his fire, she knew to her cost.

'Let you go? Not until you've apologised. Properly,' he growled in her ear.

Jen, a silent tear now running down her face, nodded grimly. She was glad she hadn't had time to turn the kitchen light on. The darker it was while she did this deed, the better.

TWO

Back at her own tiny house later that evening, after dropping off Belinda's boys and nobly declining a glass of Chardonnay the size of a goldfish bowl, Beth settled down on the sofa, laptop open.

Despite the Wyatt's job, she still had several freelance projects on the go. It was a terrible nuisance, in many ways, keeping them alive, but Beth was too anxious about the long term to put all her eggs in the school's basket. Having something to fall back on was crucial. It had been this which had been lacking in her bleakest days following James's death. After all, it wasn't possible to have another husband to fall back on. She never wanted to go back to that desperate sense of abandonment and sheer soul-aching loneliness again. Belt, braces and plenty of extra buttons, too, were her way every time, with everything.

Her black and white moggy, Magpie, climbed aboard the sofa with a less-than-graceful scramble. Beth looked at her fondly, and stroked the velvet-soft fur. While she now sometimes picked up their groceries at the Morrisons superstore on the way to or from tutoring, Magpie expected only the finest cat food and would accept no substitutes. Own brands didn't cut it, and certainly nothing that was ever on special offer in Camberwell. At this rather unflattering angle, Beth could see the result in lots of furry, snowy white undercarriage. Smaller portions in Magpie's bowl might be the way forward. For a second, the cat locked eyes with her, challenging bright green meeting serious grey.

'Oh, all right then, Magpie. You win. Again.'

Beth wrenched her mind from the ruinous price of cat food and was delving into her least favourite of the freelance chores, when she heard a noise up above. Curious. Jake had always been a brilliant sleeper, and she thanked her stars for it. Surely, that couldn't be? But it was. He was calling for her.

A full hour passed before she collapsed back onto the sofa, and this time she did succumb to a glass of wine. Not one quite as enormous as Belinda's proffered crystal goblet, but enough to make the freelance work impossible, even if she'd still had the oomph to get on with it. She could count on the fingers of one *finger* the times Jake had had trouble sleeping recently. A naturally buoyant and lively little chap, he wore himself out in the playground every day and was normally more than ready for bed by eight each night, though he regularly protested he wasn't tired and, indeed, had never been tired in his entire life.

But tonight, something had changed. He'd woken up and been unable to get himself back to sleep. Even with Beth reading a heavy dose of the soporific start of *Charlie and the Chocolate Factory*, featuring endless descriptions of the ancient grandparents before the golden ticket flutters excitingly into view, it had still taken ages to get him soothed.

Beth wished she didn't know what the problem was. But there was only one culprit looming large in her mind. The tutoring. It was the obvious change in their routine.

True, Jake had also just moved years at school, and there had been the usual reshuffling of the pack that was his class at the start of September, including the very conspicuous absence of his former friend Matteo. That entire family had upped sticks and rejoined the expat community in a hurry, after some grisly goings-on in the summer. Beth wasn't sure what she felt about that. While there was a lot to be said for avoiding the social embarrassment of encountering a psychopathic child poisoner and his parents on the streets of Dulwich, it was far from ideal that the menace had just shifted country. But as he had been under the age of criminal responsibility at the time of his crime, he was a problem Beth had no choice but to leave to Interpol.

Jake had been at the Village Primary from reception onwards, and Beth dearly loved the little Hansel-and-Gretel, redbrick state school in the heart of Dulwich. He didn't seem to miss Matteo, and she'd thought he'd settled back into school routine after the long summer break. Most of his friends – no, who was she kidding? *All* of them – had been tutored for years, so it wasn't as if he didn't know the ins and outs of the business. But that had been as a spectator. Had Beth given Jake the misleading impression that he was somehow above getting extra lessons? That he didn't need them?

She really wasn't sure if he did need them or not. It was at times like this that she missed James, as a sounding board as well as a husband. It would just have been nice not to have to make every major decision alone. All right, maybe she actually meant it would have been great to have someone else to blame, if things seemed to be going a bit pear-shaped. One disturbed night wasn't shouting major psychological damage, true, but she didn't want that to be even a faint possibility.

She put down the now-empty glass and found her phone, lodged under a bit of Magpie's spreading embonpoint. She scrolled down to find her mother's number. It had been over a week since they'd talked, ridiculous really when they lived so close. But her mother had a full Bridge schedule to maintain, and Beth... well, she was always running around with Jake, work and the rest of the cavalcade.

'Mum? It's me. I'm a bit worried about Jake. Do you think tutoring is too much pressure?'

There was a pause. Beth could imagine her mother, Wendy, putting down her English Bridge Union magazine with a sigh. Beth made it a rule not to trouble her too much, and when she did, she often wondered why she'd bothered at all. Her mother almost never managed to say what she wanted to hear.

'You know, Wyatt's isn't the only school in Dulwich, darling.'

'Does that mean you don't think he'll get in?' Beth shot back.

She pictured Wendy sitting up a little straighter in her high-backed, velvet-upholstered chair, next to the fake gas fire that she insisted was just like the real thing but so much less trouble. Her nightcap of sherry would be at her elbow, on a dear little occasional table that had belonged to her grandmother. Wendy was only in her late fifties, but she had somehow catapulted herself on, lifestyle-wise, into far later years. Beth saw it as a defence against being asked for too much help with Jake, or providing any sort of emotional support for her daughter. Now, for example, she would be itching to get back to her magazine, and away from this tricky conversation. Beth could picture her regaling her Bridge friends tomorrow with tales about the endless demands her daughter made, and how utterly exhausted she was as a result.

'Not at all, darling,' Wendy continued, her voice tremulous. 'You know I think he's as bright as a button. I'm just saying, you need to register him for the state schools as well. And then there are some grammar schools not that far away. Liz at the Bridge club was saying they're *terrific*, and of course they're free...'

'You think I haven't thought of all that?'

'Darling, I know you'll have it all in hand. It's just that *I* haven't thought of it before. I'm only thinking out loud. Of course, you know I'd do anything, if there *was* something I could usefully do, though heaven knows what on earth that would be... but you have my total support in whatever you choose to do. You don't need to worry about that, you really don't.'

Beth, now rigid on her sofa, almost snorted with the ridiculousness of this comment. Her mother, who'd lost her own husband without too much effort or pain many years ago to the then-fashionable executive heart attack, had been thoroughly cosetted by everybody ever since and had certainly not troubled herself over-much with fruitless anxiety. And hadn't she been right? Things had turned out just fine. Beth's father's large life insurance policy had paid out handsomely; his pension rolled in as regularly as the tide; and the house was mortgage-free. And both Wendy's children were independent and relatively well balanced, thought Beth, brushing swiftly over her brother Josh's inability to commit and her own terrier-like enthusiasm for dangerous puzzles.

Besides, worrying was what Beth did best. Telling her not to do it was like instructing her not to breathe. She closed her eyes and counted to three. 'Thanks, Mum,' she said heavily.

'Any time, darling. Just call whenever you need to chat. I'm always here,' said her mother quickly, putting the phone down with evident relief.

Alone again with her thoughts, Beth decided that yes, she was right to press on with the tutoring. Jake *was* as bright as a button – her mother was right on that front at least – and with any luck that could mean a bursary and the end of her agonies for good. Or some of them, at any rate. But however much she attempted to suppress the thought, Beth knew perfectly well that Dulwich was stuffed with clever little boys who'd all be sitting the entrance exam together. And more, many more, would be bussed in from all over London and the surrounding counties to have a pop at it. The chances of Jake trouncing all of them were slimmer than an After Eight mint, on the Dukan diet, posing sideways in Spanx underwear. And if she got Jake into the school without the financial ballast of a discount behind her, she would just be setting herself up for massive stress every time one of the termly accounts whacked onto the mat or thudded into her inbox.

* * *

Katie wasn't the only one to spot the bags under Beth's eyes the next morning at the school gates, but she was the only person brave enough to mention them. As usual, her solution to the problem was more yoga. Now running a slew of successful stretch classes based at the most fashionable exercise studio in the village, Katie had less time for hanging out and coffees than before, but could still spot a friend in need at fifty paces.

'OK, well, if you won't sign up for a regular class, then you're coming with me to Jane's, right now,' she said, steering Beth away from Belinda McKenzie's orbit and back towards the epicentre of the village.

One of the few things Beth and Katie really disagreed on was Jane's – still the most popular café in the village two years after its arrival had frothed all rival cappuccinos out of contention. Beth was not foolish enough to pretend you'd get better coffee anywhere else. It was just that she didn't always want to be swimming in the Dulwich goldfish bowl. At Jane's, you were pretty much guaranteed to have everyone you knew sitting within earshot. Katie, blessed with a sunny temperament and a firm belief in a benign universe, didn't really care who heard her woes, if she ever had any, and certainly did mind about whether she was drinking a reasonable latte or not.

This morning, with Beth at a low ebb, Katie was able to manoeuvre her into the one relatively discreet table in the place, at the back, near the loos, without much more than a token protest. After submitting with her usual cheery good grace to the chaotic queuing system, Katie made her way back to the table with her spoils – a brace of cappuccinos and two enormous, golden pain au chocolats as large as rolled-up carpets.

Beth's protests that she'd already had breakfast were half-hearted at best, and she was soon covered from chin to knees with light, flaky crumbs, and had a happy but slightly guilty smile on her face.

'I needed that!'

'I know, hon. So, what's up? And don't say, "Nothing." I know there's a problem. It's all over your face.'

Beth sighed. 'Great. That's all I need. Oh, it's Jake, of course. The tutoring. Am I doing the right thing? What do you really think? Does he actually need it?'

'I know you've got some ingrained doubts about it all.' Katie was still nibbling at her pain au chocolat. Most of it was finding its way to her mouth, not the surrounding area. Beth looked at her a little jealously. *God's sake*. Katie even made marshalling supremely flaky pastry look easy. 'Maybe think about it this way. Is it likely to do him any harm?'

'Well, he woke up screaming last night.'

'That could have been anything! Honestly, the time we've had lately, it's a wonder we don't all wake up yelling most nights. And it's much more likely to be, you know, that whole business last term, rather than anything else. A couple of maths questions after school aren't going to cause a massive hoo-ha, particularly for a smart kid like Jake. He gets on OK with Belinda's boys, doesn't he?'

Beth gave it some thought. The two youngest McKenzies were always lumped together as an alliterative pair – Belinda's boys, Bobby and Billy. It was hard to define any distinctive characteristics to separate them. They were a bit like the *Two Ronnies*, except not as funny, or the *Chuckle Brothers*, but much funnier. Robust, verging on porky, with jolly, round faces and the sort of physique which meant the rugby pitch was already singing a siren song, they probably did have personalities of their own, but you'd have to get to know them really well to work them out. When yelling at them to be quiet from the driving seat, which happened regularly on the trip back from Camberwell, Beth didn't bother trying to work out who was doing what any more. A quick shout of, 'Billy! Bobby! Shush!' seemed to suffice. Not that they were a problem. It was just like having a carful of Labrador puppies.

'I doubt it's them. They're actually sweet boys,' said Beth. 'Maybe I'm just getting this a bit out of proportion.'

Katie smiled at her over the rim of her cup. 'It's been known.'

'OK, OK. I'll calm down. I probably just need something else to focus on. I need to get my head down at work, really sort out these display boards. Did I tell you I'm doing another mini exhibition to go with all the Christmas concerts?'

'You didn't. Sounds great, nothing better than a bit of slavery to go with all the tinsel. Sorry,' Katie said, as Beth winced. 'That was an awful thing to say, really insensitive. But I think you need something else to take your mind off work stuff as well, something that's just for you...'

Beth thought for a second. 'I suppose there's always that redecorating. I got those tins of paint ages ago, and I meant to get round to it over the summer, but...'

Katie rolled her eyes a little. 'I mean something that's not more slog for you. There's no way you'd hire someone to do the painting, so you'd just use up all your spare time getting gloss paint stuck in your hair. That's no fun, Beth. You need a distraction, something enjoyable.'

'I enjoy DIY,' Beth remonstrated. 'Well, the idea of it. To tell the truth, I'm just really sick of having those cans cluttering up the place. They've been in the hall all summer. It's got to the point where we're using them as makeshift storage units. Jake keeps his school shoes on top of one tin and my bag goes on the other. If I'm not careful, they'll become a permanent fixture.'

'Yes, well, it's fine, if that's what you want to do, but it's not for *you*, exactly, is it?'

'What do you mean? It would be for me. Well, for me and Jake, but definitely for us. I'm not with you?'

'When was the last time you did something that was just for you alone? Not you and Jake, not for the family home, for the good of everyone. Something for *you* only.'

Beth sat and thought for a while, starting to brush the stray patisserie crumbs into a pile. 'Well. I got some new boots last week.'

She watched Katie take a cursory look at her feet, though she didn't really need to. Beth had been wearing the same style of pixie boot for as long as they'd known each other.

'You ordered those online in ten seconds, in between making supper and doing five freelance commissions, don't tell me you didn't. And if you hadn't ordered them, they probably would have sent them automatically. You've been getting those exact same boots every two years for about a decade.'

Beth withdrew a little. 'So? I know what I like, that's all.'

'I'm not criticising. I love those boots, too,' said Katie, flashing an encouraging smile. 'I'm just saying. Don't neglect yourself. You deserve to have fun, to have a life too. It can't all be about Jake forever.'

'What do you mean? Of course it's all about Jake. He's my son, I'm all he has.'

'That's not true, Beth. He's got a granny, and an uncle, and friends, and me, and a whole world, and one day he's going to be off and making his own way.'

'Well, I know that, but he's still ten now, and he needs me.'

'He absolutely does. I'm not disputing that for one second. But you both need *more*.'

'More? What kind of more? This is all there is,' said Beth, genuinely perplexed. She looked round the café, rammed now with enough mummies wearing jaunty Breton tops to crew the entire French navy, not to mention clutches of chattering au pairs, tangles of buggies and several fully loaded high chairs.

'It so isn't, Beth, and you know that. There's a whole big world out there that you've been ignoring for too long.'

'What are you saying, Katie?'

'I'm saying that you need to start dating, Beth.'

THREE

After Katie's bombshell in the café, Beth had taken some time to regroup. She'd been stunned at first, her lower jaw flopping open unattractively. Once she remembered to close it, she'd been very tempted just to get up and walk out. But, however irresistible the urge, she knew that would be unfair to Katie. She might not want to hear what her friend was saying, but Katie had steeled herself to come out with it, too. Her hands had been clutched so tightly round her cappuccino that her knuckles had been white.

A few days had passed since that very sticky moment in Jane's. Days in which Beth had churned the idea of dating over in her mind. Eventually, she realised she was working through the five stages of grief all over again.

First, denial – dating was a crazy idea, full stop. Then anger – how dare Katie suggest this? What right did she have to be telling Beth what to do and how to do it? Bargaining followed. If Katie would just shut up about this, they could carry on as before. And maybe Beth'd think about it all in a few months' time, if that didn't seem too upsetting. Depression then fell on her like a dark, dark grey blanket. She spent the weekend getting through the usual football practice even more on autopilot than usual, trudging through Court Lane and never even noticing the spectacular zing of the acer trees lining the pavements near Dulwich Park, their leaves showing every fiery red from chilli pepper to pillar box in the weak September sunshine.

She sat through a full Sunday lunch at her mother's, insulated by the dreariness of her thoughts. And while that might have been a mercy, as they got through the long afternoon without a breath of discord, it wasn't quite normal.

Jake eventually punctured her self-absorption, but not until they were on the way back home. 'I hope you're not going to be like this all week, Mum. It's boring answering all my own questions.'

'Hmm, definitely,' she said absently – then his words registered. 'I'm sorry, darling, haven't I been answering? I've been listening, of course I have,' she said, mentally crossing her fingers.

'OK, what have I been talking about for the last billion years?'

Beth thought rapidly and hard but, though a billion years for Jake was five minutes for her, she couldn't recall a single thing he'd said. Football? School? Computer games? Christmas? Nope, nothing. She could wing it, but she was quite likely to be wrong. And nobody liked to think they weren't being heard.

It gave her the check she needed. She had to snap out of this state, stop being so silly, and reach the final stage of grief – acceptance.

'OK then. I'm sorry, Jake. Race you home?'

Later, once Jake was upstairs, his head on the pillow, his soft dark hair a little long but reminding her so much of James that she couldn't bear to get it cut, Beth took stock on the sofa.

Perhaps it really *was* time to move on.

It had been seven years, no, eight, since James had died. A few headaches had, terrifyingly, meant a one-way ticket to the hospice for him and the lonely path of single motherhood for Beth. In all the time that had passed since, she felt as though she'd barely had a moment to consider meeting someone else.

True, she'd accidentally met that policeman, DI York... Oh, who was she kidding? She knew full well his name was Harry. And she'd be lying if she pretended she hadn't felt something. But, more often than not, the 'something' was boiling rage. Was that normal? Wasn't attraction supposed to be pleasant?

She couldn't remember ever wanting to hit James over the head with a frying pan, even though he must have done all the usual annoying man things in the time they were together. He'd liked football, which had been a bit dull, but he'd been pretty good at DIY, which had seemed to make up for it. He hadn't been a saint; he'd been flesh and blood and fun and love and everything to her. Had she airbrushed her own history, made him into too much of a paragon? That probably wasn't terribly good for Jake. They did talk about his dad. Not in a hushed-voice sort of way, but when something he'd liked came up, Beth would always mention it, in what she hoped was an everyday sort of tone.

Nowadays, it was a lot easier to talk about James without a tremor in her voice and without the over-bright sheen of tears in her eyes. She didn't want Jake to feel he couldn't ask anything about his dad or say his name for fear that she'd collapse. But had Beth gone too far the other way? Did she big him up too much, make it impossible for her son to live up to a perfect image? She really hoped not.

Somehow, Beth realised with a jolt, she'd moved from the scary prospect of considering dating to chewing over problems with Jake, which was no novelty at all. She had to focus, to think really hard about this whole meeting-people business, and not let herself drift off into comforting patterns that were far removed from a potentially terrifying new world.

She supposed the odd frisson – even the rage – she'd felt with Harry York, did prove she wasn't emotionally dead, however handy that might have been. But did she and Jake really have time and space for another person in their lives? Their tiny house would struggle to accommodate anyone even slightly larger than Beth herself and little Jake. There was the fact the dining table was so diddy, she decided, conveniently forgetting they'd shared meals there with Harry before, and it had been fine. The sofa, well, that was perfect for two, not so great for three. And her bedroom...

She didn't really want to think of anything that might go on up there.

Becoming a widow seemed to have catapulted her into a state of Victorian prudishness about matters of the flesh. Though she'd had the odd yearning, she never expected to feel the passion she'd had with James. No, what she was worried about in the bedroom was the duvet covers. She only had hyper-floral, Cath Kidston-type bed linen, which she adored. But surely no man would consent to spend a minute under such a flowery bower? Again, Beth firmly shut her eyes to the fact that a bit of sex usually reconciled men to anything, even girly pink patterns.

Maybe she just wasn't ready to date. Maybe the fact she was worrying more about her duvet covers than her underpinnings meant it wasn't the moment. Or maybe, as usual, she was wriggling furiously when she knew she ought to be doing something but just couldn't get her head around it.

She flicked on the TV. Some of the mums at the gates today had been discussing a show called *First Dates*, where couples got matched up to have dinner together at a swanky central London restaurant with, the producers hoped, hysterical results. The format was slick, the French maître d' was full of gnomic pronouncements on love in an accent thicker than crème fraîche, and it certainly looked as though the diners were enjoying their meals, if not always each other. But the girls with their Tango tans, laminated eyebrows and killer heels? The men with their tattoos and bulging muscles? Well, actually, now you came to mention it... Beth found herself enjoying the episode, though more as though she were David Attenborough peering in on the antics of an exotic species indulging in arcane mating rituals, than as a potential participant.

What would she have to offer a partner? She had no banter; no piercings; quite normal eyebrows, which never saw the light of day anyway due to her fringe; her heels, despite her height, remained resolutely flat; and she firmly believed that black rubber was best used as a playground surface, not an excuse for an outfit. She was not *First Dates* material.

But there were other means out there. Tinder? Match.com? Plenty of Fish? Were any of these any good? She was going to have to do some research. But that, in itself, was not easy in Dulwich, capital city of coupledom. She was literally the only singleton in the village. One of the reasons she had been so close to Jen was that, for a time, they had both been lone working mums. Then Jen had gone and ruined it all by finding Ted. Well, that wasn't quite what she meant... but the end result was that Beth had been left all the more of an anomaly in her surroundings.

Even Belinda McKenzie had given up trying to matchmake on her behalf. A couple of painful evenings, which had truly put the 'awk!' into awkward, had seen Beth sitting as the odd one out in a long line of perfectly matched couples arranged around Belinda's sweeping dining table. Most Dulwich residents had scrapped their separate diners and incorporated them into eat-in kitchens, or turned them into studies – usually infested with children trying to wrench screen time from each other. But Belinda's Court Lane house was massive enough to have a kitchen the size of a church hall, a brace of studies and this boardroom-style temple to fine dining as well, with its highly polished oak furniture and gloomy oils of ancestors that Beth rather suspected belonged neither to Belinda or her husband, Barty, but had been knocked down as a job lot at Roseberys, the West Norwood auction rooms.

Beth, who'd felt as though she was attending a doomed job interview each time she'd caved in and accepted Belinda's invites, had had to sit through lengthy evenings of showing off. She wasn't sure if it was peculiar to the area, or the generation, or the sex, but all the men could talk about was how theirs was so much bigger than everyone else's. Whether it was cars, salaries or even lawnmowers they were discussing, Beth couldn't care less. There was little hope of it being anything more visceral, and even if it had been, she still wouldn't have been tempted. The women, meanwhile, seemed content to look nice and provide backing vocals when required, like the other two in Destiny's Child, while a roomful of male Beyoncés dominated the stage. The ladies' real views would come out only when they were swapping vicious stories over a latte or three while their men were safely at work.

On both occasions, a recently divorced or newly widowed chap was wheeled in, oh-so-not-casually, to sit next to her in the hope that, like giant pandas, they would overcome timidity and fastidiousness and get it on, while their audience gawped and fed them the posh equivalent of bamboo shoots – currently dishes involving lots of beetroot and leathery duck breasts.

Needless to say, both the attempted matings had failed, and Beth had trailed back to Pickwick Road each time, abashed by the grandeur of Belinda's dos and more convinced than ever that she was a total social failure doomed to go solo forever.

But it was finally the moment to put such maundering thoughts to bed. She needed to get out there, not just because Belinda and her cohorts deemed that it was mandatory to be coupled-up, but because she had a sneaking feeling that it might actually be good for her. She was getting a mite set in her ways. She didn't want to end up like her mother. Having to live with others was healthy, wasn't it? Compromise, consultation, joint action. They all sounded good but were things she hadn't attempted for almost a decade.

And, as usual, at the back of her mind, Jake was her motivation. Didn't she need to show him what partnership was all about? If she ever wanted any grandchildren, she probably should model a relationship so that he wouldn't be entirely at sea when he eventually got to that stage himself. It wouldn't be long, unbelievable though the thought was. Puberty was lurking round the corner, like the bad fairy at the christening. It would change her soft-skinned, gorgeous boy, with his luxuriant eyelashes and ready smile, into a gangling, bristly, spotty giant that she would scarcely recognise or want to acknowledge. And from being a cherished mama, she would no doubt become a massive embarrassment and liability, popping up at inopportune moments in front of his friends to mortify him by asking him to wipe his face or change his trousers.

Ah, there was a lot to look forward to. And there was no doubt that it would be nice to have someone with her, to laugh about it all, if nothing else. Beth sighed. She was going to have to work on this dating business, and no mistake.

Once Beth put her mind to something, she was nothing if not wholehearted. Over the next few days, while nominally sorting out materials for the Christmas exhibition, she sat in her beloved executive chair at work and peered at a strange new world on the internet. When she'd first got to Wyatt's, the school's firewalls had confined her horizons strictly to her own job and the perusal of the term's snooze-worthy rugby fixtures and extracurricular clubs, but it hadn't taken her long to leapfrog over the IT safeguards, with a bit of help from Jen. Nowadays she spent quite a lot of time guiltily online, renewing her car insurance and comparing rates for holiday cover, like most employees. Today, however, she was looking at something rather different – a questionnaire that seemed to be never-ending, which she had to fill in completely before she could join the dating site eRelationships.

Once upon a time – and still, as far as her mother's genera-tion was concerned – meeting a partner online was tantamount to declaring to the world that you were a weirdo. Now everyone – well, Katie – kept reassuring her that what she was doing was absolutely normal. But Katie then rather spoiled that by being transparently fascinated by the whole process. A lot more riveted than Beth herself was.

eRelationships seemed to be asking her the same semi-intru-sive questions a hundred different ways. Beth was instantly wary. Were they trying to trick her? Would they see that she was accidentally contradicting herself? Would this mean that they'd classify her as a liar, and only match her with men who had a similarly loose relationship with the truth?

But Beth wasn't a fibber. She just couldn't remember whether she'd given 'romantic meal for two' as an answer for her perfect date three pages back, or whether she'd said 'country walks'. And if so, whether she'd given walks a five out of five and meals a four, or the other way round. She wasn't even sure if she really liked romantic meals, anyway. Did that mean the kind of cheesy Italian restaurant with flickering candles and an annoying violinist playing 'That's Amore'? And how could she go on a country walk round here, deep in the suburbs, anyway? There was the park, but she'd definitely be bound to bump into everyone she'd ever known in Dulwich there with their dogs, and her fledgling romance would be the talk of the village before they'd even got as far as the pond.

There wasn't a scrap of real country for miles. They'd have

to go on an endless train journey through the rest of south London to reach any, clanking past the backs of tumbledown houses, car-crushing yards and warehouses. And that was once they were actually on the move. First, there'd be the endless announcements about delays, being vigilant about terrorism and crackling Tannoy excuses about 'person under train'. God knew, there was nothing less romantic than a trip on Southeastern railway, unless it was having your fingernails removed by a real live torturer.

Beth looked up from her laptop with a sigh. Perhaps she wasn't in the right frame of mind for all this. Just as she was staring into the middle distance, wondering what on earth she could do to galvanise herself for what she was starting to call the love hunt, there was a discreet tap on her door.

She barely had time to say 'Come in' before Janice popped her head round the door. Janice, who'd been school secretary when Beth first started at Wyatt's, was now uber-manager of everything and had not only shimmied into that enhanced role as though born to it, but had also pulled off the amazing feat of marrying Dr Grover into the bargain. It said a lot for Janice's enormous likeability that she'd detached the head from his previous wife – quite a famous actress – and married him herself, while still remaining hugely popular both inside and outside Wyatt's walls. Janice's blonde prettiness was all about Thomas Hardy, her perfect English milk-maid looks set off by the faintest tinge of red in her blonde hair, hinting at an unscheduled Viking tumble an ancestor might have enjoyed behind a hedge about a thousand years ago.

Now, as Janice edged into the room, the final seal on her glory announced itself in the shape of a pronounced baby bump, which was proudly sheathed in her trademark pink cashmere. This baby was so cosy already that it was hard to imagine it would ever want to be born.

'Sit down, Janice, how're you feeling?' Beth said, standing up and ushering Janice to a comfy chair.

'I'm completely fine, slightly wishing everyone would stop treating me as though I'm made of spun glass,' said Janice with a smug smile.

'Oh, you love it. Anyway, make the most of it. When you really need the attention, once the baby's born, everyone will be cooing over it instead of you and you'll miss the fuss, believe me,' said Beth.

'I'm sure you're right,' said Janice in tones which belied her words. It was hard for her to imagine a time when she wasn't going to be the cynosure of all eyes. 'Just thought I'd stop by and see how you're getting on with everything. I can't seem to settle today; I'm just drifting around picking at things.'

Beth, who'd reluctantly come to realise in the past few months that she was the world's greatest prevaricator, certainly recognised that pattern. She shut her laptop with a snap and abandoned any pretence at proper work. 'Jan, can I ask you something rather... well, personal?'

Janice folded her hands demurely across her cashmere bump, almost as though covering the baby's ears. 'Of course.'

Beth leant forward, glancing from side to side to make sure they weren't being overheard, which was ridiculous in the confines of her own office. She lowered her voice and Janice leant forward to hear. 'Have you ever done any... *online dating?*'

Janice sat back and giggled. 'Honestly, I thought you were going to ask if I'd ever been dogging or something,' she said. 'And the answer to that is no,' she added quickly, as Beth looked at her in astonishment. Even Beth knew that wasn't to do with cockapoos in Dulwich Park. Although...

But Janice was continuing. 'Of course I've done some online dating. Who hasn't?'

'Well, me. People keep telling me it's time. But I honestly have no idea what I'm doing.'

Instantly, Janice was all business. It was as though they were discussing lower school budgets, or planning the upper sixth Christmas party. There was nothing the woman loved better than a clear-cut project.

'First, you'll need to download Tinder. But let's think for a second about what you're putting in your profile. What kind of men are you hoping to get?'

'To *get*? Lord, you're making it sound like organising an Ocado delivery. Can I really be that specific, just order what I want?'

'Well, of course you can. But as with most of these things, it's how you present yourself that will determine the sort of men you'll get a response from. You'll have to nail that down first.'

Beth started to fiddle with the stapler on her desk. 'Hmm,' she said doubtfully.

'Don't look so worried, Beth. And definitely don't chicken out at the first hurdle.'

Beth put down the stapler and wondered how Janice had known exactly what she was thinking. 'Maybe this is all too much hassle and I should just wait until I bump into someone the natural way.'

'And you've been on your own now for, what? Nearly a decade? And how many great men have you actually bumped into during that time?'

Beth's eyes flicked off to the right and, unbidden, a large policeman appeared foursquare in her thoughts. Ruffled dark blond hair; a direct blue gaze – usually through cross and rather narrowed eyes; a big, navy blue peacoat; and, for some reason, whenever she thought of him he was carrying a takeaway cup of coffee. But could she describe him as a *great man*, as Janice put it? A potential date, a possible stepfather for Jake, for heaven's sake? When he was always so annoying? And usually very cross with her? She couldn't remember their last exchange, but it was something along the lines of her being a total idiot, with a death wish, who wasn't safe out alone. Hardly hearts and flowers. No, whatever form of dating she ended up doing, he was one person who was never, ever going to answer her ad, or click on her profile, or swipe her – or whatever the terminology even was.

'Beth? Still with me? What exactly are you looking for?'

Beth dragged herself back to the present. 'Well, two legs, I suppose, the normal number of, ahem, other things... I've basically no idea. I don't think I've given this enough thought, have I?'

Janice was looking at Beth with a fond smile. It made Beth all the more aware that she was on the nursery slopes of dating, whereas Janice had been a black run girl for a few years, before pulling off the master stroke that had taken her off-piste once and for all.

'Come on, Beth. Let's get some lunch – and I'll talk you through a few things.'

By the time Beth was tidying her desk that afternoon, she had the virtuous glow of one who had done a good day's work. True, her inbox was a lot emptier than when she'd started that morning, and she also had a sketchy outline of the Christmas exhibitions she'd be putting before the bursar and the head in the next few days – tasks she was pretty proud of. But the real reason for her satisfaction was that, having talked things through with Janice, she felt she was a lot closer to making a proper decision about dating and the sort of partner she might be interested in.

In many ways, the whole process of online dating seemed completely antithetical to love, as she understood it. It really was a little like shopping. Janice had briefly resuscitated a few of her own dusty online profiles to show Beth exactly how the systems worked. And, being Janice, she'd managed to make the whole thing seem eminently sensible, easy, and an excellent idea to boot.

Beth was now willing to give the whole thing a try. But she hadn't lost sight of the fact that Janice, despite her skills on Tinder, had actually met her new husband in the flesh at work, and not via any old app at all.

Surely there was more hope for a relationship that was forged in real life, and real time, not something that only existed in a theoretical ether and might never make its way out into daylight? But then, where were the suitors for her hand? The only men she met on a regular basis were the deeply married staff at the school, or the extremely wedded daddies of her various mummy friends. Her brother, Josh, was probably the only unattached man she knew, and there was absolutely no chance of him waltzing up the aisle any time soon.

A little voice continued to whisper that Harry York was single too. But then, where was he? Probably busy shouting at someone else or, even more likely, dealing with some awful crime in another part of south London. Their paths weren't likely to cross again.

And that was the whole point with online dating. As both Katie and Janice had pointed out, you increased your chances of meeting the right person exponentially just by putting yourself out there. The pool of eligible men she'd meet by sheer chance was tiny. But the selection of men online was almost infinite, and it was up to her to set her own parameters, specify exactly what she wanted from her Prince Charming.

But even a convert like Janice didn't pretend all the men out there were saints. She'd warned that sometimes she would seem to have clicked beautifully with one of these online chaps, they would have a lengthy and increasingly romantic and/or amorous spate of messaging or emailing, and then suddenly the man would just drop the contact, for no apparent reason. And there would never be an explanation.

The person would just vanish back into the ether, perhaps because they'd entered another lengthy and intense cyber-relationship with someone else. Or maybe even because they enjoyed dumping a woman without giving a reason, knowing she was likely to spend far too long trying to work out what on earth had gone wrong. It was a brave new world, but a very strange one, too, with some definite odd-bods in it.

This disappearing act, called 'ghosting', was something Beth had to be braced for, Janice had said. She also had to be ready to weed out players and chancers, but luckily Janice had promised to help her with this undoubtedly onerous task.

Beth felt as though she were standing on the edge of a precipice, about to taking a flying leap. It was terrifying, but exhilarating too. She just hoped there'd be a nice bouncy safety net to catch her at the bottom.

FOUR

'Of course, Belinda. Yes, yes, no problem, see you tomorrow, bye,' said Beth, holding her phone a little way from her ear. She wasn't sure if it was because Belinda McKenzie didn't trust her to understand instructions unless they were screamed at her, or whether it was part of the woman's posh, outdoorsy, country-woman persona, but she was incapable of having a telephone conversation without acting as though she was at one end of the grouse moor and Beth was right at the other.

Beth sighed and dropped her mobile back onto the sofa, where Magpie promptly draped herself over it.

Jake was upstairs asleep, last week's restlessness thankfully turning out to be a one-off. Beth had been settled in front of the fire, proofreading a freelance project one last time before sending it off, when Belinda had rung to micromanage the arrangements for the Camberwell tutoring tomorrow, even though they were identical to the arrangements last week and the week before.

Beth looked at her laptop, considering doing a bit more of her freelance work, then smiled to herself and fished her phone back out from underneath Magpie's fluffy tum, and opened up the Tinder app. She was still only at the lurking stage, not yet having the confidence to contact anyone or do anything with all the profiles she was peering through, but she had to admit she was getting a little addicted to flicking through all the images of men, apparently dying to meet her, night after night. Some of the profiles just made her giggle; some gave her pause for a second or two. None seemed quite right.

It was a very odd thought that some of them actually appeared to be round the corner from her right now. They could stay where they were, for sure. But if she were ever really, really desperate for companionship, it was mildly comforting to think that Stephen, 42, was only a mile away and gagging for it – or so he (not very alluringly) said.

But wait a minute. Suddenly her restless flicking to the left stopped, and she paused, electrified. Here was someone she knew. She leant into the little window of her phone, turning it this way and that, trying to make the picture bigger, almost willing herself to have made a mistake.

It couldn't be, could it? But yes, there, smiling out of her phone, was a big bear of a man with rumpled dark hair and a look of rueful amusement, all cuddly in a gorgeous sweater.

It was Jen's new husband, Ted.

What? Wait a minute. This didn't make any sense at all. They'd just got married, for heaven's sake. She'd seen them only, how long ago? A week, barely, and they'd seemed so happy.

Yet here he was. And that lovely sweater he was wearing? If she wasn't mistaken, that was the special jumper that Jen had bought him from the ludicrously expensive boutique in Dulwich Village as a present, in their whirlwind courting days only a few months ago. Beth had actually been with Jen when she'd decided to splurge all her money on the gorgeous silver grey, two-ply cashmere. She'd thought at the time that she'd have to love someone an awful lot before she bought them a jumper costing as much as two or three weeks' groceries, including wine and even cat food.

Somehow that was the bit that Beth was finding hardest to get over. If you were going to attempt cheating, some part of her mind was telling her it was more acceptable if you were wearing clothes you'd chosen yourself, not a sweater that was a love token from *your new wife.*

Wait a minute, thought Beth, pulling herself back from an abyss of worry. Maybe this was just an old profile, and a jumper that was oddly similar to Jen's splurge purchase. On a phone screen it was impossible to tell whether it was one hundred per cent cashmere or totally acrylic.

How had Jen met Ted, after all? Maybe they'd hooked up on Tinder in the first place? Beth couldn't even remember now what Jen had told her about it all. One minute, she'd been her reliable single friend in the playground, always ready with a wink when all the couple-talk about where 'we' were going at the weekend and what 'we' liked on telly got too nauseating. Next it was *Brides* magazine, a simple yet stunning knee-length white satin shift dress, a bouquet of syringa and roses, and an exchange of vows that had seemed so heartfelt and sincere that Beth hadn't been the only person at the ceremony reaching for her tissues to mop moist eyes. Ted had seemed to blow in from nowhere, sweep Jen off her feet and whisk her to Camberwell before anyone could turn round.

Yes, the more Beth thought about it, the more she decided that had to be it. It was just a Tinder throwback. She was already finding out that once she'd signed up to these dating sites, they mimicked the neediest of partners and would not let you go. She'd decided against eHarmony and Match.com, but they were still bombarding her with pleading emails, asking her why they couldn't just be friends. Tinder was bound to be the same – easy enough to get into a relationship with, but nigh on impossible to wriggle your way out of.

And the little line of type under Ted's name, saying, 'Active fourteen minutes ago'? Hmm. Well, maybe he was just looking at his profile for *auld lang syne,* reminding himself of faraway bachelor days.

Beth got up rather crossly. All she needed was another thing to worry about. It was bedtime, though, and she was determined to push this whole business as far to the back of her mind as she could. First thing tomorrow, she was going to find out what on earth was going on.

As usual, Beth's best-laid plans were destined to go awry. She had been slow to abandon her very old-fashioned digital alarm clock, something she'd bought with James at John Lewis way back in the mists of time. It had been cheap and functional all those years ago, but, like everything that had distinct happy memories attached to it – James had rather hopefully teased her that he needed the insistent siren to fight off her sexual demands in the morning – she hadn't been able to part with it. It seemed so long since she had had even the vaguest frisson of a sensual feeling, let alone felt insatiable desire. She refused to acknowledge the spark she'd felt when Inspector York's hand had brushed hers accidentally, all those months ago.

The battered plastic clock was a symbol of a different life, a relic. But even they eventually let you down. After the dissolution of the monasteries, enough pieces of the one true cross were burnt in Britain to make up a forest, while there had been sufficient saints' foreskins knocking around in the churches to reupholster every Jewish man in the world. The alarm clock proved just as unreliable. One morning, its red numbers beamed out proudly to the world; the next, its display had gone forever blank. Though Beth would have liked to have got it repaired, there was no one in Dulwich who did anything nearly that useful. It had to go in the bin. Since then, she'd fallen back on her phone alarm.

Somehow, maybe due to all her swiping last night, her phone had died in the night and now they were hideously late up. It was only the sound of her neighbour crashing around with his wheelie bins outside that finally roused her from a restless tangle of dreams involving sweaters, looming faces, a laughing circle of mummies and a sense of pervading unease.

Having started the morning on the back foot, it wasn't until they were just about to rush out of the door that Beth realised Jake's hectic flush wasn't all due to the hurry of cramming down two Weetabix and finding his football kit in forty seconds flat. He had a fever. She put a worried palm to his forehead as they hovered in the hall, bags in hand. Mm. Hot. But how hot? She didn't have time to get what they called the 'earometer', the device she always rammed in his little lughole to get a quick temperature reading. The trouble was, she had a busy day on at work. She couldn't leave Jake sick at home all day. She couldn't get her mum to come over at such short notice – she needed a run-up of about six weeks for all major excursions – and Katie had a full programme in the yoga studio. Oblivious to Jake's protests, she stuck her hand back on his forehead and willed him to be well.

'Get *off*, Mum, I'm fine,' he protested.

'That's *Mummy* to you,' she said automatically, picking up her bag and keys in relief. If he was well enough to be obstreperous, he was well enough for school, she told herself.

She didn't love being this sort of mother, the type who fudged things when they were inconvenient and landed the school with a potentially sick child who would be as generous with his germs as he was with everything else. She knew a lot of people would condemn her roundly for her actions. But what choice did she really have? Her usual babysitter, Zoe Bentinck from next door, was at school herself during the day. Of the

mummies who were around all day, she supposed the closest –
geographically at least – was Belinda McKenzie, though her
way of being a stay-at-home-mum was as exhausting as running
a major company. Belinda had to boss her extensive staff of
gofers around all day, supervising, fault-finding and upbraiding,
and also continue with her mentoring programme for her
hapless acolytes, not to mention coordinating a timetable of
extracurricular activities for her three children that made the
average NASA moon landing look like a walk in Belair Park.
Beth was pretty sure that leaving Jake at Belinda's all day could
potentially traumatise him a lot more than a few hours feeling a
little bit rubbish at school.

Leaving Jake at the school gates, Beth was relieved to see
that he'd been pretty much restored to normal by the short walk
in the chill autumnal air. He gave her a happy wave and scam-
pered off, and she turned away with a smile. Nevertheless, her
first task was going to be sorting herself out so that tomorrow she
could work from home if she had to.

Looking up from her laptop a few hours later, Beth realised
she'd had a thoroughly productive morning. Tasks that had been
looming for weeks had been crunched into neat little folders,
and Gordian knots of correspondence that she'd been frankly
swerving had been cut through with a few decisive and carefully constructed emails. She raised her hands above her head,
linking the fingers and pushing upwards in a semi-yoga-ish
manner that she felt sure Katie would thoroughly approve of,
loosening up shoulders that had been hunched over her screen.
Best of all, she'd sorted everything out so that tomorrow she
could take the day off – oops, she meant work from home – just
in case Jake wasn't able to get over whatever had ailed him that
morning.

She definitely deserved a nice, long lunch break now, and

what's more, she was certain this was going to be productive, too.

She was in luck, though at first it really didn't seem that way. Strolling into reception to check whether Janice would be up for a sandwich from the canteen, she found her nattering furiously with Lily Winter, her new replacement as school secretary, and Sam Moore, who'd just joined the bursar's staff. Both women were straight out of the Wyatt's mould: attractive; polished; and to Beth, who still hoped to grow out of her shyness one fine day in the distant future, highly intimidating.

Once they were all seated round the table in the staff dining area, Beth realised that, as usual, she'd done the new girls a disservice. They were lovely. Yes, they were chatty and confident, but they both admitted they found the school big and confusing.

'I get lost every day,' said Lily.

'I can't remember anyone's names,' confided Sam. 'Who are you again?' she said to Janice, and they all laughed.

Chit-chat was general for a while – a new branch of Frost, the posh frozen food store, had just opened up in the village, and Janice confessed she'd bought a couple of square foil tins of the chicken chasseur and passed it off as her own at a dinner party at the weekend.

Lily chimed in. 'I was thinking of doing that, but I need to get in early, before everyone eats their way through the repertoire and recognises all the dishes.'

Everyone nodded solemnly. Even cheating had to be finessed in Dulwich.

'How's that, um, research going, Beth? You know, the, erm, new dossier?' said Janice, raising her eyebrows sky-high at Beth. This, Beth knew full well, meant Tinder. If Beth decided she didn't want to talk about it, she knew Janice would drop the subject and move seamlessly on. But once she'd taken on a project, Janice would not be able to resist checking up on her progress at regular intervals.

Beth didn't really want to broach her personal life with these strangers, however nice they seemed. But she sensed that, as thirty-somethings who did not appear to be wearing wedding rings, both Sam and Lily might well be useful sources of information.

'I'm thinking about starting dating,' said Beth, her cheeks flaming. 'It's been a while...'

'It's been *forever*,' Janice clarified. Beth gave her a sharp glance, but it was impossible to be cross with Janice, hands resting on today's turquoise fluffy bump, seraphic smile on her pretty face.

'I've just done a profile, but I haven't put it out there yet. I've just been having a look...'

'Ah yes, the candy store,' said Sam with a giggle.

'Looks good, doesn't it? Or some of them do. I've been quite lucky, but there've been times...' Lily rolled her eyes.

'It's all completely new to me. I'm not really sure it actually works, does it, to find true love?'

'True love? That might be a tall order. But you can certainly find something to take your mind off the futility of the search.' Lily smirked.

'Do you know what happens when you've met someone? Can you just take your profile off the system, or does it have to go on being there?' Beth leant forward a little. They were getting to the stuff she wanted to know.

'Oh, you can erase it all. They still send you emails, but you don't have to be on the app for a minute longer than you want to be.'

'Mind you, there are people who just stay on there, even when they've hooked up.' Sam made a moue of distaste. Maybe she knew this from personal experience.

'And then you hear stories, don't you, about people going

back on literally seconds after they've split up with someone?'
said Lily.

'Happened to me,' said Sam.

'No!' the women chorused.

'Swear to God. I'd just literally told him it wasn't him, it was
me – though it was actually *soooo* him. I got back home, started
looking through – just to keep my hand in, you know – and
there he was, bold as brass. Right back on, same profile as when
we'd got together.'

There was a general tutting at the fickleness of mankind.
Then Beth piped up. 'And if it says, "Active fifteen minutes
ago", what does that actually mean? Have they been on their
profile, or have they been on a date, or what?'

'Oh, it doesn't tell you when someone's been out dating,
though that would be interesting information to have,' said Lily.
'"Active however long ago" just means they were on the app
then.'

'Just looking at profiles? Or messaging, or something?'

'On the app, for sure. Who knows what they'd be doing
there? Why, what's on your mind?'

'Oh, just checking something,' said Beth vaguely. But,
beneath her fringe, she was frowning.

Later that afternoon, the kids safely delivered to their tutor by
Belinda, and Jake apparently much the better for his day at
school, Beth parked in front of Jen's door. She still had an hour
to go before pick-up, but as usual she'd rather have time in hand
and enjoy a cup of tea with a friend than trust the South
Circular to disgorge her at the right moment if she left later.

She had the wedding present safely in her handbag this
time, as she pressed the doorbell, looking up and down the little
street as she heard the peal dying away inside the house. People
were coming and going as usual, walking up the Grove to

Denmark Hill Station or down towards Camberwell Church Street and its innumerable bus stops. The street lights cast a yellow glow and Beth tried to imagine what the road would have been like in its heyday, echoing to the clopping of hooves, gentlemen lifting their hats to ladies swishing by in lampshade skirts.

Moments passed. She looked back at the front door, which remained resolutely closed. That was funny. Where was Jen?

Beth pushed the bell again, a little harder. And waited. Nothing. She waited a little longer, then leant down a little – not too far, thanks to her short stature – and prised open the letterbox, peering in tentatively, feeling like an intruder. She certainly didn't want to be caught squinting through the flap like a total busybody, but on the other hand, she wanted to know what was going on.

The hall, what she could see of it, was empty, the house quiet as the grave. Adjusting her position, she could see a scattering of junk mail on the doormat, even flopping out onto the original encaustic hall floor tiles which were one of the prettiest features of the little house. To Beth, it looked like more than a day's worth of pizza delivery leaflets and taxi cards. Maybe Jen hadn't signed up to one of those sites which promised to remove your name from databases. Or maybe she was just away? A little odd, in the middle of term, and the middle of the week too, come to that.

Beth racked her brain to see if she could remember Jen's daughter Jessica being in the playground today or yesterday, morning or evening. But no. As ever, Beth'd been in a mad rush, and recognising and scooping up her own child had been enough of a feat.

She pressed the bell, hard, for a third time, but by now had given up hope of an answer. The house had a deserted feel.

How very strange. Why would Jen have suddenly gone off

like that? Unless she was just out shopping or something, and hadn't cleared the post from the mat?

Then Beth realised with a sinking heart that she hadn't confirmed she'd be over. She'd said last time that she'd love to come, and Jen had seemed fine with that, but they'd not been in touch since. A lot could happen in a week. She'd been so busy and quite anxious today about Jake's state of health, so just hadn't got round to sending Jen that line of text that might have made all the difference. Feeling deflated, she turned round and went back to her car, putting the present back on the passenger seat. She weighed up her options.

Unlike Dulwich, Camberwell was not exactly overflowing with tempting coffee emporia to waste a peaceful hour in. Parking on the high street was hard, and not something Beth was feeling brave enough to even attempt. It was one of the capital's red routes, meaning that all the roads were lined with two parallel scarlet lines, warning cars not to stop on pain of being towed away. There were so-called 'red boxes' where you could leave your car for half an hour, but of course these were always full. As a consequence, all the bays off the main drag were usually taken as well.

Her best bet was to leave the car here and wander down to Camberwell proper on foot. There was the Greek bakery on Camberwell Church Street, though anything left at this hour would be well past its prime. Or she could pop into Superdrug, there was always a tempting new shower gel or some toothpaste to pick up there. It wasn't quite the chat over a cuppa that she'd been looking forward to. But, in some ways, it let her off a very large hook indeed. She'd been chewing over what she would or wouldn't say to Jen about Ted.

What on earth was the etiquette, if you thought someone's husband of a couple of months might, just might, be gearing up to cheat on them? Or may have already cheated? Or might just be emailing or texting someone with a view to cheating? Whatever situation she'd accidentally stumbled upon, it was going to be a ticklish one to bring up. But if she didn't ever mention it, she would feel very guilty if something came out later and Jen realised she'd known all along. Maybe, now she thought about it, that was why she hadn't got round to asking Jen if she'd be at home today. It was always lovely to see Jen, but it wasn't so great to deal with a whole bundle of nightmare options brought about by her husband. She tried to shrug it all from her mind, and marched off to the shops.

Three-quarters of an hour later, Beth returned to her car, having found a plethora of bargains in Camberwell. The little shopping centre had all the practical stores which Dulwich sorely lacked. There was a branch of Iceland – the cheap freezer and grocery store that had brand names at rock bottom prices, and was the polar opposite of Frost in Dulwich village. There was a key-cutting place, the Morrisons that she was already becoming fond of, and even a pound shop, which she'd been completely unable to resist. Inside her gaily striped plastic bags, Beth had treasure: what looked like a lifetime's supply of cotton wool buds; shampoo and conditioner; two giant Toblerones (one of Jake's favourite treats, since his Uncle Josh often brought them back from the duty-free shops of the world's airports); and some fancy rubber gloves which might, just might, make washing-up less of a chore.

She was opening up the Fiat and slinging her finds inside when, with a jolt, she spotted Jen and Ted coming down the street. Ted was in front, head down, fumbling for the house keys, moving fast for such a big man. Jen seemed to be trailing behind, listing slightly to the left, due to the large canvas bag slipping off her shoulder. Well, that was a mystery solved. They'd been away, but they were back.

Beth shut the boot and turned to greet them brightly.

'Hi there! I was wondering where you'd got to, Jen,' she said with a smile.

Startled, Ted gave her a sharp look which turned into a lower-wattage version of his usual smile. He opened the door quickly and disappeared inside, raising a hand in greeting and farewell, seeming preoccupied. Beth looked after him, a little surprised. He was normally so friendly.

Jen came up to her and dropped the bag at her feet. 'Phew, that's heavy,' she said, her dead-straight hair pushed behind her ears, make-up-free face flushed and shiny in the dwindling light. 'Sorry, were we meeting? I'd completely forgotten. Um, do you want to...?' she gestured towards the house.

Was it Beth's imagination, or was the invitation just a little reluctant? She felt a tiny stab of hurt, but then reasoned that time was ticking on anyway and Jen certainly looked as though she had her hands full. The bag was bulging, no doubt full of washing after their trip, and Ted didn't exactly seem to be in an open-house mood. Besides, from the way the light was starting to fade, Beth knew she should be getting a move on to fetch those boys.

'I never confirmed, did I? I just got caught up in the week, you know how it is. But you've been away?' she said.

'Just a quick break, a chance to... well, you know...' Jen tailed off.

Beth wasn't sure she did know. A chance to do what, exactly? They were fresh from their honeymoon. But maybe that was one of the joys of newly married life, being able to take off when you wanted to, just enjoy each other's company. Although, unless her antennae were way off, Jen and Ted didn't seem that lovey-dovey. And Jen also had her daughter to think about, though there was no sign at all of little Jessica.

Beth looked towards the front door, ajar, and saw a shadow move restlessly. Ted was in the dark hall, silent, waiting, just beyond the pool of light from the streetlamps. Jen's head jerked towards the door. She'd seen him, too.

'Look, I'd better dash. See you in the playground?'

'Yes, of course,' said Beth, relieved they'd somehow got back onto surer ground. 'Tomorrow?'

'Well, not tomorrow. My ex still has Jess. But soon. Let's catch up really soon.'

'Absolutely,' said Beth. 'That'll be lovely.' She got into the car, sliding behind the wheel as Jen walked up the path. Was she imagining it, or was her friend moving very slowly? The door shut with a soft click and Jen was gone.

As Beth was about to start the car, her glance flicked to the passenger seat. Her handbag had toppled over, and lay half-on, half-off the wedding present, its silvery paper gleaming. Damn. Not again, she thought. For a few moments, she contemplated getting out and ringing the doorbell. There was a lot to be said for just getting rid of the thing. It had been hanging around for far too long. But no. It definitely didn't seem like the right time, for reasons she couldn't quite fathom.

Oh well, maybe she'd give it to Jen in the playground? Though it would be nicer to deliver it to Jen and Ted together. If she handed the gift over in front of the other mummies, Jen might feel under pressure to open it there and then, and Beth wasn't sure that she wanted it seen by all and sundry. It wasn't expensive, but it was something she was sure would mean a lot to Jen. It was personal. And just a tiny bit quirky. Certainly not the sort of item you'd find on the average wedding list.

Beth made her decision. The present was staying where it was, for now. She moved the car into gear slowly, then signalled to move out, checking up and down the road. It was a shame. But never mind. There was always next week.

* * *

Jen knew she had a few moments before the explosion. Ted surely wouldn't do anything while Beth's car was still outside, while there was a danger of being seen or heard. She hesitated just inside the front door, her hand on the latch. Should she throw the door open again and run up the path to freedom? She could take this bag with her. It only had enough clothes for a couple of days, and they were already dirty, but Beth would let her wash them, wouldn't she? And her friend wouldn't complain about the way she ironed or folded them. She wouldn't snipe at her cooking, or the way she dressed, or her make-up – or lack of it – or her hair, her figure. She wouldn't find endless fault.

How had this happened? she'd asked herself a hundred times. No, a thousand. From the moment she'd met Ted on Tinder, he'd seemed perfect. She'd been on dates since Tim; she'd had to move on after all the scars he'd inflicted on her psyche with his see-sawing between her and Babs. It had done her ego no good at all, but what had worried her, then and now, was the effect it was having on their daughter. The whole experience had been so damaging for Jess. She knew her daughter still dreamt only of her parents getting back together, but that would never happen. Tim had lied too often to be trusted again.

Ted, though. He'd seemed so truthful, so honest, so open. He'd been hurt, too. His ex sounded a nightmare. She'd been a female Tim, it seemed – constantly flirting with other men, tormenting this kind bear of a man, inflicting terrible pain. And then his wife had gone a step further and left him. He'd been devastated. He was still hurt, and maybe it was too early for him to be dating, he'd admitted to her. But something about Jen had caught his heart.

Everything he'd said echoed her own pain. She felt for him. She'd believed him, and she'd fallen for it. All over again. She couldn't believe how stupid she'd been. Standing here now, with her hand still on the cold, smooth metal of the latch, she felt every kind of fool. She prided herself on being sensible, practical. And she wanted to show her daughter a good example.

Yet she'd been suckered by Tim, taking him back time after time, despite the broken promises, believing it was important to keep the marriage together if she could.

And now. Could she really face the embarrassment of admitting she'd done it again? That out of all the men in the world, she'd picked another stinker? And what was more, someone worse even than Tim? Someone who didn't just chip away at her sense of self with lies and cheating, but someone who... well. Someone with a very dark side.

Look before you leap. Marry in haste, repent at leisure. These phrases repeated in her head relentlessly as she spent her time trying to avoid Ted, and trying to placate Tim who was jibbing at having Jess so much. But she had to keep her daughter away from this mess. She had made a mistake, and she was paying for it. But there was no reason her daughter should, too.

She could call time on it all right now. She could run and start again. She could bolt and choose freedom. Yes, Dulwich would judge her harshly. Every mother in the playground would be talking about her. They'd think she was a total idiot. It would be hard to hold her head up. But she'd still have her work, and Jess. She could weather the gossip. Was it the right thing to do, though? Was there no hope of turning things around with Ted? If she just did things the way he wanted, would he relax, would everything go back to the way it had been at first?

They'd been so in love. He'd been wonderful. She'd felt she'd discovered the other half of herself, at last. He was a patient listener, a caring stepfather, a tender lover. But somehow, somewhere, everything had gone wrong. She wasn't sure what she'd done, but he'd started to have that look in his eye. Disappointment. Disillusionment. Then he'd made suggestions. If she could just... why didn't she... he'd told her before... he wouldn't tell her again...

How had he travelled from love to loathing so fast? She didn't understand what she'd done wrong or how to get things back on track. She wanted to try, she really did; she wanted her marriage to work, but maybe it never could. His expectations were unrealistic, and she had had enough. Her fingers went to the latch, she shouldered the bag again and turned.

The hand slammed into the door, a centimetre above her head. Ted's palm was heavy, immovable, holding the door closed, his body leaning into her so she was crushed up against the jamb. His scent was in her nostrils, the animal male smell she'd once loved, now rank and threatening.

'Where do you think you're going then, Jen?' he asked very, very quietly.

Outside, Beth's little Fiat sparked up. Then the headlights swung in a wide arc, driving away from Camberwell, into the night.

FIVE

What was it about this time of year, Beth wondered. The days and weeks seemed to start merging into one another and moving past faster and faster, like pages of a diary caught in a high wind. Autumn was a kaleidoscope of conkers, fallen leaves, Hallowe'en costumes, bonfires, dark nights and darker mornings, until they were on a slippery slope into winter, with huge quantities of tinsel and baubles mounded up to catch her at the bottom. The 'C' word. After a certain point in October, all roads seemed to lead inexorably to Christmas.

It wasn't that she was anti-Santa. She loved the idea of snuggling up with Jake, opening his stocking, filching half his chocolates, then enjoying an enormous lunch cooked at a snail's pace by her mother, and usually ready at about five in the afternoon. It was just that an unfeasible amount of preparation seemed to be involved in getting them to that stage. Presents without end had to be sourced and wrapped; decorations unearthed from the spidery loft; a tree dragged home from the little charity stall at the school. Beth always bought in every single bit of food herself, even if they ended up eating it round at her mother's. Wendy insisted on seeing online shopping as tantamount to entering a pact with the devil and, left to her own devices, would have cooked her usual single chicken breast and been very surprised when it didn't stretch to feed Beth, Jake, Josh and whichever girlfriend was briefly in tow that year.

It was all lovely, yes, but it was a huge amount of extra work and expense. And perhaps worst of all, it reminded Beth so strongly of James and everything they'd lost. He'd loved Christmas and never seemed to see it, as she did, as a mildly entertaining inconvenience that was basically not really worth the bother. He'd kept a childish sense of wonder over fairy lights, cards, baubles and glitter, so the house had always been full to bursting, like a tiny festive grotto dumped in Dulwich. In fact, Magpie's fur would be twinkling away for months after Christmas, as she had a penchant for removing ornaments from the tree, then batting them all around the house and rolling around on them for good measure. Needless to say, none of their decorations were glass.

The weeks were spinning by, and it wouldn't be long until it was time to unearth the battered boxes of goodies from their hiding place. At least James's mad splurging years ago meant she hadn't had to shell out an extra penny on decorations over the years, thought Beth, knowing she was becoming more Scrooge-like by the day.

But she did always have to count the pennies. It was hard, budgeting alone, and although her precious Wyatt's job got her through, there always seemed to be additional expenses to grapple with, looming up out of the blue like obstacles on one of Jake's PlayStation games. The tutoring, for example. It certainly didn't come free, perhaps because the rate had been negotiated by Belinda McKenzie, who thought economy was vulgar. Beth just hoped it would be worth it.

Already, the weekly trip to Camberwell had become an established routine, with no more broken nights. The three boys seemed to get on brilliantly, if boisterously, and the tutor –

made of much sterner stuff than Beth – appeared to cope. If
they were as bouncy during the sessions as they were in her car,
then the man deserved several medals and all the money that
Belinda could throw at him.

Beth had no idea whether this effort was being translated
into improved academic performance. There was no homework
at the Village School, apart from a few desultory spellings now
and again, and Jake was fine on those when he could be bothered to look at them – but that had always been the case.
Certainly, at the last parents' evening, the teacher had not
remarked that Jake had suddenly catapulted himself into an
entirely different league of attainment. But neither had she
informed Beth sorrowfully that the class hamster was brighter.
Her son was no doubt somewhere in the middle, as he'd always
been, and it was probably all a big waste of time and money.

Never mind, the end was in sight. Jake had already sat the
eleven-plus exam for the various grammar schools over the
county border in Kent, which was a sort of warm-up for the
private school exams in January. She would have loved it if he'd
won a grammar place, but the system made that very unlikely.
Thousands of children did the exams, and only the top two
hundred or so each year got a guaranteed place at the grammar
school of their choice. The rest, if they passed the test (and over
a thousand would each year) and also fulfilled the crucial catchment area criteria, were in with a chance.

But Beth and Jake lived miles from most of the schools, and
bright though she knew him to be, he'd emerged from the exam
with a dazed look on his face. Later, under her gentle cross-
questioning, it had emerged that he'd left the last *nine* pages of
the Maths exam blank, and had no clue what the comprehen-
sion passage was about either.

'It was a whale, or maybe a dog, with some people fighting
or maybe hunting. Anyway, it was really boring. Then there
was another test even after that. Then the weakest orange

squash ever and one biscuit. One! What *is* non-verbal reasoning, anyway, Mum?'

'Don't call me Mum,' Beth had said automatically, but her head had been spinning. It seemed so unfair, making such a young child jump through these hoops. Mind you, she'd had to do it herself at that age, and had survived. And there was no alternative. She loved the Village Primary, but it didn't go on past Year Six. Much as she'd love to keep on taking Jake there, just rocking up with him every morning, meeting the same mothers at the gate and watching him play with the same friends forever, it wasn't an option. She dearly wanted to keep him safe in his little primary bubble, where the biggest crises he'd ever encounter were sleeping through the alarm and half-baked school projects. But it was all coming to an end. Next September, none of his class or their mothers would be at those gates. They were all moving on. Big School was calling.

Like it or not, life changed, nothing stayed the same, and her beloved Jake, her beautiful child, with his guileless eyes so much like James's, had to grow up.

And, talking of growing, Jake badly needed new trousers. The pair they'd bought at the end of the summer were already showing enough ankle to have a Victorian gentleman swooning. Beth hated that Oliver Twist look, and was planning to rectify it tomorrow with a swift trip to the Peacocks near Camberwell.

That reminded her: she needed to text Jen to see whether she was free. After that mix-up, she was careful now to plan ahead. A couple of times Jen had been tied up. They'd had one more cup of tea, but it had been a bit strained; Jen had been on edge. Ted had been out, so Beth had hoped they'd have a proper natter, but Jen had jumped every time there had been a noise outside and the conversation had never really flowed.

The wedding present had been forgotten yet again. Beth had been so cross with herself when she'd driven off that last time that she'd shoved it out of the way into the car's glove compartment so it couldn't reproach her from the passenger seat, and the glitzy paper was now getting scuffed.

She slid her laptop to one side, fished her phone out from underneath Magpie's fluffy petticoats, and quickly pinged Jen a message. If she was around, then Jake's trousers would just have to wait. Friends took priority, even over her son's chilly ankles, and Beth was seriously concerned about Jen.

It wasn't until she was having a quick catch-up coffee with Katie the next day that she finally put her worries into words. They were in Jane's, but due to Katie's extremely careful scheduling, the place was only a third full so they could talk without every word reverberating around SE21. Fed up with the vile dishwater at Aurora round the corner, Katie had put in some diligent research to find the best possible Jane's window to appeal to Beth's highly developed sense of privacy. She wasn't the least bothered herself – but then she spent her working life in skintight Lycra, bending over with her bum high in the air. Concealment wasn't an issue.

The movements of mummies and au pairs in the area were as mysterious as the progress of spawning salmon – governed not by the tides but by the timetable of the Monkey Music sessions at St Barnabas parish hall, Baby Rhyme Time at Dulwich Library and, of course, school pick-up. While pick-up was immutable, all the other fixtures were subject to last-minute alteration and were on a need-to-know basis only.

To her excitement, Katie had discerned a distinct chink of light at about 11.15 every weekday, when the area's babies were napping after a hectic morning of socialising, older children were locked in school, and mummies and nannies had an hour or so of downtime in which to book their next holidays or apply urgently for other jobs. Beth and Katie were both supposed to be busy at work, but it was amazing how flexible schedules could become when they had to be. Anyway, it was only a super-speedy coffee, wasn't it?

Beth stirred hers absently, not sure whether she was right to voice her doubts or not.

'Come on, Beth. Tell me. You've got something on your mind, I've seen that look before,' said Katie, over the rim of her own delicious, hard-won cappuccino.

'I feel a bit bad even mentioning it. But have you noticed anything with Jen these days?'

'Jen Patterson? I've never really known her that well. Charlie isn't great mates with Jessica. She does seem lovely, though,' Katie tacked on. Finding people lovely was her default position.

Beth nodded. Of course. If your children weren't friends, then you weren't all that likely to know the mother well. It almost felt disloyal, being chummy with someone who'd produced a child who your own special boy or girl, blessed with innate perfect taste, wasn't keen on. Jessica and Jake hadn't initially been big pals, but as Beth and Jen had grown closer, the children had too. In fact, Jessica was the only girl Jake really liked. After a certain age, kids tended to play more with their own side, as it were. This would continue for a few years until the two sexes spectacularly coincided again with a bump, in the teenage years – an event widely dreaded by mothers for a whole variety of reasons.

'Jen really is lovely. She had a hard time when Jessica's dad upped and left. She was on her own, but made it work. Then all of a sudden, Ted appeared,' explained Beth.

'Yes, I remember that,' said Katie.

Beth wasn't surprised. It had caused quite a stir in the playground when Ted had first trooped up with Jen to pick up Jessica. They'd been hand in hand, Jen wreathed in a Ready Brek glow of sexual contentment that was hard to ignore – and difficult not to envy a little, if you were either in a long-running

Dulwich marriage, with all that entailed, or single in a wintry sort of way like Beth.

The effect of this unveiling had been an intense level of scrutiny and speculation from the mums, which hadn't let up even when Jessica had been safely scooped up and led away that day. The fact that the little girl seemed entirely happy with the arrangement, not resentful or jealous of her mother's new love interest, was chalked down as a big tick for Ted, who'd clearly taken time to win over the entire mother-and-daughter package.

Ted's shock value had dwindled, slowly but surely, as he became a fixture and as Jen's aura subsided from radioactive to normal levels of contentment. That wasn't to say he didn't have his flirtatious fans. Once it became known that he was great at DIY, a fair few radiators burst around the parish, and Jen was invited to double the usual number of coffee mornings in hopes that she'd tell her spellbound audience more about her dating triumph. Jen took it all with good grace, knowing that living vicariously was a sport played to Olympic levels locally.

'Have you seen her recently in the playground? Something's a bit adrift.' Beth frowned at her coffee. It was so hot it burnt her tongue.

'Haven't seen her for ages. Jessica always seems to be in the classroom already by the time we get there.'

'Her dad's been dropping her off and picking her up a lot; she's been staying with him loads,' said Beth, raising her eyebrows. Everyone disapproved of Jen's ex, Tim Patterson. It wasn't just that he'd run off with someone else – that happened; look at Janice. But he'd tried to keep his options open for years, stringing along two women and lying determinedly to both to keep his ménages on track.

Jen had taken him back several times and had her hopes dashed, until she'd finally drawn a line under the whole episode. Even then, there had been toe-curling scenes at the school gates, in front of Jessica, when he'd cried and begged to be allowed home 'for the sake of his daughter'. For a sensible, no-nonsense woman like Jen, it had been agony, and what it had done to Jessica was anyone's guess.

'I really felt for her over all that stuff with her ex. God, that wasn't great,' Katie remembered.

'She really didn't deserve all that. Tim was an utter tosser to her, kept promising it was all over with the other woman, then she'd find receipts for hotel breakfasts for two when he swore he was on lonely business trips...'

'I don't really understand why a man would do that. Why go to the lengths of promising you'll change and all the rest of it, and then *still* keep on seeing the other woman? He must have known he was bound to be caught out.' Katie looked genuinely perplexed.

Beth rolled her eyes. 'Sometimes people seem to think they can just get away with things. Do you remember when the boys were little, if we were playing hide and seek, they'd hide behind their own hands and be really surprised when you saw them? Some men don't seem to grow out of that at all. It's really odd, isn't it? Especially when Jen's so clever, and you can't fool her for a minute.'

'Maybe he liked the excitement of walking the tightrope between the two of them,' Katie suggested.

'Maybe he was scared of both of them, more like. He probably told Jen what he thought she wanted to hear when he was with her, but was too weak to refuse when the other woman wanted to see him.' They looked at each other, realising this might well be the closest they'd come to understanding the pattern.

'A cake-and-eat-it situation.' Katie nodded.

'And let's face it, who doesn't want more cake?' Beth smiled. 'Do you think our boys will be like that?'

'Of course not,' said Katie, shocked. 'We're showing them a better way.'

'Well, you are, with your lovely stable marriage,' said Beth. 'But I'm not sure what my life is showing Jake. I'm on my own, my mum is too. Look at his Uncle Josh – no sign of him ever settling down, unless a very large shotgun is pressed to his head. And even then, he'd somehow get on the next plane to a major crisis and escape again. My brother, the commitment Houdini.'

Katie gave Beth a meaningful glance. 'You've just come up with yet another reason why it's time for you to get out there and date, you know.'

Beth snorted. 'All right, all right. But can we stick to dissecting someone else's relationship this morning? Seriously, I'm worried about Jen. That whole business with Tim was why it was so lovely when Ted first came along...'

'I know you, Beth. Sounds like there's going to be a "but".'

'You're right. *But* something seems to have happened. Something I can't put my finger on. Something's gone wrong.'

'Have you tried asking her about it?'

'No! It's one thing asking strangers intrusive questions when I really need to know the answer, you know, like those times we've had recently. But personal stuff? With someone I know? It's so tricky. You know me. I'd rather go to Belinda McKenzie's next Valentine-themed dinner party, and you know what they're like.'

Even Katie looked shocked at the thought of Beth at one of those. It was typical of Belinda to have hijacked a private, and possibly even romantic, occasion and made it an annual extravaganza of red roses and fairy lights that could be seen from Crystal Palace.

'Actually, I went to her last one and it was really fun,' Katie confessed sheepishly. 'Michael was thrilled; it let him off buying a card. Belinda had done everything, and we all went home with party bags with heart-shaped pralines and those little Love

Heart sweets. I really don't think you'd have liked it. We had to play those Mr and Mrs quiz games and guess each other's partner blindfold, which was a bit odd. But seriously, if you think Jen's not happy, shouldn't you just ask?'

'You're absolutely right, I really should. But they've only just got married. I don't feel I *can* just come out with it. They can't really have problems, can they? So early on? And is it really any of my business if they have?'

'Well no, but when has that ever stopped you?' said Katie, smiling. 'But listen, I didn't come here to fret about poor old Jen. What about you?'

'What *about* me?' blanked Beth.

'Come on, Beth. You know exactly what I mean. The dating. How are you getting on? If you get lucky, you could even bring your new man to Belinda's next Valentine soirée.'

'Well, that's definitely put me off the whole idea.' Beth laughed, and took a long swig of coffee. Thank goodness, it had reached drinkable temperature now. 'And besides, didn't we just agree not to talk about it?'

Katie smiled, but gave Beth a long look. She wasn't about to let her friend off the hook. Beth sighed. 'You know, I'm really not sure if it's for me.'

'Come off it, Beth. You can't chicken out now. You're braver than that, I know that much for sure. Give me your phone and let's have a look.'

'Um, I may have deleted it.'

'*You've deleted Tinder?*' Katie's squawk was loud enough to grab the attention of the few customers scattered around, munching surreptitiously on Jane's delicious sausage rolls or grabbing a quick coffee in peace.

Beth, scarlet, withdrew completely behind her fringe as all eyes converged on their table. All that could be seen was the mulish straight line of her mouth, and two cross grey eyes glaring at her friend through a curtain of hair.

'Sorry, sorry,' Katie said, leaning forward and whispering to placate her friend. 'But you shouldn't have done that! You haven't even got started.'

'I know. But it's what I found,' said Beth, twisting uncomfortably in her seat. 'I was looking at it one evening and I saw *Ted* on there.'

This wasn't strictly the reason she'd given up on Tinder. She'd finally removed the icon from her phone several days later, when she'd realised that, for all her flicking through, she had no intention ever of swiping right. But she'd been meaning to tell Katie about the Ted business anyway. And it certainly got the desired result.

'No! Ted was back on Tinder?'

'Back on it? You mean that's how he met Jen in the first place?'

'Well, I just assumed. I think it's the thing everyone uses nowadays, isn't it? Though I'm no expert.'

That was the trouble, thought Beth. People her age were out of the loop on all that stuff. Well, certainly if they were in relationships or happy enough on their own.

'That's what I've been wondering. Do you think I should mention it to Jen?' said Beth, crinkling her nose at the very idea.

'Well. *There's* a question. It's one thing asking lightly if everything's OK, it's a whole other thing to say, "Actually, did you know your husband is on Tinder?" What would that do to the marriage? And do you know what he was up to on it?'

'It just said he was "active". That sounds bad enough, but according to some of the reception staff at school, that could just mean going on his profile without, you know, arranging anything.'

'So I should hope! But he shouldn't be on it at all, should he? Let's face it, the only thing he should be doing with Tinder these days is deleting it, pronto. Poor Jen.'

'You won't breathe a word, will you? I can't decide what to do, but I'd hate it to get out.'

Katie sat back, a little affronted. 'When, in all the time you've known me, have you ever heard me gossip?'

Beth smiled widely. 'Well, there was that time when Belinda's au pair-before-last put hair removal cream in her shampoo...'

'Oh yes. But that was different. It was funny. This really isn't. But maybe we're reading too much into it. Maybe he was just on it to get rid of it, and that shows up?'

'Maybe,' Beth agreed but, much though she wanted to believe that, something told her there was more to it. 'So, you think I shouldn't say?'

Katie stirred her cappuccino for a moment, considering. 'It's so hard, isn't it? You don't want to be responsible for causing a huge rift. And what if it's something completely innocent? Then you'll have interfered for no reason, and she might not forgive you for that. On the other hand, if he is on Tinder and hooking up with people, then she definitely ought to know.'

'I wish I'd never downloaded the bloody thing in the first place. I knew dating was a really bad idea,' said Beth glumly.

'Wait a minute, you can't lump these two things together. The whole thing with Jen, that's a mess. But *you* should definitely get back out there, no question.'

'What? When there's men out there like Ted, who seem fine but are trying to cheat the moment your back is turned?'

'Well, we don't know that. And you wouldn't pick a man like Ted anyway, not in a million years.'

'So you think there's something funny about Ted, too?'

Katie paused. 'I suppose I do. I'd never thought about it before, and Jen has seemed so happy. But I always felt, well, maybe that he was too good to be true? Do you know what I mean?'

'The way he just slotted right in, and was so great with

Jessica? That's really a shame if we find that suspicious. But you're right. It all seemed very neat. And so fast. One minute she was single, like me; the next minute they were married. And now this, with the app. And before you even say it, it's not that I'm just a bit cross that the only other single person in Dulwich found someone.'

'Beth! I'd never say that. I hadn't even thought it. You've had your reasons for being on your own, the circumstances were completely different for you and you haven't been ready. But over the past few months, well, I've thought you might be moving on a bit.'

Beth studied Katie carefully. This was interesting. Did she want to know more? She decided to risk the question. Head on one side, she asked, 'What makes you think that?'

It was Katie's turn to think for a moment, clearly weighing up the pros and cons of honesty. Beth knew that one of her flaws was being prickly, but although she was already feeling wary about what was coming next, a little corner of her psyche was alarmed that even her best friend didn't dare offend her. Was she really that oversensitive?

'Maybe someone should say it, and no one's closer to you than me...' Katie said tentatively. 'Well, here goes. Don't shoot me, but that policeman—'

'What about him?' Beth snapped, sitting up a little straighter, trying to resist an overpowering urge to leap to her feet and rush straight out of the café, trampling any stray toddler or nanny in her way.

'I said keep calm! There just seemed to be a little... something, that's all. On both sides. There, I've said it now. Don't be angry.' Katie held her hands wide and looked imploringly at Beth. 'I really think he likes you. And you, well... I think you might like him a bit, too.'

Beth took a deep breath and felt her racing heart calm down just a little. She gripped her hands round the sides of her chair and the reassuring feel of the wood, solid and smooth, made her feel more grounded and a bit less panicky.

'I'm sorry I'm so frightening. I'm not angry. It's just that... it's complicated. I feel guilty about James. I know it's been a long time, in your eyes, but to me it's all still yesterday. Or maybe the day before yesterday, now. And then there's Jake. And then the policeman, well, *Harry*, he's always shouting. James and I never shouted. I don't know if I want to argue all the time, and I don't want Jake to see me in that sort of relationship. And anyway, I haven't heard from him since that whole business with Matteo, ages ago now. It's just, you know, a lot.'

For Beth, it was a very long speech. It left her flushed and pink. Katie looked at her with a fond smile. 'So, you're not denying the spark bit?' she said impishly, head tilted slightly to one side.

'Hmm. Isn't it your turn to get the coffees?' said Beth, suddenly aware of her flaming cheeks. There was a tinny beeping noise. 'Oh, that's my phone.' She fished it out of the depths of her bag, and studied the screen for a calming few moments longer than she needed. It was a text from Jen, saying they were on for a cup of tea that afternoon. 'Looks like I might have a chance to find out what's going on with Ted later,' said Beth, and the conversation was successfully turned.

SIX

Sitting in traffic later on, inching over to Jen's where a cup of tea had her name on it, Beth wondered exactly how on earth she was going to broach the more-than-ticklish subjects of dating and infidelity. She had parked the question of her own feelings for Inspector Harry York, to return to at some very long-distant moment when she had nothing else pressing on her mind. Which, as she well knew, was quite likely to be never.

As soon as Ted opened the front door and ushered Beth in, with an affectionate kiss and hug, she realised that any deep discussion with Jen just wasn't going to happen today. Ted showed no signs of disappearing off upstairs to work this time, and was positively bouncing with bonhomie.

He led her straight through to the stylish little kitchen where Jen was pottering about. To Beth's relief, her friend seemed happy and smiley today, with no trace of the slight tension she'd detected on previous visits. Perhaps whatever had gone awry had been straightened out.

Ted had a new project on the go, they explained – getting the garden in order. It was badly in need of taming, Ted said with one of his stage frowns. While Jen had been brilliant at keeping everything moving as a single mum, she had never embraced her inner Alan Titchmarsh, even when she'd lived in Dulwich. Beth couldn't really remember ever seeing what lay beyond the kitchen windows here in Camberwell, and had never ventured outside.

The scrubbed pine table was heaped with books on garden design and the back door was open, Jen's little tabby cat Meow lurking rather anxiously on the threshold. She didn't look too keen on having her exclusive domain invaded by Ted. The tangle of shrubs beyond was hard to make out in the gathering dark. Though it wasn't even five o'clock yet, it was promising to be a gloomy evening, with the sort of autumnal mistiness in the air that made you shiver. Despite that, Ted insisted on taking Beth outside to explain the plan while Jen put the kettle on.

'So, there'll be a line of beds here, we'll do away with all that overgrown stuff,' he said, waving at what looked like a forest shielding the garden from the neighbours. 'And here at the end,' he said, striding away into the darkness, 'will be the pièce de résistance.'

'Ted. Ted,' came Jen's anxious voice from the house. 'Be careful of the pit. Don't take Beth down there.'

Something in Jen's voice made Beth stand stock-still. Pit? What did she mean? Unearthing her phone from her jeans pocket, Beth quickly flipped on the torch mode and played the greenish light over the tussocky damp grass, studded with a couple of mysterious dark shapes which revealed themselves to be forlorn, deflated footballs, mouldering like windfalls. Maybe they belonged to whoever had owned the place before Jen. Otherwise, there was nothing much to see, except a narrow but surprisingly long and wild garden stretching all the way down to a high wall, beyond which must be the railway track running to Denmark Hill. Yes, suddenly she heard the chug-chug of a train passing, gathering speed to a metallic scream, wheels grating on the rails. Ted was right at the end of the garden now, rooting about near the high concrete wall.

Suddenly Jen was at her elbow.

'Glad you didn't go all the way down. There's a dirty great hole at the bottom of the garden. That's one of the reasons I hate it,' she whispered. 'I don't really want Jessica out here. I even worry about the cat. Come on, let's go inside.'

Beth followed Jen back to the house, glad to return to the brightness and warmth of the kitchen and to sit at the table, warming her hands round a very welcome mug of tea. The ankles of her jeans were unpleasantly damp from the wet grass, and she felt herself blaming Ted.

'What *is* this pit? I don't understand,' she asked.

'Oh, it's not really a pit exactly, I just call it that to make it sound less intriguing to Jess. It's actually an old bomb shelter. An Anderson shelter, you know?'

'Really, left over from the Second World War? That's rather amazing.'

'Ha, that's the historian talking. I should have known you'd love it. You'll have to come round in the daytime, and have a proper look. You can't see a thing when it's dark like this. Honestly, it's a death trap. I can't wait for Ted to sort it out. He's great at stuff like that, so practical.'

'It must be brilliant to have someone around who can do all that,' said Beth, thinking that if she ever did really get going on Tinder, which would now involve the added bore of downloading the app again, it would be to find a handyman as much as a lover. Could you specify you wanted someone who had his own spirit level and knew how to use it? That reminded her, unfortunately, of the difficult subject she needed to tackle.

Just as she was about to say, 'Talking of dating...' Ted burst in through the garden door, his chunky jumper festooned with bits of twig and leaf from all his rummaging, his jeans wet, too. Jen jumped up to brush off his shoulders, smiling indulgently at a pile of detritus which would have had Beth tutting and vacuuming in her own home, as he wandered off to change. Jen was obviously a lot more understanding with messy males than she was. Beth instantly felt a flash of guilt for all her nagging of Jake to wipe his feet and wash his hands. Not that he seemed terribly scarred by it, as he never took a blind bit of notice.

Jen slid a casserole into the oven and they sat chatting for a few minutes, as the rich smells of beef and tomatoes started to tickle Beth's nose and remind her that she still needed to pick up Jake and organise their own supper.

'Jessica with her dad again?' she asked Jen. She thought a touch of sadness passed her friend's face as she nodded.

Ted, sauntering back into the room in sweatpants and another comfy sweater, slapped a hand down heavily on his wife's shoulders. 'Yes, she's got it easy. Just me to look after tonight.'

'Surely you'll be looking after Jen, too?' said Beth lightly.

Ted frowned for a second before sitting down heavily, stretching his legs out wide under the table and ostentatiously looking at his watch. 'Sun over the yardarm yet? What do I have to do to get a drink round here?'

'Oh, time for me to be on my way,' said Beth, jumping to her feet.

'Can't you stay for a quick one?' said Jen.

'Driving, and late as usual,' said Beth ruefully. 'But I'd love another cup of tea next week, if it suits you and you're not busy?'

'Course, I'll look forward to it,' Jen was saying, when there was a crash from Ted's side of the table. He'd been moving the tower of gardening books, and one had caught the edge of Beth's mug and sent it flying. Luckily, the tea was almost all gone, but the china cracked into three neat pieces on the patterned tiles.

Jen ducked down to pick the bits up. Beth got up to help

her, but once Ted had leapt up as well and was getting out two plates and glasses, the little kitchen seemed full to bursting.

'Listen, you've got your hands full, I'll leave you two to it, I've got to rush anyway,' she said.

Jen, who'd ducked into the cupboard under the sink to get out a floor cloth to wipe up the splashed tea, smiled at her and started to get up to see her to the door. But Ted, laying the table with a clatter, called out, 'Yep, just let yourself out. See you soon, Beth.'

She clicked the door shut and trailed up the street to her car, a tiny frown on her face as she zapped the lock with her key and slid into place behind the wheel.

* * *

The next morning, by dint of setting her phone ten minutes earlier than usual and putting their entire morning routine on fast-forward, Beth had pulled off the monumental feat of getting to the playground early. Once his initial surprise at not trailing in after everyone else had worn off, Jake quite enjoyed the feeling of being first on the equipment and lord of all he surveyed. Beth, hanging about on her own in the morning chill and glancing at her watch every five seconds, wondered if all the effort had been in vain.

But just as she was cursing herself and her bright ideas, Jessica burst into the playground at a run, spotting Jake and making straight for him over on the slide.

Beth craned her neck to see if she could see Tim. Sure enough, there he was, just loping away into the distance. With his gangly, slightly stooped figure and hangdog air, it was very hard to believe that this was the lothario who'd had two Dulwich women on the go at the same time. Heartbreakers came in all sorts of packages, Beth thought with a mental shrug, and to be fair, Tim wasn't facing stiff competition. The daddies all seemed to relax visibly once they'd snared their life partner, reproduced and got mortgaged up to the hilt. They developed comfortable paunches, bald patches and entrenched opinions about the niftiest route round the South Circular before you could say Jeremy Clarkson.

She shouted a quick farewell to Jake, who barely took any notice of her, and sprinted out of the gate, catching up with Tim just as he made to cross the road up to Calton Avenue. He was in a suit, a smart but dull tie slightly askew, under a battered khaki raincoat.

'Fancy seeing you here,' said Beth, a little pink in the face.

Tim, who'd been minding his own business, waiting for the lights to change, started visibly, his glasses slipping a little on a long, thin nose, sandy eyebrows raised in alarm, face becoming slightly mottled. It had been months, if not years, since one of the mothers had addressed him.

'Er, just dropping off Jess,' he said tentatively, as though he were being accused of something.

'It's great that you're around so much for her at the moment,' said Beth, nodding to signal her sudden approval of Tim and all his doings.

Though seeming a little taken aback, he immediately started to smile with a bit more confidence. It apparently didn't take much to restore him to his usual unwarrantedly high opinion of himself. Perhaps it was this that women found strangely attractive.

'Just helping out, you know. While Jen is so snowed under with this huge work project. I like to do what I can,' he said, shifting his battered laptop case from under one arm to the other. He had the faintest twinge of a Scottish accent.

'Fantastic that you can really give her a hand,' said Beth, marvelling that the man believed he was bestowing a huge favour on Jen by pitching in with his own childcare arrangements for a change.

'Yep, well, she's working twenty-four/seven at the moment. Luckily, Babs – that's my, er, partner – is fine with getting Jess from the after-school club.'

Right, thought Beth. The whole of the school knew Babs – by reputation anyway – and the word that Jen had often used to describe her, in turbulent pre-divorce days, was definitely not 'partner'. It looked as though Tim was actually only doing the daily drop-off, and lumbering Babs with pick-up and presumably entertaining Jess until her dad got home. Not quite as heroic an effort as he thought.

Beth wondered if Babs, who from memory was mid-thirties, childless and rather Amazonian, was enjoying having sole custody of Tim these days, with all that it suddenly entailed.

She also wondered what on earth Jen's terribly important IT project was. There'd certainly been no signs of flat-out striving last night, unless it was over Ted's garden revamp. Beth knew that Jen's workload could suddenly get intense – as a freelancer herself, she was well aware that it was impossible to turn down commissions for fear one would never be asked again – but Jen hadn't seemed at all busy last night. And last week, hadn't she just gone off on a little midweek jaunt with Ted? She'd never do that with deadlines looming.

As Tim chuntered on about his own job at one of the large accountancy firms in the city, Beth suddenly saw the light. Jen, fed up with Tim's years of perfidy and his constant weasel-like behaviour, was merely playing him at his own game, getting a bit of free childcare and a break into the bargain. But a break from her beloved daughter? They'd always been inseparable, as close as any mother and daughter she'd seen. To Beth, lying to Tim seemed fair enough, in the circumstances – a little bit of payback for all that had gone before. Sidestepping her own daughter was odd, though. There was no escaping it. There was definitely something up with Jen.

. . .

The thought nagged at her throughout the morning at work, but Beth was honest enough with herself to know that probably meant she was just trying to avoid thinking about something else. In this case, she was pretty certain it was what she was beginning to call the Dating Issue.

She had a lot of problems with the whole idea, but there was one stumbling block above all that she really couldn't clamber over. Meeting someone online was so unromantic. All the great love stories featured a 'meet-cute', where the heroine was spurned by the hero at a ball, or spotted him playing piano in a bar and couldn't get him out of her mind. Her own story was nearly as good as they came. She'd first met James at sunset, on Blackfriars Bridge, when she'd dropped a satchelful of papers and he'd helped her scurry about and gather them up before they blew into the Thames.

Waterloo Bridge would have been even better. For her, it had the finest view in the world, with the London Eye and the Oxo Tower, the South Bank and National Theatre, all lit up like showgirls on a night out. It had also had a song written about it. But she'd take Blackfriars; it had been quite magical enough for her.

She'd had an awful day at the newspaper she'd then worked for, being shouted at by the news editor for getting scooped on a story by a rival. But meeting this kind stranger had turned that, and the rest of her life, around. It couldn't have been a more promising beginning. She'd been a damsel in distress, he'd definitely been her knight in shining armour, and the little thank-you drink she'd insisted on buying him in a seedy bar on The Strand – an act of very uncharacteristic boldness on her part – had led to all this. And to Jake.

'I swiped right as soon as I saw him' just wasn't going to cut it. It was hardly a story to regale the grandchildren with.

On the other hand, when did she ever meet a single man? Everyone in the vicinity was taken, and she couldn't remember the last time anyone had even looked at her in that certain way.

Although a little voice in her head did keep squeaking, 'What about when Harry York walked into Wyatt's on the day of the murder, and everything seemed to stand still?'

That had certainly been one of the most memorable mornings of Beth's life. Though whether that was because it had involved a freshly slaughtered corpse, or the commanding figure of Inspector York – his blond hair ruffled and the collar of his peacoat turned up – she couldn't say. He'd definitely given her a few smouldering looks over the course of their acquaintance. But mostly when he was livid. He'd also given her some glances that suggested strangling was much too good for her, and done his fair share of shouty-crackers yelling as well, which she definitely wasn't at all keen on.

No, things had never got off the ground with York, which was a shame, because Jake had thought he was marvellous – until the last outbreak of shouting, anyway. And he'd seemed to be fond of the boy in return. York did look as though he might actually be capable of doing DIY as well.

But it was no good thinking about him. That window, if it had ever even been open a crack, was now firmly closed and thoroughly double-glazed over. It was ages since their last encounter, and it was extremely unlikely they'd ever run into one another again. She certainly wasn't about to bump anyone off to get his attention, put it that way.

The sad truth was that if Beth wanted to date, she'd just have to stop hoping for romance, and approach the whole thing in a more matter-of-fact way. That might mean some of the twinkly magic was gone, but it might just help her to get the job done. Then maybe everyone would get off her back.

With a new, professional attitude, Beth strode off at lunchtime to get more help from her guru, Janice. As she'd hoped, Lily and Sam were already in the staff dining room, munching away at the excellent sandwiches and chatting animatedly, and they told her Janice was on her way. As soon as she plonked her tray down, Lily asked her, 'So? How's it going?'

'Yeah, great thanks, you?' she said.

'Yes, yes, but how about the dating? Met anyone?'

'Well, not yet. It's early days, isn't it?'

'Not really, Beth. You can get a date in minutes on Tinder. How long have you had the app, exactly?' said Sam.

Under this sort of scrutiny, Beth started to blush. 'To be honest, girls, I've had a tiny bit of a setback.'

'What happened? Not a pervert? What was he, a boob man?' Sam leant in to get all the details.

'Toe-sucker?' said Lily understandingly.

'No, *no*! Does that happen? God, I hadn't even thought to worry about *that sort of thing* yet,' said Beth, shrinking away in alarm. 'Although I suppose the problem is a bit foot-related. But it's mine that are the trouble.'

The girls looked at her blankly.

'Well, they just got a bit cold,' said Beth, laughing delightedly at her own joke, then realising no one else was joining in.

The pause that followed told her she was definitely on a different humour wavelength from the two girls. They finally smiled weakly, then started to remonstrate with her. 'But you've got to go on, Beth! You never know. The perfect man could be on there right now, and you're missing him.'

'Well, yeees,' said Beth, about to reveal her new resolution to plough on no matter how unconvinced she was that Mr Right was lurking in her phone. But she didn't get a chance. Both women started to speak at once, just as Janice sat down.

'What's all this?' she asked, looking from girl to girl.

'Beth's only chickening out of Tinder,' said Sam with a shrug.

'I'm not, I'm just... regrouping,' said Beth. 'I admit, I did temporarily delete the app, yes, but...' She started to explain, but was drowned out again. 'Look, don't worry, I can get it back,' she said.

'You certainly can,' said Janice, unceremoniously taking Beth's phone and stabbing away at it. 'Here we go,' she said. Magically, Tinder descended from the Cloud, and the icon popped back up on Beth's phone.

'That's much better, isn't it?' said Janice, as though a life-threatening crisis had been averted.

'Honestly, I don't know why you're all so bothered – though it's lovely that you are,' Beth added quickly.

'We just want you to have a happy-ever-after. None of us grows out of that, do we?' Janice said, while Lily and Sam nodded sagely.

'Do you think we actually get brainwashed by all those fairy stories, or do you think we'd want that ending innately anyway?' Beth, who'd adored Cinderella as a child, and felt she'd got her version of the story with James, always wondered how deep the programming really went. Was it her biological destiny she was after, or a Disney story? Both were equally beguiling, that was the trouble.

Janice, Sam and Lily just looked at her as though she were mad.

'Look, it's nearly time to get back to work. Let's not worry about all the whys and wherefores, let's just try and get you a date,' said Janice firmly. 'It's all very well you uploading the app again. But you've been there, done that. Now you need to stop playing about and actually pick someone to talk to, doesn't she, girls?' she appealed to her sisters in crime. Lily and Sam agreed fervently.

'Oh, it'll take ages to redo my profile...' Beth prevaricated.

'Oh no it won't,' said Janice, inexorable as a panto dame. 'If you've just restored it, then it'll all still be there from before. Look,' she said triumphantly, opening up Tinder and waving the phone around. 'Now, let's find someone really *good.*'

'Don't you mean really *bad*?' said Sam with a wink.

'Absolutely not, not the first time anyway,' said Janice reprovingly. 'And remember, Beth, you're just going for a coffee. It's like an interview, really, to see whether you like each other and whether it's worth going on an actual date.'

'You mean I've been hesitating and hesitating, and it's not even real dating at all, just some sort of pre-selection process?'

'Well, exactly,' said Janice. 'Absolutely nothing to be scared of, is there, girls?'

Was Beth imagining it, or did Janice give Lily and Sam a swift warning glance? If she did, it worked, and both girls were suddenly nodding vigorously. 'Couldn't be easier.' 'Nothing to it,' they chorused.

'All right then,' said Beth tentatively. 'Who do you think looks nice?'

'Well, that's up to you, honey. One man's meat, and all that,' said Janice with a twinkle, knowing full well that in her own husband she'd got the whole of Dulwich's favourite prime cut.

'Hmm,' said Beth, scrolling. 'I don't know. They all look, sort of, I don't know... needy.'

'Well they are, of course,' said Sam smartly. 'They need *you*.'

Beth looked up at her, but Sam's expression was so innocent that she let it go. 'Well, I suppose this one looks sort of OK,' she said tentatively, showing the screen to the others.

Immediately, a chorus went up. 'Not him!'

'Why on earth not? He doesn't look too bad – all his own teeth, look at that smile.'

'Well, yes, but...' Lily winced.

'The thing is...' said Sam.

'He's not bad-looking, though, is he?' said Beth, surprised at the lack of enthusiasm.

'*Not bad-looking*? Do you know who that is, Beth?' said Janice, sounding a little exasperated. 'Oh come on, don't you recognise Ryan Gosling when you see him? Someone's just using his picture. You can bet he looks nothing like that at all.'

'Oh,' said Beth, deflated. 'That explains why I actually thought he was quite attractive. I should go to the movies more. The only things I see now are superhero films with Jake. He's ten,' she explained apologetically to Sam and Lily. 'I don't think I've seen a man who isn't wearing a mask and a Lycra bodysuit for years.'

'Well, you can probably find loads just like that on Tinder,' said Sam. 'Joking!' she added swiftly. 'We should go on a girls' movie night, refresh your cultural references a bit. But that's only *after* you've done a bit of dating.'

Why did Beth feel as though she was being made to do a painful bit of homework, with no treats until she'd finished it to these three strict teachers' specifications? Surely dating was meant to be fun? Or was she just hopelessly old-fashioned about the whole thing? On second thoughts, she didn't really need an answer to that. It was quite obvious she was stuck in some sort of Jurassic dating past, whereas these women – and probably everyone else she knew – had moved into a sleek cyber-future where the worry was not how you met someone, but whether you liked them enough to progress beyond a hot beverage. Luckily, the bell rang, signalling the daily stampede back to the classrooms after lunch.

'OK, Beth, so next time we meet, you're to have gone on at least one date, and we want to hear every detail,' said Lily.

'That's everything, mind,' said Sam.

Janice lingered a little after the others had rushed away, gathering up her things in a slow and stately fashion and using both hands to push herself up from the table, bump ascending first. 'You know you actually don't have to do this, if you don't want to?' she said, kind as ever. 'But it *is* probably time, isn't it?'

'I suppose it is,' agreed Beth with a sigh, and made her way back to work.

SEVEN

For once, Beth managed to get through loads of work that afternoon – because she had got to the part of her research which revealed much more about Sir Thomas Wyatt's appalling deeds in the colonies. It was such an emotive and difficult issue, and she was determined to handle things carefully. She knew it was her responsibility to draw attention to the topic and display the information in a digestible way, without glossing over its horror.

She was using a rich new source of information about Thomas Wyatt's Caribbean activities, in the form of the ships' manifests from his fleet. This fleet ferried not only coffee and tobacco back to Britain but also, horrifically, snatched people from Africa and dragged them off to the island plantations as slave labour.

It made grim reading, but Beth knew these things needed to come out into the light of day. She was planning to have the original handwriting – the beautiful curling copperplate of Sir Thomas's meticulous head clerk – blown up in size and reproduced on boards, leading visitors round the exhibition space. There weren't many surviving artefacts she could use to punctuate the mass of words, but she'd found pictures of comparable ships, like the tea clipper, *Cutty Sark*, which was in dry dock at Greenwich. They would also have glass cases breaking up the display, containing samples of sugar, coffee and tobacco – Sir Thomas's key money-spinners. These would obviously not be authentic; Beth was planning to stock up on own-label, modern-day versions on one of her trips to the Morrisons in Camberwell. But the fact that commodities like these were now so cheap and plentiful was, in part, due to the heinous activities of men like Wyatt developing trade routes and methods of intensive farming – at huge cost, of course, to those he'd exploited so cruelly.

In another display case she was planning to show replicas of some of the glass beads that, according to the ledgers, were used to entice people onto the ships and into a life of slavery.

She was so engrossed in the sombre, chilling and emotionally demanding work that it was 3.30 p.m. before she knew it. She cantered down the road towards the Village Primary to get Jake, glad to be out in the fresh air, with the blustery day blowing away a little of the miasma of guilt and pity she always felt when dealing with the worst aspects of the Wyatt's archive.

When she got to the playground, only a few minutes late, three-quarters of his class were still milling around but there was no sign of Jake. With a flash of annoyance, she remembered at last that it was his day for extra reading after class. She'd been so wrapped up in work she'd completely forgotten.

Although Jake's previous reading helper had abandoned her post at very short notice, the school had been swift to find a replacement. This time, it was a mother with kids in the lower reaches of the school, who was glad to dip her toes back into employment with a few hours here and there before looking for something more onerous. Beth was, in any case, pretty convinced that Jake no longer needed any extra work on his reading, but as she was paying a fortune for Belinda's tuition, she'd graciously accepted the school's free help when it was offered, and hoped he'd derive some benefit from it. You never knew, it might tip the scales when it came to the much-dreaded entrance exams.

Just as she was deciding what to do with the extra twenty minutes she unexpectedly had on her hands, one of the other mothers sidled up to her. 'Excuse me, are you Jake's mum?' she asked.

Startled, Beth realised that the woman wasn't a mother at all. Rather, it was Tim's partner, Babs. An attractive woman somewhere in her thirties, she had the sort of physique you only got from spending, in Beth's view, far too long in the gym. Babs also had one of those heart-shaped faces she'd always envied, allied to large brown eyes and a smooth and unlined forehead. She was dressed from head to toe in black, but it wasn't the Sweaty Betty leggings and sweatshirt ensemble many of the mums lived in. Instead, she was in chic separates – the sort that women's magazines called a 'capsule wardrobe', which Beth knew she would be incapable of mustering, even if her life depended on it. A beautiful teal cashmere scarf was looped round her neck in an oh-so-casual fashion that looked as though it had taken months to achieve. Add a small and classy handbag, definitely not big enough to stuff a school project into at the last moment, and it couldn't be any clearer that this woman's uterus had never been brought low by a passenger.

'Yep, that's right, I'm his mum,' said Beth, a little wary. For a long while, Babs had been spoken of as pretty much the Antichrist. Playground chatter condemned Tim, Jessica's father, as weak and indecisive – but then he was a man. The real villain of the piece, as far as many of the mums were concerned, was always the Other Woman. She had knowingly lured a father away from his child, and broken Jen's heart into the bargain.

Beth looked around to see who would be watching her

consort with the enemy. But then she thought, what the hell? It was all ages ago now. Jen was safely remarried – she hoped – and they all had to move on. She smiled at the woman encouragingly.

It was all Babs needed. She edged closer, no longer seeming worried that she might get a sharp kick in the shins, and smiled a little tremulously in return.

'It's just that I'm waiting for Jess, and there's been no sign of her.'

'Oh, I'm doing the same with Jake. I completely forgot he was doing extra reading after school today. I still haven't got used to the new timetable,' Beth said, rolling her eyes. 'Is Jess doing extra reading, too?'

'I don't *think* so, but she could be, I've no idea. There doesn't seem to be anyone around to ask...'

'No, the teachers do all scarper the moment they can, unless they're on duty. And they tend to keep a bit of a low profile even if they are.' Beth didn't blame them. She'd hide, too, rather than being held at bay by a mass of mummies, all with very particular concerns about their own darling offspring and no interest at all in the teacher's personal space or anyone else's child. 'Have you tried asking Tim?'

'He's in a meeting,' said Babs miserably. 'I don't really know what to do. I don't mind waiting, but if I don't know how long for... The car's in a bit of a dodgy parking spot, you see.'

Beth sympathised. The parking situation was the pea beneath the feather bed of life in Dulwich. People bought more cars all the time; it wasn't uncommon for households to have three or sometimes even four, with teenage children and nannies acquiring driving licences and cars with tiresome regularity. And there was never anywhere to put them, except squished bumper-to-bumper on every road, bursting out of every legal bay, piled up on wavy white lines, encroaching on bus stops, and even wandering onto the double yellows. It was like playing Grandmother's Footsteps with the traffic cameras.

Beth thought for a moment. 'Do you want me to give Jen a ring? See if she knows?'

Babs looked so grateful, Beth thought she might burst into tears of sheer relief. 'Oh, would you? That would be amazing. I'll just go over there, see if I'm getting a ticket...'

Beth nearly told her not to bother – traffic wardens didn't circulate any more, it was all done remotely. But Babs was probably just giving Beth the privacy to ring Jen without being overheard.

Beth dialled quickly, taking a swift glance around the playground, just in case anyone was judging her for helping Babs out. But the press of mothers had thinned, and it was just a few standing around now – parents from Years 1 and 2 who were more indulgent about allowing their kids a last go on the play equipment with their friends before home time. With no homework at all in the lower reaches of school, and with their little prodigies not signed up yet for endless extracurricular stints, they usually had time to kill. And standing chatting in a windswept playground was more fun than watching mind-numbing children's telly at home while defrosting plaice goujons (the closest to fish fingers most Dulwich mums could allow themselves to get) for the kids' suppers.

Beth let the phone ring on, then heard the click that signalled it was going to voicemail. She killed the call, and sent Jen a quick text instead. It was another mystery. If Jen was really up to her eyes in a work project, it was just possible that she wouldn't answer the phone. But most mums were pre-programmed to be extra attentive at school drop-off and pick-up times, even if they weren't on duty themselves. No one wanted a mix-up, and on occasions it did happen.

Just then, one conundrum was solved, as Jess came

barrelling out of the school and ran straight up to Beth, hugging her briefly. 'Where've you been then, missy?' said Beth.

'Had to stay behind and help clear up,' said Jessica with an innocent look which, if she'd been Beth's child, would have been the cue for a vigorous debriefing. Staying late was the closest the cuddly Village Primary got to thumbscrews and the rack for bad behaviour. Jessica wasn't a naughty girl, but there was something to be found out there, if you knew the buttons to press. Luckily for Jess, that was outside Beth's job description. Just then, Babs bustled up.

'Jessica, there you are, I was getting really worried about you,' she said in a slightly high-pitched, stagey voice. It could have been an attempt to cover up her annoyance, or maybe it was her habitual way of communicating with children. Either way, it seemed unsuccessful. Jessica, who'd been so tactile with Beth who she didn't know that well, suddenly switched into ice maiden mode and merely grunted at Babs, striding towards the school gates without a backward glance.

Babs, a little pink, watched her go. 'The joys of stepmother-hood,' she said ruefully, widening her eyes at Beth.

Beth smiled in a slightly non-committal way. She had no doubt it was tough. But wasn't that what Babs had taken on when she'd got involved with a married father? It was easy enough to say that Babs hadn't known quite what she was getting into. As she wasn't a mother herself, she could never have realised how difficult it might be to inveigle herself into the good graces of a hurt child. As Jen's friend, Beth felt a pull to judge her. But, she tried to tell herself, there were always many sides to a story. And she was beginning to think that Jen might be just as good at spinning a yarn as anyone.

'See you soon,' said Babs hopefully. Meeting a reasonably friendly face in the playground seemed to be important to her.

Beth thawed, and gave her a big smile. 'Yep, probably tomorrow. Have a lovely evening.'

Babs scuttled off after Jess, who was now a rapidly retreating form trudging towards the car. As far as Beth remembered, Tim had moved to West Norwood after the split. The extremely pretty, Victorian-terraced marital home in Hollingbourne Road, on the way down into Herne Hill but still close to North Dulwich railway station, had been sold just before Jen's wedding. It had reached a sufficiently good price to provide both the Camberwell coach house for Jen and a 1930s semi for Tim and Babs in Cheviot Road, West Norwood, which they'd been renting before. It wasn't a perfect solution for either side, as each had had to move out of Dulwich proper, but both houses had their charms. Beth had a soft spot for the big bay windows and exuberant, rounded porches of the Cheviot houses, which were on the jolly side of Art Deco – though she'd never say so to Jen, of course.

She mused on what Babs was doing work-wise while she was suddenly having to step in for Jess. Perhaps she was working from home in the afternoons. She wondered how well that would go down with her employer, then realised she wasn't entirely sure what sector Babs was in. It must be something fairly flexible, that was for sure.

Her ruminations were cut off by Jake erupting out of his literacy lesson with all the wildness of a ten-year-old who'd sat still for unfeasibly long stretches of time. Oh great, thought Beth. They were in for a rambunctious night.

EIGHT

Before Beth knew it, another week had been swallowed up and it was Monday all over again. Dropping Jake off had become a bit fraught, as she now had to dodge Tim, who seemed to be timing his trips with Jessica to coincide with hers. As she'd actively sought him out and chatted to him once, he now seemed to fondly imagine that they were best friends.

She sympathised, to an extent. He'd stuck it out for years in solitude as the playground baddie, and the way she'd shown a bit of interest seemed to have convinced him he could finally come in from the cold. But his wheedling poor-me personality was very unappealing. She also worried that, having briefly been at the apex of a love triangle, Tim had somehow convinced himself that he was enormously attractive and that Beth was the latest woman to fall for his charm. He kept favouring her with little winks that made her heart sink and her toes curl. There was also the important consideration that, even though events had moved on, mummies had memories like elephants and she was sure it wasn't doing her reputation any good at all being seen chatting with a man clearly identified as a cheating love rat.

Today, his eyes lit up when he saw her across the crowded asphalt and he started loping towards her. Beth, who was thoroughly fed up with discussing his job – he showed no reciprocal interest at all in her own work, or anything else about her – nodded to him briefly and all but galloped off.

* * *

Tim, who'd picked up a bit of speed when he'd seen that little mum dropping off her boy and had hoped to intercept her by the school gates, looked around frantically, before seeing her crossing the road by the chemist's. There were so many of these other women standing around chatting, getting in his way, as though they didn't have a care in the world. And they probably didn't, he thought angrily. Certainly no bloody job to get off to. Part of him wished he could idle away his days, doing nothing like these squawking parasites. The irony was that they all looked down on him for having done the dirty on Jen. Well, she'd deserved it. Like many of them this morning, she'd totally let herself go after having Jess. Blobby stomach, too tired for sex, nothing but jeans. No man could stand that for long.

Babs, on the other hand... Well. She still knew how to get him going. Always looked the part. Put the effort in. Not an ounce of flab, and stamina like you wouldn't believe, thanks to the gym. Well, she couldn't get there now because of all the childcare, but she had Jess to keep her fit. And though she was always banging on about having a baby of her own, she wasn't going to get one... thanks to his vasectomy. She had no idea he'd had the snip, and he certainly wasn't going to enlighten her.

As long as she didn't discuss her 'infertility problem' with Jen, he was safe. And that was never going to happen, was it? For one thing, Jen was always public enemy number one as far as Babs was concerned, he'd made sure of that. Though he and

Jen had certainly been getting on better lately, there was no reason why Babs should know.

At least Jen'd seen reason over redoing her will. He'd been a bit surprised. She'd remarried that lump of a man, Ted, in seconds flat, and Tim had been sure that would be that, he'd never get his hands on a bigger slice of the capital tied up in the Camberwell house. By rights, a lot more of it was his than hers, but thanks to that cursed divorce lawyer, who would rot in hell if there was any justice in the world, she'd got a whopping fifty per cent. All right, it was what she was legally entitled to, but morally? *Morally* she should be scraping pennies off the pavement.

Anyway, he'd talked to her a fair bit over the past weeks about how she needed to be sure that Jess got everything she was entitled to, how Ted didn't need the money and could look after himself, unlike a little girl. Yadda. To be honest, it hadn't sounded convincing even to his own ears, though he knew he usually had a way with words. But astonishingly, Jen had been receptive and had trotted off to a solicitor's – behind her new husband's back, Tim was sure. Looked like she was starting as she meant to go on – hiding stuff, sneaking around... virtually forcing a man to cheat. Well, Tim didn't care much now he'd got the estate settled.

Where was that little mum, what was her name? Bess? She could move pretty fast on those wee legs if she wanted to, he thought with a harrumph. It was annoying, because he didn't have her phone number and he'd been hoping to lumber her, well, sound her out, to see if she'd take Jess this afternoon. The truth was that Babs was getting a bit fed up with having Jess around so much, bleating about her work, as though her career actually mattered. They might be earning almost the same these days – and that was all due to pushy women's libbers, in Tim's view – but it was obvious to anyone with half a brain who was the breadwinner and who just wasn't. But still, Babs probably did need the odd break from Jessica. She was getting to a tricky age, and he didn't see why this Tess, or Bess or whatever her name was, shouldn't provide some much-needed free childcare. If only she wasn't so nippy. Oh well, he'd get her tomorrow morning.

* * *

As soon as Beth had crossed the road and got safely to Calton Avenue, a long way away from Tim's lone figure, she slowed down, caught her breath and pinged a message over to Jen, asking if there would be a cup of tea going in Camberwell tomorrow. The jaunty tone of her text was designed to disguise two things she was uneasy about.

The first was the wedding present. It now looked pretty tattered when Beth occasionally caught sight of it, stuffed in the Fiat's glove compartment, with an assortment of car detritus like empty sweet wrappers and ageing school notices shoved on top of it. She wished, oh how she wished, she'd remembered it that first time she'd called. Then, it would have been the easiest thing in the world to hand it over. Now, it was downright embarrassing because it was so late, and there either seemed to be a terrible atmosphere or Jen wasn't there at all. She resolved that this time, no matter what was going on, she'd just give them the dratted thing and move on. It was a shame. A present which she'd chosen with a gladsome heart had now become a bit of a millstone. But that wasn't the present's fault, or even her own, Beth realised. There was just something a bit off about the whole situation.

Which brought her neatly to the second issue that was worrying her. She still hadn't got up the courage to mention the Tinder business to her friend. Though she'd been on the app several times in the quiet evenings when Jake was asleep and her freelance work had bored her to a standstill, she'd not seen Ted's profile pop up again. Whether that was because she wasn't looking in the right place, whether he wasn't on it any more, or whether she was just lucky, she didn't really know.

The only certainty was that she still hadn't had the courage to swipe right. Yes, she'd finally seen a couple of guys who weren't completely hopeless. Just listen to me, she thought. *Guys* – that sounds so casual; she was making progress, definitely. She'd even considered sending them a message, fingers hovering over the letters, sentences being constructed in her head. But something was still holding her back.

There'd been a diving board at the Victorian swimming baths her primary school class was bussed to once a week. She'd never been on it. Even at that age, she'd been self-conscious, and once she realised that the overwhelmed teacher didn't really notice if not all the thirty kids in her class were in the water, she'd lingered as long as she could behind the comfortably closed saloon doors of the changing room, occasionally peering out underneath to see what the others were up to. Now, looking back, she was horrified that the teacher had never once carried out a simple head count. He could have left kids behind every week, or some could have drowned, unnoticed, and no one would have been any the wiser. But those were the free and easy days before health and safety and risk assessments. On balance, she was glad that Jake's class trips were more closely supervised than a chain gang of convicts.

Ah, she remembered those swimming sessions. The fierce tang of chlorine in her nostrils, the echoing shouts of the class, the reflections of the water bouncing on the walls, and then the ferocious splash when someone threw themselves off the diving board into the turquoise depths below. Every so often, one of her classmates would freeze on the end of the board, and either exhortations from the teacher, a crafty push from the kid behind, or an ignominious withdrawal shuffling back along the board past braver souls, would mark the would-be diver as a failure.

This was how Beth now saw herself. She knew she should plunge into the dating pool. But part of her was still shivering in the changing room, poised with the horrible, tight, pink rubber cap dragged over as much of her long hair as would fit, not at all convinced that she really wanted to dip even one toe into those chemical waters. Back at school, it had been her friends dragging her out of the cubicle, persuading her to jump in the shallow end with them, who'd helped break her free. But she couldn't expect that now. No one, not even Katie, would want to come on a date with her to hold her hand. No, she needed to face it. She was a grown-up and she had to go it alone.

It was a thought that preyed on Beth's mind all through the day and evening, and was still furrowing her brow as she drove off to Camberwell on the Tuesday to fetch Jake and Belinda's lads. She set off ridiculously early as usual, but it wasn't until she pulled up at Jen's door that she realised she'd never had a reply back from her friend to confirm their cup of tea together. She drew out her phone, stabbed at it, and looked at the text trail. Nope. Nothing. How silly of her not to have checked.

She couldn't believe she'd been caught out again. The first time, she hadn't even texted. This time, she'd done her bit, but just forgotten to check that Jen was OK with the plan, too. She'd been so consumed with her own hypothetical problems that her mind had drifted off concrete schemes for the here and now. She pressed the call button, and held the phone to her ear. It rang and rang. No reply. While she listened, she craned her head through the windscreen to look at the house. No lights visible, windows blank and dark. The street itself was deserted, a scattering of crinkled leaves here and there, the gutters piled with more. It was quite dark already.

What should she do now? Trudging round to the high street didn't really appeal. For once, there was nothing she needed from Superdrug, and if she went to browse just to fill the time, she'd inevitably be tempted by fripperies she could manage without and didn't need to waste money on. The dwindling light meant it would be hard to sit and read alone in the car until the hands of the clock inched round to collection time. And, to her annoyance, she'd left her book at home anyway, so that wasn't even an option.

She weighed things up. She could just go early to the tutor's house and ask to sit there, but then she'd have to start listening to Billy and Bobby's high-spirited chat before they even got in the car for the drive home. She wasn't sure she could face an extra hour of that, which was possibly harsh, but she did have a headache coming on which definitely wouldn't be helped by more time in their boisterous company. Jake seemed to cope with them all right, but he was a boy, and their age to boot.

Maybe, just maybe, Jen had a problem with her phone? Granted, the house looked deserted, but maybe not as dark as some of the others? Was there the faintest glow coming from somewhere? Maybe a light at the back? Her eyes now becoming accustomed to the gathering gloom, Beth peered more closely at Jen's house.

She unbuckled her seatbelt, cracked open her car door and got out onto the pavement, looking up and down the street. It was quiet, dark, and the air had that autumnal tang that betokened Hallowe'en and Bonfire Night just round the corner. She walked up to the front door and rang the bell. As she'd more than half expected, there was no reply, the sound echoing in the empty hall. The house seemed to be breathing with her, waiting. But for what? Beth turned away and was contemplating marching back to her car and finding a café somewhere, when one of Jen's wheelie bins caught her eye. It was out of alignment, a bit further forward than usual, and drew her attention to the garden gate.

Jen's house was semi-detached, with a narrow alleyway running alongside and into her back garden. The house on the other side was the same – another coach house tacked to its neighbour, and with an identical passageway running parallel to Jen's. In Dulwich, these side returns had all but disappeared, their valuable square footage absorbed into extended kitchens, playrooms and garden rooms, adding countless thousands to asking prices. In Camberwell, where budgets tended to be tighter, little places like Jen's had their square kitchen and bathroom boxes tacked on at the back, yes, but the original design was intact in all other ways and the alleyways remained, useful for storing bicycles and bins but not good for much else.

Beth, suddenly feeling very naughty, wondered if she should pop through into Jen's garden just to check if there really was a light on anywhere. Maybe both the doorbell *and* Jen's phone were malfunctioning? OK, she'd actually heard the doorbell reverberating in the hall, but say Jen had had earphones in for some reason? She might be listening to music while doing this 'huge project' that Tim had been banging on about. Beth sometimes did that when she was at home. She could be oblivious to everything when she did.

In fact, Beth remembered only last week she'd been concentrating really hard at the kitchen table, listening to some music, and Magpie had leapt up onto her lap and almost given her a heart attack. Definitely taken years off her life. Was Jen doing that right now? She could be in her kitchen, working away, none the wiser that her friend was getting seriously chilly out here.

It was worth a tiny peek, wasn't it? And better than sitting in her car doing nothing.

Conscious she was probably crossing a line, and half hoping a sturdy lock on the garden gate would put paid to both her wanderings and her wonderings, Beth tiptoed forward. But, far from being securely fastened, the garden gate seemed to give at Beth's first tentative touch. It couldn't have been latched at all, which in itself was a bit odd round here, where burglaries were not exactly unknown. Maybe Ted had forgotten to lock it from the other side?

She moved forward gingerly, once again scanning the street to make sure there was no one clocking this bit of trespass. She didn't want to get mistaken for a burglar herself. But no, everything was quiet. Deserted. The only things moving were the leaves being pushed by desultory eddies of cold air. She strode forward a little more boldly now, and shoved the gate. It swung inwards with an agonising creak of protest. Again, she looked quickly round in case anyone had heard. Nothing. Nobody.

Two seconds later, and Beth was in the silent, narrow alleyway. All was dark and quiet. Shivering a bit, and not just from the afternoon chill, she stepped forward carefully. On one side was the brick wall of the house, and barely an arm's width away was next door's rickety wooden fence. She'd never been down this little passageway before, but it contained everything you'd expect. A couple of ratty-looking brooms, no doubt to sweep the patio area in better weather; the snaked coil of a garden hosepipe; and a metal bucket, catching the few gleams from the street light. An old rounders bat, probably belonging to Jess or left behind by the last owners, lolled nearby. So far, so ordinary. But the narrowness of the pathway made it dark and somehow much creepier. Ridiculous. In daylight, she knew she wouldn't have hesitated to stride down it. But it was a relief when she stepped round to the garden proper. She straightened her spine and looked around.

The mustiness of leaf mould and long, damp, neglected grass was much stronger here, out in the open. Maybe her sense of smell was more acute because of the fading light. The garden was subsumed in that grainy, grey evening darkness, but she could make out far blacker shapes massed at the end, down near the railway tracks, which she definitely wouldn't be investigating. It looked as though Ted hadn't got very far with his garden clearance plans. With a shudder, she remembered Jen's warning last time about the pit.

She turned to the house. She'd been right. Somewhere, deep inside, there *was* a gleam of light; she could see the faintest of glows. Which room was it coming from? The excitement made her abandon caution, and she walked briskly over to the blocky extension, pressing her nose up against the cold glass of the kitchen window and unashamedly peering in.

The light wasn't coming from the hall, or she would have seen it from the front of the house. Nor was it the kitchen, which Beth could dimly see into. There were dishes in the sink, the table cluttered. It certainly didn't look as though they'd gone away. The light was coming from elsewhere. Could it be the sitting room? Jen scarcely used it, preferring to work in the newly decorated kitchen – the heart of her home. Had Beth ever actually been in it? She remembered an undistinguished blue sofa, the usual shelves of books, a tiled fireplace, which no doubt had been described as a delightful original feature when Jen bought the place.

Beth's breath was rapidly misting up the window as she squinted this way and that, trying to work out was going on. She stepped back a little to wipe the condensation down with the sleeve of her coat. Suddenly, a twig snapped somewhere behind her in the dense mass of dripping darkness that was the garden. In the quiet, it was as loud as a gunshot going off. She clutched her chest. Her heart had started pounding. Was it a fox? Or maybe Jen's beloved cat, Meow? She knew from Magpie that sometimes you could see cats' eyes glittering in the darkness. She swung round, suddenly supremely conscious that she really shouldn't be here. But there was no sign of a cat, or anything else. Thank goodness. She turned back again.

Instantly, there was a flurry of movement right behind her. Then pain exploded through her skull, as something hard and heavy connected mercilessly with the back of her head. Her final thought, as she sank to the ground, was that she hoped she wasn't going to be late to pick up the boys.

NINE

Beth looked down at the washed-out blue coverlet and felt a powerful sense of déjà vu. But this time it was her stretched out in a hospital bed, not a lifeless teenager. She moved her head a centimetre to check her surroundings, and pain seemed to pour in on her from all directions. She became aware of a large, uncomfortable bandage on the back of her head, pulling her hair, feeling as big and as unwieldy as a paperback book stuck to her skull. She stopped moving and the contents of her head seemed to settle down, the white-hot stabbing replaced with a dull, regular throb. She was gasping for a drink of water. And the light was so bright.

'Ouch,' she whined, shutting her eyes tightly.

Instantly, she heard the creak of a plastic chair and a large, warm hand came down on hers. She opened her eyes a crack, only to then find them widening so much that *that* hurt as well. 'What... what are you doing here?' she croaked.

'Well, hello to you, too,' said Detective Inspector Harry York of the Metropolitan Police, with a big and – if she wasn't mistaken – extremely relieved smile.

'What happened?' she said faintly. Even the movement of

her jaw sent waves of pain upwards through her head, making her nauseous.

'Here, have a sip of water,' said York, holding out a plastic cup with a straw.

Gratefully she gulped down a little of the lukewarm liquid, trying to angle her head so it didn't hurt so much. It didn't really work. Every time she moved, a new bit of pain prodded her with a sharp stick. She subsided back down onto the pillow, exhausted.

'Wait, did someone pick up the boys?' she said, moving her legs restlessly and looking as though she was going to try to sit up.

'Yes, yes, your friend stepped into the breach. That one with the car like a tank.'

Beth screwed up her eyes. That didn't narrow it down much. Personal space was at a premium where she lived. Once people had bought the largest houses they could manage, with the biggest mortgages they could possibly leverage from the banks, they then bought massive vehicles to match, so they could take their bubble of expensive air with them wherever they went.

'What did she look like?'

'Oh, you know, tall, shiny hair, I think she was wearing white trousers...'

Again, that wasn't really helping. York had just described every woman she knew. Beth tried to think logically who would have caught the ball she'd inadvertently dropped, but her head was hurting again.

'Oh, wait a minute, she was wearing boots. And she had one of those, you know, handbags...'

Beth looked at York through narrowed eyes. Was he doing this just to wind her up?

'...And she was extremely bossy.'

'Belinda.' She sighed with relief. Of course. Billy and

Bobby's mother was the best bet. She'd have been the first person the tutor rang when Beth herself didn't appear.

York nodded. 'All that stuff is being taken care of. Jake's with her tonight. I saw him very briefly and he's absolutely fine. Don't worry about anything.'

The news that Jake was at Belinda's was not good. Yes, it was kind of her to take him. But she couldn't imagine for a second that he'd be having an easy time there. It would all be new, and very unfamiliar. And Belinda would be in the centre of it all. Goodness knew what she'd be saying about what had happened. One thing was for sure, she'd be on the phone all night to every acolyte she had – and there were plenty. Jake was bound to overhear. The last thing she wanted was for him to be worried. She pleated her forehead, and felt the pain radiate again. Her eyes shut. She was too tired even to think about it at the moment.

'What time is it, anyway?' asked Beth fretfully.

'It's nearly three a.m. You were out for a good long while. You gave us quite a scare.'

Beth found herself warmed by the concern in York's face, despite her anxiety. And if it was 3 a.m. – and how had that happened? – then Jake would be asleep. No point worrying about him now. But instantly her mind was buzzing with questions again.

'How did you even get here? Do you have a special Bat phone that rings when something's up in Dulwich?'

York chuckled. 'It feels like that. You know I actually live round the corner from where you were found?'

'No! You live in Camberwell?'

'Lots of people do,' he confirmed with a smile. 'You were very lucky. A neighbour spotted your foot when he was putting his bins out. Gave him quite a turn. Otherwise you could have been there a while.'

Beth closed her eyes again briefly. That wasn't a pleasant

thought. It had been cold enough standing in the garden. Lying unconscious, for who knew how long – it didn't bear thinking about. But wait a minute. 'I'm sure I got hit in the garden, right by the kitchen windows... but it sounds like I was found round by the side gate at the front. They're quite a long way apart.'

York looked thoughtful. Beth was sure there was a lot he wasn't saying. But maybe it explained why her back also felt so sore. Had she been dragged down the passageway? And to what end?

'Try not to think about all that too much,' said York, attempting to sound reassuring. It was not a natural role. He was more used to exhorting people to remember as much as possible, as quickly as they could. 'I suppose it's no use my asking what on earth you were doing round there in the first place?'

'It's a long story,' said Beth uncomfortably, knowing that, again, she'd put herself on the shady side of the law. Just a bit. But all in a good cause. Which reminded her. 'There's no sign of Jen, is there?'

'Jen?'

'Jen Patterson. The friend who lives in that house. I was just checking to see if she was in,' said Beth, knowing it sounded lame.

'There are these things called doorbells, you know,' said York mildly.

'I'd tried the bell. I just wanted to check.'

'Did you have a definite arrangement, then? Is it out of character for her to be away from home without telling you?'

'Well, no, not exactly...'

'Then I fail to see what you were up to?' York was suddenly all business. He was more or less radiating rules and regulations at her, whereas a few moments ago... well, there had been something else entirely in his eyes, Beth realised, though she couldn't say precisely what. 'You could be charged with breaking and entering, you know.'

'You're not serious?' Beth screwed up her face in consternation. That was all she needed.

'Well, in this case, the householder doesn't seem to be around to complain. Luckily for you. But that was a very nasty crack on the head you got. You seem to have a very tough skull. But you need to watch out, Beth.'

'I know, I know,' she said, subsiding into apathy. What would have happened to Jake if she'd been more seriously injured or, heaven forfend, killed outright? He'd be looked after, yes, by her mother and her brother. But they were hardly the dream team. Her mother was in her own very safe little world, and her brother by contrast was always off seeking out danger zones. Neither was what a small boy needed. And that was leaving aside the whole issue of Jake being an orphan. It just didn't bear thinking about.

'Do you know who might want to do this? Any idea at all?' said York, leaning a little closer.

Beth tried moving her head from side to side, and gave it up immediately as a very bad job. 'I've no clue at all. Would it have been a burglar or something like that? Had someone broken into the house?'

'Not that we can tell. It all looks fine. Do you know where the owners are?'

'That's just the thing. They should be there. Or at least Jen should,' Beth said firmly. A little too firmly, as her head started to swim again. And then again, what did she really know about Jen's schedule, anyway? Jen could be anywhere, doing anything, and she had a perfect right to be doing all of it without informing or contacting Beth. Why, then, did she feel so worried? There was something funny going on, of that she was sure.

'Jake's been having tutoring every Tuesday, so I've been going round to Jen's—'

'Tutoring?' said York, his eyebrows going skywards.

'Don't you start,' said Beth limply. 'I've got enough doubts about it myself, without any disapproval from other people. It's just that, well, everybody does it round here...'

'Everybody also drives too fast and drinks too much,' said York censoriously. 'I don't notice you following suit on all the trends.'

Beth winced. She had been known to knock back a Sauvignon or three if she was at a sticky Dulwich dinner party and the talk turned, yet again, to the monumental problem of getting a reliable cleaner for your second home. True, she didn't drive too fast, but only because her car would fall apart at the seams if she edged over thirty miles an hour.

'Jake seems a smart little chap. Does he need extra lessons?' said York.

Beth tried to shrug. 'Well, I don't know. I think he's smart, too. But I just want to give him every chance...' Her voice was getting quieter and quieter, and she was having trouble getting to the end of her sentences. Waves of tiredness competed with the pain, both fighting to carry her away.

'I'd better let you get a bit of rest,' said York, patting her hand. Instantly, Beth's fingers clung.

'Don't go,' she said sleepily. She was in the land of Nod as soon as her eyelashes hit her cheeks. Her hair swung to one side, exposing her high forehead to view. Despite her constant worrying, the lines were smoothed out in an instant as she slept. With her penetrating grey eyes closed, she looked almost as young as Jake, and just as vulnerable. York smiled gently and stayed on.

It was 4 p.m. when Beth next woke up properly. There'd been brief interruptions to her rest, when people had taken her pulse

or given her tablets, but she'd basically slept the clock around,
like a teenager again. As soon as she surfaced, she struggled to
get upright and then waited for the pain to hit her in a wave, as
it had last night. Sure enough, there it was, but it was a little
weaker, as though the tide was turning. Thank goodness.

She looked around for the first time. She was in one of the
rare side rooms of the hospital, King's College by the looks of
things, and already there was a card propped up on the
windowsill with its dispiriting view of the railway track that
must lead to Denmark Hill Station. The card – a folded piece of
A4 with rather aggressive lettering saying 'Get Well' – brought
a lump to her throat. It was from Jake. York must have brought it
with him last night, after seeing Jake at Belinda's.

She wished she could reach out and grab it, see what it said
inside, but after all the pain in the night, she didn't quite dare.
She put her hands up slowly to her head, to feel round the
bandage. It was all pretty sore, but without the catastrophic
aching she'd felt before. Either she was healing fast, or they'd
given her some pretty strong drugs. She gingerly propped
herself up a bit higher on her pillows, which immediately made
her feel more in charge, for the first time in nearly twenty-four
hours. Whoever had done this to her had a lot to answer for.

And who could it have been? She thought back. She'd been
standing with her face literally pressed to the window. God, she
was such a nosy parker. She wished to hell she'd stopped
herself, but curiosity had got the better of her. Again. She could
just imagine Katie saying to her, 'You know what happened to
the cat, right?' Beth sighed. Well, she'd learnt her lesson this
time.

She was closing her eyes and feeling herself drift again –
what was it about an injury that made you sleep so much?
Suddenly there was a minor commotion at the door and Jake
burst in, cheeks red from the cold outside, bounding over to her
and throwing his arms around her in the biggest, untidiest hug

ever. Her eyes filled with tears, which she hastily batted away, reaching down to rumple his dark hair, which looked like it hadn't seen a brush for a week. He smelt so good, just of the crispness of outdoors, of hot little boy, and of not-hospital. How wonderful. He was as good as a million painkillers.

Bringing up the rear was Katie, with Charlie in tow. Katie's own eyes were glittering with unshed tears but Charlie, of course, was just Charlie.

'Wow, cool view of the railway,' he shouted, in what was a normal decibel level for a ten-year-old boy and was borderline eardrum-damaging for anyone over twenty-five in a confined space. Jake didn't need more prompting, but scooted over to the window with his friend, where they oohed and aahed over the trains coming into the station. Katie took a seat at the head of the bed and looked Beth full in the eyes.

'You had us worried.'

It was said gently, but Beth again felt herself tearing up. She put a hand up to her mouth. 'I'm sorry,' she said in a small voice.

'Don't be silly,' said Katie, all smiles again. 'I'm just glad to see you're all right. Or on the way, at least. Have they told you how long you'll be in?'

'I haven't seen anyone, not that I've been aware of, anyway.'

'Want me to try and find out?' said Katie, immediately looking towards the door.

'Just sit here with me for a while. How's it been?' Beth asked, gesturing towards Jake.

The boys were busy at the window, so Katie could say honestly, 'You know, surprisingly OK. Once I'd got over the shock, that is. The first I heard was when Belinda rang me last night.' At this point, Katie's eyebrows rose significantly and Beth could just imagine the conversation, or rather, Belinda's tone of scandalised relish as she passed on all the gory details. 'It was too late by then for me to go over to her place, so I thought

I'd let sleeping dogs lie for the night. I hope you're OK with that?'

Beth nodded. She knew it would have been difficult for Katie. Her best friend was well aware that Beth struggled to get on with Belinda, and managed it mostly by keeping her at arm's length, despite their current Camberwell joint venture. Beth wouldn't have wanted Jake staying there. But nor would she want to involve Katie in a massive tug-of-love by proxy on Belinda's doorstep.

'I completely understand,' she said, closing her eyes as a finger of pain jabbed her temple.

'Are you sure you're up to all this?' said Katie, gesturing to the boys whose chatter was making it hard for the women to hear themselves.

'Definitely,' said Beth with a smile. 'So you picked them up from school today?'

'Yes, and of course Jake will stay with me for as long as you're here, no question about that. Unless you'd like him to go to your mum's?'

Beth thought for a second. If she was likely to be here for ages, she couldn't impose on Katie indefinitely, so she'd have to consider her mother. That's what family was for, and her mother would have to step up and even – yikes – rearrange her Bridge schedule if need be, though that would be a feat akin to getting the graven images at Mount Rushmore to step down from their mountainside and start doing the Macarena. But Beth was already feeling much stronger.

'I'm going to be out of here as soon as I can. I'll try and discharge myself tonight, if not sooner, if they'll let me.'

'Are you sure that's wise, Beth? A head injury, after all?'

'Jake needs me, and that's the most important thing,' said Beth simply.

'He needs you in one piece. And you know as well as I do, it's a big treat for them to have midweek sleepovers. He'll be loving it,' said Katie. It was true. Now that Jake had seen with his own eyes that his mum was fine, awake, and looking pretty much as normal except for a cool bandage, he had relaxed completely. He had total faith in the world to keep on turning very much as he wanted it to. Beth hoped he kept that confidence forever.

She smiled over at him fondly, then sighed and sank back a little against the pillows. They were very comfy. And another amazing sleep, like the one she'd just had, would set her up, she knew it would. Maybe it wouldn't be the worst thing in the world to stay in another night.

'Of course, he'd rather be with you,' said Katie, but they both knew this had been tagged on diplomatically. Jake would definitely prefer an unscheduled playdate with Charlie and his state-of-the-art PlayStation.

'What about work? Do they know what's happened?' Beth, now that Jake was sorted, was straight on to her next worry.

'Yes, of course,' said Katie. 'I rang whatshername, the one who ran off with Dr Grover, lucky thing...'

'Janice,' Beth supplied with a smile.

'Yes, her. She was absolutely fine about it, said to come in when you're better. She did ask what on earth you'd been up to. And I think we'd all like to know that,' said Katie, lowering her tone a little. The boys seemed oblivious, but you never knew what they were picking up. 'Where were you? I mean, I was told it was some strange street in Camberwell, but why? I mean, *Camberwell?*' Katie's emphasis summed up all the prejudices a long-term Dulwich resident could be expected to hold against a place that was just a turn of the South Circular away, geographically speaking, but considered a different country in so many respects.

Beth thought for a second. It wasn't going to sound great however she said it, so she might just as well come out with it. 'I've been a bit worried about Jen. You know... that business with Ted and Tinder?' she said quietly, one eye again on the boys.

'Did you have it out with her? That was brave,' said Katie.

'Well, no, I didn't really get the chance. Every time I was round there, either Ted was hanging around as well, or she was out. It was impossible to talk. So this time, I was determined to do it – well, *reasonably* determined,' Beth added, to give a fair airing to all her doubts and circumlocutions. 'And I also wanted to give her that wedding present I got her ages ago...'

'You still haven't given it to her?'

'No. Well, again, there's always been some reason or another... and I've forgotten a few times as well. There's always so much going on. Anyway, yesterday, I just decided to see what was up, once and for all. Have the talk about, you know, *Tinder*, and also hand the present over at last. When I got there, no one answered the door. But I sort of had a feeling, you know, that there was somebody there...'

This was the first time that Beth had acknowledged this. Even while she'd been waiting outside in the cold, or creeping round to the kitchen windows, she hadn't quite put it into thought – although something had kept her trying.

'You know that feeling you get when you ring someone's doorbell, and they're definitely not in? The house has an empty feel. It's hard to explain, but you kind of *know*. I was there a few weeks ago, and Jen was out. Totally different that time; I knew there was no point persisting, and I went off to the high street. My fault for not getting my plans sorted out. Well, this time, although again I hadn't had a reply to my text so shouldn't really have turned up, I had this feeling that there was someone around, you know?'

Katie looked at Beth, nodding along. Beth slowed down. Now they were getting to the bit that Katie probably wasn't going to agree with at all.

'Now I look back on it, that's the reason why I, well... why I decided to make sure, by going round to the back.'

'What? You decided to break and enter?'

'No, no, not at all,' said Beth so vehemently that she shook her head and had to pause for a moment as the pain flickered back to life. 'The gate was open... She's got one of those side return passageways, and I thought I'd nip down that, just in case the doorbell was broken... or something.' She paused for a moment, looking down at her hands, where they were playing with the frayed edge of the NHS blanket. The thing was going to be in shreds by the time she'd finished.

Eventually, she looked up to find Katie giving her the sort of look she'd dart at Charlie when he'd been bad. Very bad. Both boys had also paused in their background chatter, looking curiously over at the bed. They knew, from long experience, when a telling-off was in progress. And one between adults was definitely a novelty that they wanted to experience.

'Boys,' said Katie smoothly. 'There's a vending machine right opposite this room, just down the corridor a little bit. Why don't you take my purse and see if you can find yourselves a snack?'

For a moment, the boys looked as though they might want to pinch each other. Were they dreaming? Had Katie, the goddess of health and fitness, just offered to hand over to them the keys to all the NHS could provide in terms of nutritional super-highways to diabetes, high blood pressure and obesity? Then they rushed for her bag, realising this offer would be good for one or two nanoseconds at most before normal service was resumed.

'Are you sure they won't get lost out there? These corridors all look the same,' said Beth weakly.

'It's a five-minute walk there, and the same back. They'll be fine, and I'll be able to see them out of that little window in the door if necessary,' said Katie briskly. The boys didn't need a second urging; they were off, banging out of the door, school shoes squeaking on the highly polished green lino, and already loudly discussing the merits of violent orange drinks versus artery-clogging snacks.

'For God's sake, Beth, what on earth were you thinking?' said Katie, as soon as the door closed. 'Wandering around in the dark, in Camberwell, of all places?'

'First of all, Camberwell isn't a war zone, you know. And it wasn't just anywhere in Camberwell, it was *Jen's* house – someone we know – and it wasn't the middle of the night, it was only about four thirty, five p.m. at the latest. It was dark, I grant you,' said Beth, with a slight shudder at the memory of dank shadows in the silent, watching garden. 'It wasn't nearly as crazy as it seems,' she added hastily, banishing the thoughts. 'If it had been broad daylight, no one would have thought twice about it.'

'No one, except the person who clonked you one on the head,' said Katie drily. 'They clearly weren't at all happy with what you were doing. So, I take it you were wrong, Jen and Ted were out all along, and someone else was trying to burgle the house at the same time you were poking around? Talk about bad timing. Do they have any idea who it was?'

'They're looking into it,' mumbled Beth, her colour rising. 'That is, well, um, Harry York is.'

Immediately, Katie straightened up. 'Oh? Oh, I see,' she said, trying but failing to suppress a very big smile. 'That nice Detective York again?'

'Detective *Inspector*,' said Beth, a touch defensively. She felt as though she'd leapt out of the frying pan straight into the fire. True, she was no longer getting it in the neck about her general recklessness, but she could feel a lot of unhealthy matchmaking interest emanating from Katie right now, which could well be even worse.

Katie, though, kept her own counsel, taking a moment to duck her head into her handbag, locate her phone and look extremely busy with it, before adding mildly, 'Message from Michael, sorry. Well, I'm just glad they've got someone good on the case. And someone who knows Dulwich.'

'Yes, though it turns out he was only involved because he actually, well, lives in Camberwell.'

'No! Does he?' said Katie in interested tones. Again, she said a lot less than Beth was braced for. 'Well, thank goodness he was around, that's all I can say.'

'Yes, it was Jen's next-door neighbour who saw, um, my foot...' said Beth, and the reality of the situation crashed in on her again. She'd had a very lucky escape. Who knew what her assailant had had in store for her, dragging her down the passageway like that? She felt a twinge in her back and shoulders again at the thought. She'd been unconscious, but the bruising and tenderness she'd been left with seemed to point to a speedy yank across the rough concrete rather than anything more sedate. She was probably lucky she'd been wearing a thick coat.

'Do they know what the person planned to do with you? Surely not just leave you lying there in the doorway for the bin men to find?'

'No idea. Maybe they were going to put me in a car or something? I just don't know. We'll never know, probably. It's not a great thought. Even if he'd just planned to leave me there, I think I would have probably got hypothermia, if not worse. It was a cold night.'

'Thank goodness the neighbour saw you when he did,' said Katie with a shudder. 'Meanwhile, what's going on with Jen? Where on earth is she?'

'Well, that's the thing I'm really worried about. I haven't heard a thing from her for ages. I've texted her again and again, but nothing. I could try her now, I suppose.'

'Yes, why don't you? That's a good idea. Where's your phone?'

Beth pointed to her bag, hanging on the hook at the side of her little bedside cabinet. Katie, with some difficulty, extracted the phone, accidentally disinterring a few Twix wrappers en route, which she balled up without comment and shoved in the bin.

'There you go,' she said, handing it to Beth.

She checked quickly for a reply to her texts. Nothing. Then she pressed dial. The phone rang ten, twelve times. 'Nothing at all,' she said sadly.

'Looks like we're going to be none the wiser, for the moment at least.'

'Hmm,' said Beth. Then she remembered. 'But what about Tim? Jen's ex? He's bound to be in the picture.'

'You don't want to speak to him, though, do you?' said Katie, disapproval written across her face.

'Well, I know he didn't behave that well during the divorce and so on, but he is Jessica's dad…'

'Well, yes, but,' said Katie, wrinkling her nose as though at a bad smell.

It was typical of the place, thought Beth. Much though she loved Katie, her friend was rushing to judge Tim on the basis of gossip, mostly from Belinda McKenzie. Katie had probably never spoken to the man herself in her life, and she wasn't even very close to Jen either for that matter. Yet she had definitely taken sides.

Beth was no apologist for Tim and his doings and, though she'd got to know him a little recently, she still wasn't a big fan. But there had to come a time when you gave someone a chance, and maybe this was it. She'd felt sorry for the man. He'd been so astonished and grateful that she'd spoken to him at all. The playground could be a cold and lonely place if the powers-that-be decided you were a pariah.

'The thing is that Tim will know where Jen is; he'll have to. He's been looking after Jess quite a bit but not all the time, I bet.

Maybe I should ring...' But then Beth realised she didn't have his number. It must be on a school list somewhere; she'd have it at home. 'Oh, I'll try when they let me out,' she said, lying back on the pillow. Suddenly it was all getting a bit much.

'You're looking grey again,' said Katie. 'Look, we'll find out what's going on, don't worry, and if we don't, then your nice policeman certainly will. I think it's time I got the boys off to their supper and let you have a bit of a rest. So tomorrow, during the day, I'll either pop in and visit you or give you a lift back home. Just let me know, if you're up to it, or I'll ring the ward. Get a good rest now. There's nothing going on that can't be sorted out tomorrow.'

Beth smiled weakly at Katie. It was true, she was feeling like a limp dishrag. But she wasn't sure if she agreed with everything her friend said. What about Jen? What if she needed help? What if she was in trouble right now, but just didn't have a great friend like Katie on her side, or a handy policeman like Harry York either, come to mention it?

She closed her eyes tiredly, and didn't see Jake waving through the little window at her. He looked disappointed for a second, then Charlie jabbed him in the ribs and he was off, chasing him down the corridor, while Katie followed behind, a thoughtful expression on her face.

TEN

Despite Beth's initial intention to leave hospital the moment she could, she found herself being lulled by the rhythm of institutional life. First came the absurdly early supper. She was used to eating early with Jake in theory, but because she was always rushing around doing something or other, their evening meal never seemed to hit the table much before 6.30 or even 7 p.m., which was late for a boy of Jake's age. In the hospital, Beth started hearing the commotion of trolleys of food in the corridor outside at about 4.30, and by 5 p.m. she was settled with a surprisingly good chicken korma with rice, and a nice plain apple for pudding.

When the nurse tried to bed her down for the night at about 6 p.m., she realised the whole hospital was run on a nursery timetable, putting itself to bed as early as possible then rising again with the dawn. The night, a full twelve hours long, was punctuated with as many clangs, crashes and clatters as the day, though the lights were dimmed. Presumably, the schedule made sense to someone, somewhere, and maybe kept the patients tranquil, since so many were half asleep after the endless disturbed hours.

Though Beth had still not spoken to a doctor, she found the fact curiously reassuring. No one could be particularly worried about her if she wasn't getting any treatment beyond four-hourly doses of pain medication. To be honest, she could perfectly well have taken that at home. But maybe there was method to this madness, and a strategy at work that she just didn't understand. Was this the close observation that they talked about on medical dramas, so essential after a head injury?

The only time she'd thought she was about to see a real live medic was when she'd woken in the night to see a tall, dark, white-coated figure hovering by her bed, but the man had turned away quickly and rushed off when a nurse walked in to shuffle through her charts again and write gnomic scribbles in the margins.

'Who was that?' Beth had asked groggily, but the nurse just shushed her, and now she wondered if she'd dreamt it all.

She'd resolved to ask about it again, but when someone bustled in through her door at 6 a.m. wearing the familiar blue uniform, it turned out to be a different woman entirely. The other nurse, she was told, had gone off shift hours ago.

Beth hated to admit it, but she was rather enjoying the luxury of being waited on. Even if the food wasn't quite what she'd have ordered if she'd had a free choice, it was plentiful and really not bad at all. She had porridge for breakfast, and slightly rubbery toast with those weeny plastic tubs of jam and golden folds of butter. And every time cups of tea were brought round, she was given handfuls of little twin-packs of biscuits. It was a bit like being in a rather odd hotel, where they insisted you stay in bed and shun all the sights.

Beth found herself secretly revelling in it all. Being in command every single day, always having to be the one with a plan, responsible not just for its drafting but its execution and with the outcome weighing on her shoulders, Beth had been thoroughly grown-up for years. It was knackering. But lying in this bed, tucked in by someone else, obeying the bonkers timetable, and eating food you didn't even need to chew, she could feel herself relaxing. Almost too much. She could see how long-term patients found it hard to leave.

As the pain in her head receded, and the prospect of lunch at the absurd hour of 11 a.m. loomed, Beth realised that enough was probably enough. She swung her legs out of the bed, feet touching the cold lino, and pushed herself up. Her head swam for a moment or two, and she wondered if abandoning this lovely comfy sanctuary was a big mistake. But, unexpectedly pleasant as these hours of respite had been, she did need to take up the reins of her life again.

Jake would love being at Charlie's, because it was a novelty. Whether he knew it or not, he needed the safety and security of his routine at home, with his mum, to enfold him again. And Beth herself required a lot more stimulation than she was getting in her sky blue bed, gazing at the blank walls, wondering when her next cup of tea would trundle along. It was time to find a doctor.

Shuffling down the corridor, passing the vending machine where Jake and Charlie had made free last night, Beth was having to stop every few steps to wrap her hospital gown more securely around her. Why did they make them like this, flapping open at the rear? What on earth was that all about? Surely the majority of people in hospitals were not there to have their bottoms operated on. For whose benefit was all this unintended buttock-flashing?

The relaxing effect of her stay had mostly worn off by the time Beth found the nurses' station, an island of paperwork in the middle of a labyrinth of beds. There were no nurses there, but a few pimply medical students were snorting with laughter at something at one end, their suspiciously fresh-looking lanyards giving away their status as total newbies to this hospital, and to healing in general. There was no one else to ask, so Beth approached them.

'I was just wondering when I'd see a doctor?'

'You're seeing four now,' said the tallest of the bunch, a strapping lad with a lugubrious face and curly dark hair.

'Are you qualified?' asked Beth pointedly, and the boy had the grace to look abashed, staring down at his shoes.

'We need practice, ask us anything,' said another of the group.

Beth gave him the sort of look she reserved for Jake when he was at his most annoying. Then she addressed the girl in the gang, who had long, straight, fair hair and was wearing a sensible Fair Isle jersey that would have made Beth sweat buckets in the hospital heat. She was clutching a biro and a clipboard and looked ready for just about anything – except Beth.

'When are the ward rounds? I'm in a room just over there,' Beth gestured.

'Um, well, that's, well, probably...' the girl stuttered, already outside her area of expertise and they hadn't even got anywhere near illness or symptoms.

Beth was just about to roll her eyes when, thank goodness, a nurse appeared. She threw herself on her mercy. 'Could you tell me when I'm likely to get seen by a doctor? I'd like to be discharged,' she said.

'Ah, the kind of patient we like best,' said the nurse, her apple-cheeked smile infectious. 'Don't worry, Mrs, er...?'

'It's Beth Haldane, I'm in that room down there,' she said, pointing.

'Ah. OK then, Beth. Let me just check my notes...' It was clear that Beth's name had prompted a caveat in the nurse's memory. She shifted round to get behind the desk, poking at the drifts of files everywhere across the surface, picking up first one then another. 'Ah, the handover notes. They don't like to make things too easy, the night team.' She smiled again and Beth found herself following suit.

The medical students, thankful now to be off the hook, seemed to edge further away and were soon laughing again, the Fair Isle girl standing an inch apart. Beth felt for her. It was never easy to be the clever, try-hard girl amongst a gang who made things look easy; she knew that all too well.

The nurse, running her finger down a page of the file, stopped and read intently. 'OK. I see. So, you'll need to be seen by the consultant before we let you go. Head injury, you know. Can't be too careful. And you'll have medication to take at home, so we'll need the discharge nurse to go through that with you.'

'Medication? Really? I don't think I'll be needing anything major, it's hardly hurting at all now.'

'Well, that's good, but we don't want to take any chances, do we? Now, at the moment you're on four-hourly paracetamol, no problems on the dispensing front there, so that could end up speeding things up a lot for you,' she said and smiled again.

'If it's paracetamol, I don't need anyone to tell me how to take that, I've been doing it myself for years.'

The nurse shrugged. 'Safety protocol,' she said, as though that explained everything. And in many ways, it did.

'Um, did a doctor see me during the night? I remember waking up and seeing someone in a white coat in the room? Would that be noted there?'

'It would if they made any observations but,' said the nurse, running her finger down the entries again, 'I don't see any note here of a doctor being called to see you. Normally they wouldn't come in the night unless there was an issue. Did you call for a nurse, or ask to see the doctor?'

'No, definitely not. I just woke up and he was there.'

'Hmm,' said the nurse, giving her a beady glance. Beth wasn't sure whether that meant the nurse thought she was naturally a fantasist, or whether the head injury itself had caused delusions. She turned back to the file and seemed to see something confirming her doubts. 'And I see here, there's a police interest in it all?'

It was Beth's turn to use the non-committal 'hmm'. She wasn't going to go into all that now, on the open ward, with the fledgling doctors probably listening in feet away, and who knew how many patients with nothing better to do than eavesdrop as well.

'Well, if I could just see the doctor? As soon as possible? I'd love to get home.' Beth tried an ingratiating smile, but it seemed the nurse had turned against her. She gave her a glance that seemed to suggest she'd be held at the hospital until the nurse herself was good and ready, which wouldn't be any time soon. 'There must be loads of pressure on beds, after all?' said Beth raising her eyebrows. She would have thought they'd be only too happy to turf her out onto the street as soon as possible.

'Look around you,' said the nurse. 'We're not busy. Not too busy to make sure you don't go home before you're good and ready.'

Suddenly, it sounded like a threat. Beth retreated back to her bed. By the time she got there, her legs were a bit shaky and she was grateful to lie down. But after an incredibly early lunch of a grated cheese sandwich on white bread, a banana and a cup of tea – during which she was beginning to wonder whether her teeth would fall out due to disuse if she stayed in the hospital system much longer – there was a sudden commotion at the door. The apple-cheeked nurse appeared with a whole cluster of white coats – some of the students from earlier, with a few extra thrown in for good measure.

Beth sat up a bit in her bed and looked at them expectantly. They all shifted about from foot to foot, in silence, avoiding her eyes, while the nurse noted things down in her chart and took her temperature. Then there was a swirl of motion from the door and the consultant was there – a tall, sturdy woman in her mid-fifties, with business-like salt and pepper hair in a geometric bob, and mauve half-moon glasses that she peered over. She gave Beth a surprisingly shrewd glance from cold blue eyes before holding out an imperious hand for the notes. The nurse mutely handed them over, the consultant adjusted her glasses and raked her eyes down the line of squiggles, and pursed her lips.

Beth wondered whether the vertical lines scored above them meant she was, or had been, a smoker, or whether she just existed in a permanent state of mild disapproval. 'And how are we feeling, Mrs... Haldane?' she said crisply, timing the question so that she'd flipped the folder to the name on the front just in time to ask her question seamlessly.

'I'm fine now. Tiny bit of a headache, but I'd really like to go home,' said Beth.

'That's the spirit,' said the consultant, with a swift glance around at the band of white-coated minions, who tittered sycophantically.

'Well, it looks as though I'm your fairy godmother today, Mrs... Haldane,' she said, with only the briefest of glances down to refresh her memory on the name. 'I'm going to make your wish come true. You're looking a lot better than when you came in, that's what we like to see.'

'Oh, did you see me when I was admitted?' said Beth with interest.

'Well, no, just a form of words; the notes tell the story. The important thing is that you're feeling fine in yourself, no signs of concussion. No dizziness? Weakness? Light-headed at all?'

'Not at all,' said Beth, blithely skipping over the odd muzzy moment. She'd be fine when she got home.

'Well then. You're good to go. Matron here will arrange for the discharge nurse to see you and then you'll be on your way.'

'Oh, is that really necessary? I mean, I understand it's just a question of taking painkillers...'

'I'm afraid so. Guidelines,' said the consultant with another sharp look at Beth over the mauve glasses, and that was that. 'Onwards and upwards,' she said sharply to her little crew of white coats, who bustled after her like tufty goslings in the wake of a large, sleek Canada goose.

Beth was left realising that she hadn't even asked about the doctor who'd appeared in the night. Something told her she'd just have earned one of those dismissive glances over the mauve spectacles, but she was still kicking herself. She hated an unasked question almost as much as an unanswered one.

Two hours later, the unanswered question was definitely where on earth was the discharge nurse? Was there only one servicing the whole hospital? And was Beth the only person who had to stop herself giving a slight snigger every time the poor nurse's job title was announced? *Discharge.* Ick.

The joke had worn very thin by the time 4 p.m. came around. There was a sudden bang at her door, which she hoped was the nurse at last, but it was even better. It was Jake, hurling himself at her in an action replay of yesterday. Katie and Charlie followed, wrapped up against the cold outside and already rosy from the tropical temperatures on the ward.

'How are you feeling?' said Katie, giving her a slightly off-balance hug. The height of the bed, the bandage, and Beth's slight reticence about public displays of affection, all combined in a nexus of awkwardness.

'I can't believe I'm still here,' said Beth. 'I've been trying to leave since this morning.'

'Right,' said Katie. 'We'll see about that.'

Half an hour later, they were back at Beth's little Pickwick Road house, with Beth ensconced on the sofa with a piping hot cup of tea in her hands. Katie's sunny optimism had cut through all the red tape associated with the simple action of leaving hospital as effectively as a hot knife through royal icing. They even had a plastic bag of paracetamol tablets with endless instructions on how to take them, as though they were the deadliest poison on the planet.

'I wonder if they're just trying to protect themselves against being sued, and that's why they make it such hard work to get out?' mused Beth.

Katie raised an eyebrow. 'Oh, it's just silly. Let's not worry about it. I'll nip down the road later, get a takeaway from Olley's, and we'll watch *Strictly* on catch-up – how about that?'

'Bliss,' said Beth happily. She adored the fish and chips from the shop down in Herne Hill, and it was even more of a treat as they'd had to foreswear fast food since Jake's tutoring started soaking up every bit of spare cash. She was usually slightly allergic to *Strictly*'s sequins, but they were just what she needed tonight.

They were all snuggling on the sofa, watching the nail-biting red-light moment when one of the contestants gets stripped of their fake tan and has to head back into the real world, *sans* glitter, when the doorbell rang. Beth instantly stiffened. She might be feeling a hundred per cent better, but she was still jumpy.

Katie gave her a glance above the boys' heads, then went to the front door. Moments later, she was back with a smile. 'Time for us to go now, Charlie,' she announced brightly, to groans from both boys.

Beth was about to join the chorus of protest, when she saw Harry York looming behind Katie and doing his usual trick of making her home seem like a doll's house.

'Oh, chips,' he said, falling on the remnants in one of the Olley's bags on the floor, then installing himself on the sofa and grinning widely at Beth and Jake. 'Yum.'

For the first time in what seemed like forever, a man shepherded Jake up to bed that night. Beth was still tired out by the whack on her head, and as night fell she was very grateful to have the suddenly clingy boy bundled off by someone who wouldn't take a lot of nonsense. She tried to bestir herself and at least collect up the plates, chip papers and Jake's inevitable ketchup, but the effort seemed too much. Instead, she gazed blankly out of the sitting room window into the darkness. It was a little like the view she'd had into Jen's kitchen that night. An indistinct reflection, lights, distorted shapes.

Wait a minute, had she actually seen her attacker, fleetingly? Did she have a vague recollection of someone reflected in the window – tall, wearing a hoody...?

But that hardly narrowed it down. Almost everyone in the world was taller than her, and half of them probably had hoodies, too. She gave up puzzling and applied herself to her cold cup of mint tea instead. Katie had made it just before she left, and it was a wonderful antidote to the slightly overstuffed, greasy feeling left after the fish supper, delicious though it had been.

York bounded down the stairs moments later, and plonked himself next to her on the sofa, rooting around in the bags and wrappers for any spare chips that hadn't been guzzled. 'You could go and get some more, if you like, it's not far away,' said Beth mildly.

'I've already eaten. This is just a lovely dessert,' said York, munching contentedly. He made the bonanza discovery of half a packet of chips in the corner of one of the bags.

Must have been Katie's, Beth thought. Only a yoga teacher could pass up the total deliciousness of a crisply fried Olley's chip.

'So. Remembered anything about your injury?'

'Funny you should say that. I was just thinking, well, something did come back, while I was looking at that window.'

'Yeah? Anything useful?' said York indistinctly. He'd now

hit a motherlode of battered cod, undoubtedly left by one of the boys. Even deep frying couldn't make fish much of a rival to chips, chips and yet more chips, in Jake and Charlie's estimation.

Beth passed him an unsqueezed lemon quarter from her plate, but he looked at it, baffled, before carefully putting it to one side on the arm of the sofa. 'Got any ketchup?' he mumbled. With a sigh, Beth handed it over. It looked as though Jake had a rival in the epicurean stakes.

'I have the oddest feeling that it was someone I know. And the only person I can think of, who'd be hanging around the house at night like that, would be Ted.'

'Ted?'

'Jen's new husband. Well, not that new,' Beth added. Quite a few months had gone by now since the wedding. And immediately her thoughts went to that bloody wedding present. Where was it? Still sitting in her car? And where, come to think of it, she thought with a prickle of panic, was her actual car?

'Oh yes, Ted Burns,' he said indistinctly.

'Is my Fiat still outside the house, you know, in Camberwell?' said Beth in horror. Although she knew it was silly, she really didn't want to have to go back there to collect it, even in broad daylight.

'Don't worry. Give me the key and I'll bring it over for you.'

'You're not insured to drive it, though?' said Beth, worried grey eyes raised to his amused blue gaze.

'It'll be OK. Give me the name of your insurers and I'll sort it,' he said, patting her hand with his own slightly sticky one.

The fleeting touch of his fingers was warming and, notwithstanding the grease, she felt instantly reassured. But the physical contact seemed to have introduced a new element and she suddenly felt all gawky, sitting there on the sofa, and struggled into a more upright position. York, too, was staring rigidly ahead. Had a line been crossed? She wanted to get back to the ease they'd had a moment ago.

'Peppermint tea?' she said, a little desperately. She'd like a warmer cup herself and it would give her an excuse to get away. She thought she was feeling up to a bit of movement now.

'What? Haven't you got any good old builders' stuff?' he said, eyebrows reaching his thick blond hair.

She laughed, and they were back to normal. She levered herself out of the embrace of the saggy sofa and wandered slowly to the kitchen, picking up the Olley's debris as she went. She'd leave the white paper carrier bags by the front door, and dump the rubbish in the wheelie bin outside before going to bed. There was nothing worse than coming downstairs in the morning to the smell of elderly cod.

She brought the mugs back in – one peppermint, one builder – and asked, 'So, will you be questioning Ted?'

'Already tried to get hold of him. No joy yet. And no sign of your friend, either.'

'What? You haven't been able to trace Jen?'

York shook his head. 'Not so far. But don't worry, we'll find her.'

'What about her ex, Tim? Doesn't he know where she is?'

'He had some story about her going away to finish a huge work project. But we've spoken to her current, or I should say, last, employer, and she's up to date with everything for them.'

'That's really weird,' said Beth. 'She didn't say a word to me about a big project anyway, that came from Tim. And I thought it was odd that I didn't see any sign of her having a huge deadline or feeling the stress.'

'Does she normally confide in you?'

'Confide? I'm not sure about that. Well, work isn't a secret thing, anyway, is it? So it's not really a question of *confiding*. But yes, we do talk about work because we're in similar fields. Well, Jen's gone more IT these last few years, but we both started off in journalism, pretty much in related areas. The trouble is there isn't really enough of that work to go round, so everyone diversifies.'

'But you just work for Wyatt's, don't you?'

'I actually do other bits and pieces on the side as well,' admitted Beth. 'Not much. Probably not as much as I should, but it's hard to turn down and I like to keep my hand in, just in case.'

'Just in case what? They love you at Wyatt's. Fancy new institute and all that?'

'Well, yes,' said Beth modestly, her cheeks feeling warm. 'It's been going really well. But you never know, do you?'

York glanced over at her, but said nothing.

'I like to have a back-up plan,' she admitted, holding the tea up to her lips.

'I've noticed that. Unless it's really dangerous, in which case you just steam in like a nutter.'

For a second, Beth sat up straighter, ready to leap to offence. Then she sneaked a look at York and saw his smile curving. He was only trying to wind her up.

She laughed. 'I'm a reformed character. I'm going to be tiptoeing around, not getting into any more hot water, I promise,' she said.

'Believe that when I see it,' muttered York into his mug of tea. 'So, what's the next bit of your cunning plan?'

'I'm not sure I have one. You mean, the plan to find Jen? Or whoever clonked me on the head? Or my life plan?'

'Do you actually have a life plan?' asked York. 'Love to hear that.'

'Well, it might be a bit sketchy... things keep changing,' Beth said, dodging the question. She suddenly felt shy in front of this big virtual stranger. If she confided her hopes and dreams to him, he'd probably laugh. And besides, some of them were so tentative that they'd go pop, like soap bubbles, if she exposed them to the light of day. Far better to think of something else entirely. 'But you've just given me an idea. A mad one, but still. Do you think *Jen* might have hit me?'

'Why would she have done that? Had you had a row?'

'Not at all. I just can't think of anyone else who might have been there to do it... apart from Ted, of course.'

'We keep coming back to him, don't we? And to answer your question, no, I don't think it can have been Jen, unless she's built like a navvy. I haven't met her but I'm guessing that's not the case?'

Beth shook her head. Jen was of middling height, and slight.

'It was probably, but not definitely, a man who hit you. It was quite a hard blow; you were lucky not to have cracked your skull. Looks like you moved at the last second and the force just glanced off to the side,' said York, peering at Beth's head with the professional detachment which came with years of studying messy crime scenes. Beth's hair, with a bandage still clinging to the soft dark strands, was now one of these. 'Otherwise, well, if he'd hit you full on...' York didn't elaborate but Beth went cold for a second.

Then she decided she just couldn't afford to get caught up in might-have-beens. She'd had a narrow escape; she should be thanking her stars.

'So it wasn't Jen. That's a relief. I didn't seriously think she'd do it, but I'm glad she's ruled out. But Ted. He's the obvious suspect. And I've got a feeling about him. I can't quite put my finger on it, but there's *something*, a sort of suppressed anger, if that makes sense? Jen's odd, when he's around.'

'Odd? In what way?'

'Oh, I don't really know. But she's a bit wary, as though she's worried about saying the wrong thing all the time.' Beth shook her head. 'Look, I'm probably imagining it. Take no notice.'

'No,' said York slowly. 'Your instincts are good. If you think something's off, I'd put money on you being right. But we can't steam in there and arrest him for making his wife polite. Even if we could find him.'

Where on earth was Jen? Beth sighed. She'd been worried before. But now she was really anxious. And where was Ted, for that matter? They couldn't both have vanished off the face of the earth. Could they?

ELEVEN

Beth had roses in her cheeks the next morning as she towed Jake along to school, and not just because it was one of those gorgeous crisp wintry days that allied blue skies and bright sun with biting sub-zero temperatures. She was hugging a secret bit of knowledge to herself that made her feel as fizzy inside as Christmas morning. York, when he'd eventually left late last night, had shrugged his coat on in her tiny narrow hall and, after an awkward moment, had bent down and deliberately planted a brief kiss on one of the very cheeks that now glowed so pinkly.

She could still feel the imprint of his lips – gentle, maybe just the tiniest bit tentative to start, but becoming firmer, while the prickle of his chin had rasped her soft skin in a bracingly male way. His hands had briefly clasped her shoulders. She knew this was to steady himself; he had a long way down to bend in order to reach her. But still, it had felt possessive, even passionate. Rather delicious. And as he'd leant in, she'd smelt the faint, lingering whiff of a nice citrusy cologne, battling on from his morning routine hours before, overlaid at this late stage in the evening by the stronger, more masculine scent of a man who'd been on his feet all day, keeping the world safe.

He'd straightened up. He'd looked down, she'd looked up, their eyes had met in a smile, and he'd said, 'See you.'

Then the door had banged and he'd been gone.

All night, she'd deliberated. Yes, she'd been kissed on the cheek many times since James's death. Mostly by women friends. Sometimes by elderly men at Christmas or at get-togethers, occasionally by other people's husbands. They were kisses that were either instantly forgettable, or memorable for all the wrong reasons.

This kiss, though. It had been nice. More than that.

Special. She wasn't imagining the spark between them. She couldn't be. Her knees had sagged when he'd gone, and she'd had to lean against the hall wall for a moment or two. And it wasn't just the blow to her head. Had he also faltered on his way, or had he just gone striding off back to Camberwell? Once her heart had stopped hammering, she'd heard his measured tread receding down the quiet street, and had to assume he'd beetled home as though nothing had happened. But that didn't mean he wasn't affected by their kiss.

Their kiss! She ought to listen to herself, she chided mentally. She was getting completely carried away about noth-ing. Almost nothing. Well, a bit more than nothing, really. In fact, it had been really something.

She had to face it. She'd wanted more.

But what had it meant? Did a kiss on the cheek mean the *friend zone*? Was that as far as they were ever going to get? Did a man kiss a woman on the cheek because he didn't want to kiss her anywhere else? Or was it a prelude to more kisses, some-where more interesting?

She had spent an hour or two, once she'd got to bed, wondering if she could have been more receptive, more enthusi-astic. But what would that have even been like? If she'd just grabbed him – well, for one thing it was something she would never, ever do, in a trillion years. And for another, what if he'd run a mile?

Then she'd spent a further chunk of the quiet night thinking about what various of her friends would have done in a similar situation. Katie would probably have hugged him back. Belinda McKenzie would have munched him up and spat him out the next morning. Jen... what would Jen do? She couldn't quite picture it. Something eminently sensible, probably. Though, look at her with Ted. She'd fallen for him in seconds flat, and then married him almost as quickly. Jen would probably have dragged him upstairs as well. Maybe that's what Beth should have done herself.

She had tossed and turned all night, finally dislodging her bandage. After the clout to her head, she knew she needed her sleep even more than usual, which of course made things worse. There was nothing like lying awake, thinking about how much you needed to be unconscious, to ensure total insomnia. And it wasn't as if she had any outlet to discuss this kiss situation. Normally, she'd discuss any issue that was worrying her with friends. But this, no. It was too... well, her cheeks flamed just thinking about it. It was everything. And nothing. She didn't dare bring this up. She'd just have to think it all out for herself.

That hadn't worked well overnight, and when the morning finally came, Beth was still in turmoil. Perhaps it was time for her to admit to herself that it had been a long time since she'd felt this way. A long time – even before James had died. She'd never delved into it, it had seemed so disloyal, but her relationship with James had been very... well, placid, before his death. It was partly that having Jake had changed things, as a baby always does. But had it been even before that?

Sometimes, the fireworks she felt with Harry made her question the tranquil waters she'd drifted into with James. Too much peace could be as bad as too little. Had they become more like brother and sister than lovers? While that bond was really close and truly comforting, she did already have a brother. Maybe, even, that was why she hadn't noticed he'd got ill?

The suddenness of James's decline and death still shocked her. It had proved to be little more than three months from codeine to coffin. Had there been much more, which she just hadn't noticed because, well, they weren't living in each other's pockets? But it was ridiculous for her to take all the blame. James could have said if he'd been feeling ill. He'd been an adult, responsible for himself, ultimately. It had just been a particularly aggressive form of tumour; the consultant had said so. That didn't exactly make Beth feel better, but she needed to keep things in perspective, if she could. She and James had been close, and loving. They just hadn't been in the first throes of passion by the time he died – but who was, with a toddler in tow?

Beth looked up guiltily from her thoughts. They'd reached the school railings, and Jake was running ahead, bursting into the playground, impervious to the cold and just pleased to be with his friends again. Why couldn't everything be so uncomplicated?

Out of the corner of her eye, she saw Tim edging towards her. Mentally, she sighed. Oh well, maybe listening to his endless work stories would give her a break from the turbulence in her head. She turned to him with a gentle smile.

'Morning, Bess,' said Tim with a sycophantic smile. 'Lovely to see you.'

'*Beth*,' she corrected automatically. 'How are you? I've been meaning to ask, have you heard from Jen lately?'

'Jen? Oh, she's fine, I think, still working away on this huge project. It's really keeping her busy. So much so that we've been a bit stuck with Jess recently...' said Tim, pouncing.

'Really? Stuck? With your own daughter?' said Beth. She tried to keep her voice neutral, but she could feel disapproval seeping out of every pore.

'Well, it's just that Babs is forging ahead with her career. I'm all for supporting women in that, totally behind equality in the workplace, all that stuff,' said Tim smarmily.

Hmm, thought Beth. She'd found that the men who waved their feminist credentials around most enthusiastically were often the most misogynistic.

'But of course, it makes it hard for her, having Jess every afternoon while she's trying to get on with things, and I can't get away any earlier than I do...' Tim faded out on a pleading note, letting the sentence hang heavy in the air.

Realising full well what Tim was up to, Beth toyed with making him spell it out. But what the hell, it might be nice for Jake to have someone to play with tonight. All right, she'd only just got out of hospital with a head injury, but she couldn't expect Tim to know that; she hadn't mentioned it. And she felt absolutely fine. She could easily take Jess for a couple of hours. And she might be able to find out something about Jen from her daughter, if she proceeded cautiously.

She waited a couple of beats longer, just enjoying watching Tim squirm, then offered magnanimously, 'Well, I could pick her up tonight if that helps? Babs can fetch her about six thirty. What's your number? I'll send you my address.'

Tim, having got what he wanted, was off and out immediately – a familiar pattern, as both Jen and Babs could have attested. 'That's great,' he said, reeling out a string of numbers that Beth hastened to get down on her phone. 'Just send me your address, see you soon,' he said, sprinting for the gates.

Beth was left smiling ruefully. Fine, let him think he'd played her. She was happy to give Jess a bit of respite from Babs, whom it was plain she had not gelled with, and even to give Babs herself a bit of a break. But if Tim thought he was going to make a habit of this, he had another think coming.

. . .

By pick-up time, Beth was regretting her decision. Her sleepless night had caught up with her, her head was sore and pounding again, and the day's work she'd put in was lacklustre at best. If she'd been doing her own performance review today, she'd have sacked herself on the spot. When she hadn't been mooning hopelessly about the kiss, which had now grown into a moment to rival Rodin's sculpture or Klimt's shimmering golden clinch, she was revisiting painful truths about her marriage and alternating that, just for the sheer fun, with pointless worrying about Jen's whereabouts. She was thoroughly fed up with herself, and was willing to bet that two ten-year-olds were going to be much more than her frayed state could manage this afternoon.

But, as usual, Jake confounded all her expectations. It would have been wrong to use the word 'gallant', exactly, about the way he treated Jess that afternoon, but he certainly showed her a consideration and thoughtfulness that was absolutely never accorded to Charlie. And that, to Beth's astonishment and baffled guilt, reminded her strongly of poor James. He'd really been the loveliest man, and she'd been so lucky. If she'd ever found him predictable, that just showed what an awful, shallow person she really was, she fulminated, shaking her head at her painful thoughts.

'Are you talking to yourself again, Mum?' said Jake, bombing into the kitchen with Jess to get snacks.

'Of course not, I never do that,' she said quickly, sitting up straighter and smiling mechanically at the children.

'Don't worry, my mum does that all the time, too,' said Jess, taking a large handful of crisps from the bag Jake had just ripped open.

'Does she?' said Beth slowly, then turned to Jake. 'And did I say you could have crisps?'

The boy shrugged. 'You didn't say we couldn't,' he said, with all the insouciance of Garry Kasparov moving into checkmate. If Kasparov had ever spoken with his face exploding with crisps, that is.

'Don't talk with your mouth full,' said Beth, and turned to Jessica. 'So, how is your mum?' she asked, somewhat tentatively. She didn't quite want to come over like the inquisitor in the painting, asking, 'When did you last see your father?' But that was exactly the sort of question she wanted to put to the girl.

'Fine,' Jessica said with a shrug, hands deep in the crisp bag. It was a race against time if she wanted to get a fair share. Jake was now on auto-chomp and showing no signs of slowing down. Being nice to girls was all very well, but he didn't often get away with opening a family-sized bag of crisps before dinner, and he wanted to make the most of it while the going was good.

'You're spending a lot of time with your dad at the moment,' Beth said, hoping that a slight upward inflexion would mean she didn't sound as if she was cross-questioning but would still elicit a reply.

Jess nodded, and carried on munching.

'Babs seems nice,' said Beth, trying again. This time Jess just rolled her eyes and stuck her hand in the bag again.

Beth racked her brains desperately. She could ask about Christmas plans, which were always fraught in divorced families, but for kids this age, the festive season was still as far away as the planet Pluto. 'What about this weekend? Going to see your mum?'

'Dunno,' said Jess, but she looked as though she was thinking about the question at last. It was a start. Beth didn't want to distress the girl but, on the other hand, she needed answers.

'I've got a wedding present for her in my car, but I keep forgetting to give it to her, and sometimes she's out. Do you think you could give it to her?'

'A present? Cool!' said Jess. At last, thought Beth. She'd hit on something that might work. 'Yeah, I could give her that, she'd really like it.' The girl looked so eager at this tempting bait, a sure-fire way of pleasing her mum, that Beth felt yet another guilty pang; as if she hadn't overdosed on them already today.

'I'll just go and get it,' she said, making for the hall. York had dropped the key through the letterbox earlier, with a scrawled note saying where the Fiat was parked. She turned back at the door. 'You two will be fine for a second, won't you?'

Jake and Jess looked innocently back at her, faces lightly encrusted with crisp crumbs and the orange powder residue of the paprika flavouring, which was no doubt full to bursting with horrible toxins. No two children could look saintlier. It was worrying, but Beth thought it was worth the risk of popping out just in case she could finally get somewhere with Jen's disappearance.

The car was just down the street, near the junction where Pickwick Road turned into the wider, grander thoroughfare of Dulwich Village itself. On the way to it, she bumped into all her neighbours, from lovely Zoe Bentinck – her sometime babysitter – to Jean Pepperdine, a retired English teacher from the College School. Mrs Pepperdine was a Bridge rival of her mother's, and had plenty to say about their last encounter over the green baize cloths of the Dulwich Bridge Club.

By the time Beth had been to the car, fished the parcel out of the glove compartment, and brushed off a few boiled sweets, used parking stickers and various urgent briefings from school that she really needed to read carefully one day, ten minutes had ticked by. When she let herself back into the house with a cheery, 'Hello,' she wasn't that surprised to be greeted by silence.

A quick tour of the downstairs confirmed that Jake and Jess had probably gone up to his bedroom. No doubt, in a few years' time, a discovery like this would lead to all kinds of moral panics about teenage goings-on, but today Beth wondered briefly whether she could just leave them to it, crack on with the supper and then use the gift as a bargaining tool to get Jess to open up later. She hesitated, her hand on the smooth grain of the oak newel post, looking up the stairs to the dimness of the landing beyond. It was quiet up there. Too quiet.

With a sigh, she trudged upwards, then swung open Jake's door. Sure enough, both children were there, sitting on Jake's floor, with no fewer than three open giant-sized bags of crisps, as well as a bar of Cadbury's Dairy Milk that Beth had been planning to smuggle into her work stash, and the half-eaten box of Marks & Spencer chocs that neither Jake nor Beth loved – a present from her mother's last visit.

Jake's face was a picture. There was the horror of discovery, the guilt of the theft, the surreptitious pleasure of all this contraband, and the unmistakable flush of a sugar overload. Plus, the camaraderie of suddenly finding himself in a gang of lawbreakers, i.e. Jess. Added to that, the paprika beard he'd acquired earlier now had unmistakable chocolaty additions. Jess herself, meanwhile, just grinned impishly up at Beth. Maybe her own mother would be able to decode all the meanings behind that smile, but Beth certainly wasn't going to bother trying.

'Well, you two have been busy,' she said sternly. 'Jake, I'm not impressed. *At all*. And Jess, well, I don't know what your mother's going to say about this,' she said.

'Are you going to tell Mum? Do you think she'll come round and get me? She hates me eating too many sweets,' said Jess, now with unmistakable eagerness written all over her face. Aha, thought Beth. Is that what this had all been about? An attempt to get her mother involved?

'I'll certainly ring your mum right now. Do you want to talk to her?' said Beth, not even trying to keep up the cross act. Jake looked as though he was still waiting for the axe to fall, but Jess was transparently eager to get on the phone to her mum, even if she thought a ticking-off was coming. It was heartbreaking.

'Come on downstairs then, and bring that lot with you,' said Beth.

Jake jumped up immediately, gathering up the contraband, glad to have been given something to do that looked reassuringly like a punishment. Jess followed at Beth's heels and they were soon settled at the table, Beth tapping the dial icon. The phone rang and rang. Jess, who'd looked as keen as Magpie expecting a cat treat, gradually slumped across the table, ending up lying with her cheek pressed against the scrubbed oak. Beth tried again, and again the phone rang out. Jess shut her eyes. Jake, shoving the crisps back into cupboards, missed seeing a lone tear trickle down Jess's cheek.

'When did you last speak to your mum?' Beth asked the girl gently, her hand on her arm.

Jess instantly withdrew. 'Dunno. Ages ago. Dad says it's because I've been playing up.' Her head was down, and the last sentence was mumbled into her jumper.

'I'm sure that's not it, Jess. Your mum's probably just away, or working really hard...' Beth thought quickly, trying to come up with something, some excuse, that would make sense to a small girl who missed her mother. But there was no reason in the world Beth could think of that would keep Jen from at least talking to her daughter, if not seeing her on a regular basis. And how mean of Tim to suggest to his daughter that it was her fault her mum wasn't around. Alarm bells were going off so loudly in her head that Beth was surprised the children couldn't hear the clanging.

At least one thing had been made a lot easier by the evening's events. 'Neither of you are going to be very hungry, are you? So we can all make our own sandwiches for supper,' said Beth brightly.

The girl might be worried, but there was nothing she, or maybe anyone, could do at the moment. So why not take her mind off things with a bit of fun? Jake, still a bit wary that a severe talking-to was imminent, instantly brightened. Sand-wich-making was one of their best things. Little did he know, but Beth chiefly brought this into play when she was too tired, for one reason or another, to make a 'proper' supper involving cooked vegetables, traditional servings of protein, and so on. Sandwiches covered these bases, but were a lot more fun all round, for exhausted cooks and small kids alike.

By the time the doorbell rang, two eager sous-chefs had done their best to convert Beth's tidy kitchen to chaos. Beth, getting up from a table festooned with small dishes of sliced cucumber, cherry tomatoes, grated cheese, bits of chorizo, and dollops of mayonnaise and Jake's inevitable ketchup, realised that it was bound to be Babs at the door. She hastily rinsed her hands and dried them on her jeans, striding to the door.

Babs stood there, pristine in a little fitted charcoal grey work suit that clung to a carefully toned figure. Over it was a camel coat of a type that Beth had long ago decided reluctantly was incompatible with everything about her lifestyle and her budget. It would have lasted two minutes in her house before becoming speckled with toothpaste or bestrewed with Magpie's generously shed hairs. The whole ensemble was topped off by a gauzy scarf in a shade of fuchsia that Beth knew would make her look both fat and gaunt at the same time, but was perfect with Babs's sleek halo of dark hair.

'Come in, come in. Sorry, it's in a bit of a state, only just finished supper,' said Beth as airily as she could. As she strug-gled with OCD tendencies, she hated others seeing her home when it was less than pristine. But short of brushing her entire kitchen under a non-existent carpet, there was nothing she could do except hope to style it out. She rattled some plates together and dumped them in the sink, wiped the table top with a cloth and automatically popped the kettle on.

'Tea?' she asked, more for form's sake than anything. Mothers almost always shared a debriefing session after a playdate, unless Armageddon had broken out and one side or the other needed to rush off and regroup.

Babs, unsure of the etiquette, hovered on the kitchen threshold, clearly transfixed with horror at the state of the place. She kept staring from the floor to Beth again and again, not managing to say a word. Beth tried to look at it through a stranger's eyes, and knew the blobs of ketchup on the floor, the grated cheese drifting across the table, and the abandoned crusts with crescent-shaped bites taken out of them, did not look good. But on the other hand, with her years of hard-won tidying experience, she knew it wasn't going to take more than a few moments to deal with this lot.

After getting out two mugs, she rushed round with a sponge and her trusty Flash spray, picked up here, there and everywhere, and by the time the water was boiled, things were down to manageable levels of chaos. The wedding present, which was still unopened and with its once-sleek wrapping now lightly encrusted with grated cheese, was shoved to the back of the work surface by the sink. It definitely wasn't the moment to be brandishing Jen's gift around, in front of her erstwhile love rival.

'Builders' or Earl Grey?' she asked. Earl Grey was the usual Dulwich option, but some people, York for example, liked to keep it real with a bit more of a tannic blast from their cuppas.

'Um,' said Babs, settling herself on the very edge of one of the kitchen chairs. She clearly thought she was risking contamination. And, Beth thought with an inward sigh, she was probably right. There was a smear of what looked like brown sauce on the back of the chair. Which was odd, as Beth was pretty sure she hadn't deployed the HP at supper time.

Beth dithered. To wipe or not to wipe, that was the question. On the one hand, she could hardly bear to see such a lovely outfit ruined. On the other, this was Jen's nemesis, the woman who had made her friend suffer for years. All right, that was through the agency of Tim's boundless twattishness, but still, Babs had to bear her share of the blame. He'd been firmly married when they'd met.

'An Earl Grey, please. Just a drop of milk,' said Babs with a tentative smile, and made as if to lean back. Despite herself, Beth swooped with her sponge and just got the blob off before at least two hundred pounds' worth of designer suiting stuck to it. Babs, aware that Beth was faffing around behind her, sat forward again and gave her a quizzical glance.

'Just making everything nice and tidy,' said Beth, knowing she was coming over as a deranged Martha Stewart-type but not caring over-much. She'd done the right thing; by the dry cleaners in the village, if not by Jen. 'Don't know where those children have got to,' she added, 'but they've been playing nicely.' She wasn't sure if that was entirely true. She was pretty certain, biased though she undoubtedly was, that Jake had been led astray in the matter of the unauthorised snacks, but she wasn't about to grass Jess up.

'How are you getting on with all the childcare stuff?' said Beth, making conversation but also genuinely curious. It couldn't be easy taking on someone else's child, at a late stage, particularly when you had no experience with kids yourself.

'It's quite... well, you know,' said Babs, clearly fearing to commit herself. 'It's certainly *different*.'

'Ha, you've got that right.' Beth smiled. 'I think it's like having pets. Better to get a cat when it's a kitten, then it can train you. Same with babies. I'd never even held one, till I had Jake. I had no idea what to do. You learn on the job. But you're brave, taking this on,' she said, smiling encouragingly at Babs, who was taking a cautious sip of the still-hot tea.

She put it down again and seemed to have made up her mind to speak.

'I had no idea it was all so tiring,' she said, then let out a whoosh of breath. 'Gosh, it feels good even to say that. I can't say a word to Tim, he's Jess's dad – and it's not as if Jess isn't great, she is, don't get me wrong...'

Beth, leaning forward despite herself, and fervently hoping no small ears upstairs were catching any of this, silently willed Babs on. There was clearly a ginormous 'but' looming.

'*But*... to be honest, I have no clue what I'm doing. Jess seems to hate me, and I'm just so fed up with getting every single thing wrong.'

To Beth's consternation, Babs put a hand to her eyes. Oh no!

To some extent, she'd been willing Babs to admit how difficult this whole mothering thing was. There was such an image these days, of gorgeous mummies gliding around baking cupcakes with one hand and French-plaiting their children's hair with the other. Making it look so easy. But the reality of parenting was, in Beth's experience, often more like a slow-motion car crash, or if not quite so catastrophic, then at least a major tug-of-war between opposing factions with entrenched views and wildly differing aims. She'd have liked Babs to have said she suddenly realised how hard women like Beth had it. Maybe they didn't have lovely little suits, maybe they just had the modern-day flak jackets of mothering that were tatty joggers and worn-out jumpers, but they deserved medals, every single one of them.

Unfortunately, Babs wasn't focusing on the wonderfulness of Beth and mothers like her, but instead, predictably, was brimming over with self-pity. Quite literally, as a tear started to dribble down her beautifully made-up cheek, taking a little fuchsia powder blush – a perfect echo of Babs's gauzy scarf – with it.

If there was one thing Beth couldn't stand, it was grown-ups blubbing in her kitchen. Unless it was her doing it, of course, and even then it should only take place in the still watches of the night, when no one, but *no one*, was around to witness it. In her view, all this touchy-feely stuff that was so fashionable had a lot to answer for, letting people dangle their feelings all over the place. OK, she'd been probing a bit. But she just wanted to find Jen. She did *not* want a closer glimpse at the darker corners of Babs's psyche.

'Oh, I'm sure you're doing a fine job. Jess seems... quite fond of you. That's better than most stepmothers,' said Beth as bracingly as she dared without coming over as totally uncaring. Anything to get the emotional genie back into its bottle. To her surprise, it seemed to be working. Babs looked up, her nose a little raw-looking, but her swimming eyes full of hope.

'Really? You think I'm better than most stepmums you know?'

Beth nodded enthusiastically. Given that the only stepmothers she could think of were the Wicked Queen in S*now White* and Maleficent in *Sleeping Beauty*, it was pretty much a dead certainty that Babs was streets ahead of the competition. That was presuming she didn't actively want to kill Jess, or keep her in a coma for a century or two; Beth was going to give her the benefit of the doubt on that. Having got to know her slightly better, it certainly seemed that Babs was well-intentioned, but out of her depth – not waving, but drowning.

Still, concern for Babs shouldn't deflect her from her mission, thought Beth. 'But what I really wanted to ask was, do you know where Jen actually is at the moment? I've been trying to get hold of her, and I think Jess is missing her.'

'We're all missing her. No one more than me,' said Babs, with heavy irony.

Beth was startled. For years, Babs and Jen had been locked in mortal combat. One or other of them would pop up at every carol concert or summer fair, but never both, for fear that the universe would implode or the gossips of Dulwich would have a real live catfight on their hands.

'Really? I didn't think you got on?' she said warily.

'I tell you, I used to yearn for the day when *poof,* Jen would just disappear. She used to be hanging around all the time, those hurt eyes, that poor-me look, making me feel really rotten, even though Tim swore to me right from the start that every-thing was dead between them, that she hated him and they hadn't, you know, had sex since 1995 or something. I'm begin-ning to think that was all a big lie. And now we've got Jess *all the time.* The joke was on me all along. Jen's got over Tim completely; she's got Ted, who's pretty gorgeous, and she gets to swan around the place, taking off whenever she likes, with free childcare laid on by yours truly. I don't even get time to go to the gym any more. My arms are getting *flabby,*' she said, lifting up her arm, rolling back a sleeve, and displaying a string of muscles which, while not quite a condom full of walnuts, would have still have done Popeye proud. 'Honestly, that woman. She's getting away with murder.'

Beth looked at Babs, startled both by her biceps and her vehemence. This wasn't just self-pity. She'd thought Babs was irredeemably shallow, but her rage certainly seemed to have hidden depths. And she seemed particularly bitter about looking after poor Jess. 'Didn't you say you wanted children?'

'I do,' said the woman simply. 'I want *my own* children. Unless you've had to deal with other people's, you just don't understand. Everyone seems to think the sun shines out of their own kids' backsides. Well, it damn well doesn't shine out of other people's, that's for sure,' Babs hissed across the table.

'Jess is a lovely girl,' Beth remonstrated.

'I bet she's lovely to *you.* She never speaks to me. I get up in the morning, make her breakfast, get her bag ready, I've already washed and ironed her clothes – after literally picking them up off the floor in her room – then I brush her hair, if she'll let me, give her a lovely healthy snack for breaktime, which she never bloody well eats, and send her off to school with her dad. Then I pick her up, make sure she does any homework, watch those bloody awful kids' TV shows with her, make her tea, try and chat to her; I even put her to bed most nights and read her a story, for God's sake. Tim always makes sure he's back too late from work. Not a word of thanks, from either of them. Tim thinks I should be happy as Larry, looking after his precious daughter. Especially as we've spent years, you know, trying for our own. He's always told me it's the best possible practice. Ha! But Jess? She's just an ungrateful little... beast,' said Babs, drawing breath briefly then bursting into speech again.

'I wouldn't mind, if she just said *something* to me. Not even thank you. Just a "hello" would do. Once a week, maybe. But do I ever get a single word out of madam? Nope. Not a syllable. Not. A. Single. Word. Ever. She literally won't speak to me, won't look me in the eye. It's like I'm a non-person. And she's pretty much as nice as pie to her dad, but when she goes up to her bedroom every night, if he's not around, she slams that door like she's going to break it off its hinges. I go in to read to her and turn off the light, but it's like I'm there on sufferance; she turns her face to the wall. I'm reading Harry sodding Potter to myself, night after night. *The Chamber of Doom*, that's her bedroom, that is. It's doing my head in, I don't mind telling you,' said Babs, even pinker in the face now than her scarf, after her tirade. She drank down some of her tea, fighting for composure.

At least anger had replaced tears, Beth was glad to see. But it did, indeed, sound like a horrible way to live. All your efforts ignored, your overtures spurned. How soul-destroying. Like living with an unrequited love, and allowing them to show you an Arctic shoulder all day, every day. Most people in this situation would break off all contact, go cold turkey for a while, and move on. But you couldn't do that with other people's children. You were well and truly stuck with them – nominally, until they were eighteen, but in truth, way beyond that. And the reason why it cut so deeply was that Babs, despite herself, had clearly grown fond of Jess and just desperately wanted the girl to like her back.

Poor Babs. Isolated and under siege at home, where she was supposed to find peace and relaxation. Meanwhile, the mums at school also treated her like a plague-carrier, and Tim, no matter how he felt about being lumbered with total responsibility for his daughter all of a sudden, would be as unenthusiastic as any parent to hear a whisper of criticism of his greatest creation.

'That sounds grim, it really does. Have you tried to win her over?'

Babs said, through gritted teeth, 'I've tried everything. Girly chats, shopping trips, craft projects. I even took up knitting so I could teach her! She said she wanted to try. Then, when I'd spent three weeks mastering casting on, she told her dad – not me – that she'd much rather ask her mum. And that was that. I've still got the sodding knitting needles cluttering the place up.'

Beth looked at her, full of sympathy. It did sound crushing. 'You need to spend a bit less time with her.'

'Tell me about it! But Jen seems to have just dumped her on Tim. Weeks, this has been going on for. I don't know what the hell is happening, I really don't.'

Beth felt prickles of unease again. 'You mean you haven't seen Jen? Not at all? When was the last time she was around?'

'I never see her, so I don't really know. She's always steered clear of me, for obvious reasons. Hates me. Detests me. Can't stand me. Well, like mother, like daughter, I suppose,' said Babs, looking suddenly defeated. If ever someone was reaping what they'd sown, it was Babs, thought Beth.

'Don't you think this is odd, though?' Beth asked.

'You'd have to ask Tim, if you want the nitty-gritty. As far as I'm concerned, it looks like she's just done a runner. Decided her evil little kid is the devil's spawn and taken off for good. Heaven knows, I would if I could,' Babs added.

Suddenly, there was a scuffle out in the hall. Beth shot out of her chair, and got to the kitchen door, just in time to see a flash of blue as Jess scarpered up the stairs as quickly as her little legs would take her.

'Christ, that's really gone and done it,' said Babs, half rising from her chair. She looked stricken. If she'd seemed miserable before, it was nothing to the way she was now. Beth plonked herself back down again and tried to cheer Babs up, though it looked like a task as insurmountable as skate-boarding up Sydenham Hill, from where she was sitting. 'Look, let's just settle down here for a bit. I'll make some more tea. We don't know for sure if she even heard anything. I'll go up in a few minutes and see how the land lies.'

'Thank you,' said Babs, her eyes brimming again. 'You're a real friend. I wasn't expecting to like you. I thought you'd be like her... you know, *Jen*. But you're a good person. I'm really sorry.'

'Sorry? About what?' said Beth.

'Oh, you know... everything, really,' said Babs, a little strangely.

Sitting across the table from the person who'd wrecked the life of a woman she really liked and admired, Beth realised – not for the first time – that things in this world could get compli-cated. Helping Babs was not top of her to-do list. Though she felt for the woman, Babs's predicament was, to some extent, self-inflicted. Hurt children lashed out where they could, and were better than heat-seeking missiles at finding the right spots to target. Jess was doing an exquisite job at torturing Babs, far better than any water-boarding rendition expert any day. But if Beth could do anything to make Jess feel happier, then her rela-tionship with Babs was bound to improve as well, and that would cheer things up for everyone around her, including, Beth fervently hoped, her elusive mother, Jen.

'Look, have you just tried saying to Jess, you're sorry her

mum's not around, you're not trying to take her place, but you'd just like to be friends?'

'Do you think that would work?' Babs's eyes were, again, as full of tremulous hope as a kitten's.

'Well, it's not going to be a magic wand, that's for sure. Nothing's going to be instant. But at least you'd be on an honest footing. It strikes me that both of you are quite angry, about different things, and pretending you're not isn't getting anyone anywhere,' said Beth.

As she took her own cup to the sink, rinsed it quickly and flicked the switch on the kettle, Beth wondered. Were the two of them actually furious about the same thing? Jen's disappearance was at the bottom of both Jess's pain and Babs's strange sense of disgruntlement. Finding her was going to answer a lot of questions. Maybe it was time that Beth really got down to working out what was going on. In the meantime, she got the milk out of the fridge, fished the teabags out of the mugs, rinsed the spoon, and then ran her hands down her jeans again. She really must get a proper towel, or at least put the tea towel somewhere she could actually find it. Then she braced herself to talk to Jess.

She slid a refill of tea over to Babs and, somewhat wearily, climbed the stairs. All this drama was a bit much, and her head ached a little. Jake's door was firmly shut. She knocked, then tried the handle. To her surprise, it wouldn't give. She realised there had to be little hands grasping it on the other side of the door, holding it closed. No prizes for guessing who.

'Jake, I need to talk to Jess, can you ask her to come away from the door, please?' Beth used her no-nonsense tone, and wasn't surprised when a muffled sound of argy-bargy from within signalled that someone had been bodily removed from the doorway. She opened the door, and peered round.

Jake burst out immediately. 'I'm, um, just going...' He clattered down the stairs, caught sight of Babs in the kitchen, and wheeled immediately into the sitting room. A few seconds later, Beth heard the theme tune of one of his beloved PlayStation games. Hmm, unauthorised screen time; he was pushing it. But, like all males, he'd use any tactics at his disposal to get out of a good old heart-to-heart. Beth sympathised with him entirely. She didn't much like them herself.

Careful to keep herself in the doorway, in case Jess should try to make a bolt for freedom, too, she smiled at the girl. She was sitting on the corner of Jake's bed, head resolutely turned away from her.

'Look, I don't know what you overheard downstairs. All I know is that Babs is a bit worried about you. She says she thinks you're really missing your mum.'

At this, Jess's head shot up and she risked a quick glance at Beth. This wasn't the ferocious telling-off she'd expected.

'Would you like me to have a word with your dad about it, when I next see him?' Beth asked. She had a sneaking feeling that offering to ring him, right there and then, would convince Jess that something was awry, and that was the last thing she wanted to do. The girl was already seriously discombobulated, hurt at her mother's continuing absence. She didn't need to be worrying about where on earth she was into the bargain.

Jess risked a glance at Beth again, and nodded her head just once.

'OK, then,' said Beth. She cautiously moved forward, sat down next to Jess on Jake's star-printed duvet, and risked putting a hand on the girl's shoulder. God knew, she wasn't into constant tactile displays, but she could tell when a child needed a hug. As she'd expected, Jess turned instantly and burrowed into her. Beth put her arms round the girl, rested her chin on her soft dark hair, and stared unseeingly ahead, deep in thought. *Oh, Jen. Where are you, when your baby needs you?*

TWELVE

It would be too much to say that she'd effected a rapprochement between Babs and Jess, but as she sat in her swivel chair at the research institute at Wyatt's on Monday, after a mercifully quiet weekend, Beth did allow herself a little pat on the back. Stepmother and stepdaughter had gone off together on Friday night hand in hand; both with their tears dried, thank goodness. Babs's wobbly smile at the front door had been full of gratitude. Beth just hoped it was warranted. There was no point in hoping that Jess would suddenly love spending time with Babs. Her stepmother was always going to be a poor second best to her mum. But the girl might be reconciled to life at Tim's house, if someone set a proper limit on her visits so she could share her time reasonably equally between her parents. And that seemed to be problematic, for reasons that neither Jess, Beth, or even apparently Babs really understood.

This morning, Beth'd managed, accidentally on purpose, to give Tim a miss. Although she knew she had to get on to him soon and sort out what on earth he knew about Jen's where-abouts, she was getting a bit sick of being in the middle of that family's problems. Her own were complicated enough.

With all the hoo-ha on Friday, the gloss had rather come off her twinkly encounter in the hallway with York. But that wasn't to say she'd forgotten all about it. It was still a treasured moment, keeping her warm, bringing a secret little smile to her face right now, as she sat in her swivel chair.

Unfortunately, that was the moment when Janice chose to pop her head round the door. One second was all it took for her to diagnose the difference in her friend.

'That's a sex look!' Janice announced loudly, advancing into the room bump first with an avid look on her face. 'You've been doing some dating. And you've had a result!'

Beth immediately sat up straight in her padded chair, feeling as guilty as a schoolgirl caught behind the bike sheds. 'What? What on earth do you mean?'

'You can't fool me,' said Janice, lowering herself carefully into the chair facing Beth's sweeping mahogany desk. 'You've met someone and you were thinking about him just now. Don't tell me you weren't.'

One part of Beth admired Janice's shrewdness, and wondered for the umpteenth time why she wasn't working for MI5 instead of the school; she had no need of truth serum, thumb screws, even simple interrogation. The other part cursed her soundly.

'I don't know what you mean. I was just thinking about the exhibition I'm putting together. It's going to be a corker...'

Janice snorted. 'No woman, ever, looked like that because of an *exhibition*. Unless it was a man, making an exhibition of himself. Come on, you might as well tell me. You know I'm going to get it out of you sooner or later.'

Beth pondered. There was a lot of truth in what Janice said. Beth was no match for her. But, on the other hand, what had happened between her and York in the hallway was such small beer that Janice would only laugh again. And she wasn't sure she could bear that. It would be as savage as a bucket of freezing cold water poured on all her poor little dreams. No, she needed to keep this to herself. For as long as she could, anyway.

Besides, she hadn't heard from York since that night, apart from that no-frills note about where he'd parked her car. Granted, it wasn't exactly a long time ago. But still. Surely he could have rung, just to check on her? Or even texted? She *had* had a head injury, for heaven's sake.

'It's really nothing, Janice. You know I'd tell you if it was important,' Beth said, the pleading in her eyes unmistakable. Janice sighed, obviously thinking the better of whatever line of questioning she'd had queued up. It would keep.

'How are you feeling, anyway? Should you be back at work already?'

'I'm fine, thank you. The bandage just fell off of its own accord, the bump's completely gone down. All the bruising must be covered up by my hair, thank goodness, otherwise I'd be black and blue. My back's a bit sore, too. Everything is tender if I prod it... but I won't,' said Beth, before Janice could remonstrate. 'They said I was lucky. A few inches higher and the head injury could have been, well, really nasty.'

'Sounds nasty enough to me already. And have they caught who did it?'

'No. Looks like there's no hope of that.'

'Where was it again?'

'Outside my friend's house, in Camberwell,' said Beth, seeing Janice's face change. 'Don't look like that, there's nothing wrong with the place.'

'I'm just saying. Wouldn't have happened here in Dulwich, would it?'

'Worse things can happen in Dulwich, as we know, Janice,' said Beth, a little crossly. Maybe she was still feeling weak. She was very tired all of a sudden.

Janice seemed to get the hint, levering herself out of the chair and managing the feat of waddling with grace as she let herself out of the room. 'Lunch with the girls?' she asked, before disappearing like the Cheshire Cat, leaving only her smile and a bit of fluff from her cashmere behind her.

Lunch with the girls was the last thing she needed, Beth thought. They'd be agog to know her adventures on Tinder, and would be mortally disappointed, and equally condemnatory, when she had to reveal she was getting nowhere fast. But maybe she should press on with it? Maybe what she'd felt in the hallway had been just a bit of silliness? She had no idea whether York felt the same, or whether he kissed all his suspects and collaborators, not that she was exactly either one or the other this time. Perhaps that was the problem. She wasn't his sidekick, that was for sure, and they didn't really have an official investigation on the go at the moment, either.

Beth sat up again. Maybe that's what needed to happen.

She had to up the status of her current obsession with Jen's disappearance, to make it official business. That way she would make some progress with it at last, and maybe – she blushed as she even thought it – make some progress on the other front as well.

She'd started to google missing persons, wondering if it always had to be a relative who logged their concern, when she realised it was a big waste of time. Why bother dipping her toe into the murk of the internet when she had the crystal clear source of all police information available to her? She picked up her phone and scrolled to York's number. Then hesitated. Was she being terminally uncool? Would this somehow count as pursuing him? Should she play hard to get, wait for him to get in touch with her? Weren't there rules about this? A three-day thing... Yes, but surely that was when you were actually dating someone, Beth told herself. A kiss on the cheek hardly counted as a full-blown romantic encounter. She was being extremely silly. And anyway, her friend's disappearance outweighed any paltry considerations about who looked as though they were stalking whom. Didn't it?

She still hesitated for a minute more, before girding her loins and pressing the button. Instantly, she wished she hadn't – but it was too late. Then, inevitably, as her heart started pounding, listening to the ringing tone, the phone clicked off into voicemail and she felt a huge disappointment engulf her. Should she leave a message? Lots of people didn't even bother listening to them now, preferring texts if they were busy. She hummed and dithered, then realised it was all being recorded, and snapped the red button to cut the call.

Well, that had been pointless. She now felt thoroughly flustered – certainly too much so to settle down to any real work. She gathered her bag crossly and trudged over to the staff restaurant to grab a coffee and a plate of sandwiches. She'd bring them back to her desk, that way neatly avoiding the third degree from Janice and her cohorts. She loved them to bits but she just wasn't up to explaining all the delicate nuances of a fleeting collision of lips and cheek, and how much that had meant to her. She could just imagine the torrents of derision that would greet her nascent hopes, and she couldn't bear it. It was something that those with simpler lives were never going to understand, and almost certainly would feel no sympathy with, either.

* * *

Janice, looking out of her window and seeing Beth trooping back to her office a few minutes later with a bulging bag, noticed the dejected droop of her friend's shoulders and wondered what on earth had caused her to crash from excitement to despair so quickly. Or rather, *who* on earth? If Janice's years of experience told her anything, it was that only a man could play havoc with a woman's emotions so quickly. Oooh!

Just then, she felt a little kick. Her hands crossed protectively over her bump. Yet another sign that she had a boy on board. She and *her husband* – and how she still loved the comforting, oh-so-respectable sound of those two hard-won words – had decided not to find out the sex of their baby. There were few moments in life, Dr Grover had said, when both options could produce equal delight, and Janice had outwardly agreed. But it wasn't going to be a surprise for her. From the way the baby kept her up all night, with no consideration for anything but its own convenience, pressing on her bladder, kicking her in what she was pretty sure equated to her goolies, complaining when she lay flat, and hating it even more when she stayed bolt upright, she was more than two hundred per cent sure it was a boy. Another little Dr Grover in the making. As long as he had his daddy's wit and charm. Oh, he'd be a heartbreaker, for sure. She couldn't wait to meet him.

But Beth, though. She deserved to feel as happy as Janice did right now. And if Janice had anything to do with it, she'd make sure she did. Just leave it to her. With a seraphic smile, she drew her phone to her and made a quick call. There. That was settled. Now all Beth had to do was thank her. Once she'd thrown her bridal bouquet into the air and set off for her honeymoon with a ring on her pretty little finger, that was.

* * *

York peeled off the thin latex gloves and leant against the front door of the little flat in Camberwell, taking some very welcome breaths of cold November air. They were at one of the few high-rises in the area. Built to be communities in the sky in the 1960s, they'd rapidly become vertical rabbit hutches, storing their human cargo in separate, isolated units, with catastrophic effects like those he'd just seen. Poor old lady. She'd been someone's mum, someone's gran – that was clear from the framed photos proudly displayed on her dusty sideboard. But somehow, somewhere, those relationships had faltered, and the old woman had died alone. Quite a long time ago.

York hated these G5 calls, as they were known. It was never good news when neighbours started complaining about the smell of drains. If only these self-same neighbours were equally ready to stir themselves before things got to the whiffy stage. If they popped in, once in a while, to see how the elderly folk around them were doing, the police wouldn't be faced with such ghastly sights. But of course, they were all busy, just like him. There were probably old biddies in his own road who could do with a visit now and then, and he'd never even seen them, let alone thought to do a bit of shopping for them.

He did pass the time of day with old Len, though, who lived two doors down from him and who was always shuffling to or from one of Camberwell's betting shops whenever they met. He made a mental note to spend a bit more time chatting with the man, maybe ask him if he needed help with his garden. From what York remembered, it was an informally curated outdoor installation featuring lager cans and ciggie packets from the last twenty years or so.

At the same time, he wondered who he was kidding. There was so much to do in his own unloved flat, with the rickety flat-pack furniture he hated threatening to collapse any day like a pack of cards, and a sofa lumpier than cold school custard. Maybe he'd be found there himself in fifty – who was he kidding? forty – years' time, impaled on a rusty spring, surrounded by a few sticks of MDF. But no, if he met his death in that place, it would be because one of his bookcases, filled three volumes deep with Golden Age mysteries, had fallen onto him. Few people knew of his addiction to Agatha Christie, Dorothy L Sayers, Margery Allingham and their sisters in crime. Perhaps it would be a fitting way to go.

Just then, the old lady's obscenely fat cat shouldered the

front door open and sauntered off to its first taste of freedom for what looked like several weeks, at the very least. York shuddered. He certainly wouldn't be offering to rehome that creature. As he watched, it sat down on its well-upholstered bottom and set to, giving its whiskers a much-needed sprucing.

This was what you got for not making proper human connections while you could, thought York. It wasn't for want of trying. He'd had that girlfriend for, what, a few weeks, last year, and they'd even been on the abortive trip to Paris. But it hadn't worked out. It wasn't him, it was her, she'd said somewhat unconvincingly. Hanging around while he broke date after date, giving precedence to all kinds of low-lifes and criminals because that's what he did, had not suited her one little bit. Dating another police officer was an option for him, though synchronising shift patterns would doubtless be a nightmare, and he just hadn't met anyone he wanted to make that effort with down at the station. Since Paris, work had been so full on. And he had loads of books to read.

As the mortuary team trundled away with their burden, York chatted with the SOCO and turned to go. With a sigh, he realised he really was on a fast track to being eaten by his pet himself. Well, that was easily sorted. He'd never get a cat.

Just then, his phone went. With the gloves still clutched in his hand, he fumbled and didn't reach it in time to answer. Peering at the screen, he saw it was Beth who'd called. He took a second to take stock. Head injury. No further information had come in about the attack. No witnesses. He'd got uniform to knock up and down the road. Nothing doing, but that didn't surprise him. In Camberwell, hardly anybody saw anything, even in broad daylight. She'd been very lucky that her friend's neighbour was on the case, though by the sounds of it he'd actually been a bit pissed off that she was in the way of his bins rather than playing the Good Samaritan.

As usual, she'd been asking for it, skulking around someone

else's garden in the night. Though it hadn't been night exactly, more late afternoon. But still. That didn't make it any better. Honestly, she seemed to have some sort of death wish. He'd never known an outwardly sensible, even respectable, young woman before with anything like her propensity to get into trouble. That wasn't to say she didn't have a nose. He was big enough to admit she'd helped him out on a couple of occasions now. She had the amateur's conviction that there was always a solution, whereas he, dealing with this stuff all the time, knew full well there were a vast number of cases that never even got close to being solved.

The Met's clear-up rate was good, and God knew they dealt with the lion's share of the crime going on throughout the country – and many of the most complicated cases, to boot – but there were limits. Not all murderers conveniently left a DNA-stained hanky at the scene of the crime, or even gave the talented amateur the kind of clue that made those 1930s plots, to which he didn't mind admitting he was addicted, work with such well-oiled precision. No, that was one of the many reasons he loved his books so much. They gave him the neat finish that was so often lacking in life, with every loose end tied into a perfect bow, and the reputation of the sleuth further burnished by their amazing deductions. It was as good as catnip to a moggy any day.

And that brought his mind back to the present. He listened to Beth's aborted message, while watching the old lady's cat sauntering off into the distance, furry arse hanging low. He was sorely tempted to kick it. Hmm. No clue what she'd wanted. It had been nice to see her the other night. He hoped her head was OK. He'd ring her back when he had a minute.

Just as he formulated the thought, his phone vibrated again. He listened intently. It was information on one of the cases he had on the back-burner, diligently relayed to him by a new member of his team who was showing promise.

'Right. On my way,' he said, pulled back to police business. He stuffed the gloves into his pocket and strode off.

* * *

Beth, hunched at her desk, finishing off the last of her sandwiches and scrolling up and down the text of one of her panels for the new slavery display, knew she should print the thing out and proofread it that way. But she was being seduced into trying to check the text on screen. She knew perfectly well this didn't work, and that typos galore would be gliding past an eye that had gone flaw-blind, but she was feeling too tired to walk all the way over to the temperamental printer. And besides, she wanted to avoid Janice, Sam and Lily, if possible. All three of them were in deranged matchmaker mode. One she could have dealt with, but a trio was a pack and best avoided. She had plenty to be getting on with here, out of harm's way – the trouble was that she just didn't feel like doing any of it.

Talking to York about the Jen problem would have been the ideal displacement activity, but his failure to pick up had put the kybosh on that. Was there anything else she could usefully be doing? She quickly skirted the school firewall to see if there was any Christmas stuff she could order online.

Jake had his eye on the latest upgrade to the PlayStation – some kind of Nintendo gizmo that promised to do just about everything except iron her shirts, for the price of a second-hand car. She debated asking her mother and brother to chip in, and getting it for him as a joint enterprise. It'd take some arranging, and she'd probably have to pay for it upfront and then attempt to recoup some money later. But that would be difficult with her mother, due to her impenetrable vagueness about everything except her last hand at Bridge, and with her brother too. Although he was generous to a fault, he was never in the country to ask.

She brought up the image of the Nintendo box on her screen. To her, it was yet another slab of plastic, festooned with annoying black wires, that would look horrible in the sitting room for a couple of years until it suddenly became obsolete. To Jake, no doubt, it represented not only an exciting bit of kit that he'd (hopefully) have before any of his friends, but also a million races with an Italian plumber, or endless chances to dodge bullets from an evil sniper. She hesitated over the 'Add to cart' button. As if she could afford a cartful of this stuff.

She read over the description one last time, then realised that the astronomically expensive box she was foolishly considering paying way too much money for, *didn't actually come with any games at all*. They had to be purchased separately, and weren't cheap either. Right, that was it. She'd have to give it a lot more thought before she took the plunge, she thought, crossly shutting down the page.

Her phone rang and, for once, she was thrilled to pick it up as a distraction from her angry thoughts about manufacturers clever enough to make fortunes out of sheer tat. No caller ID. Her heart beat a little faster. It was going to be York, ringing back at last. She took a breath. It was vital to sound casual, off-hand.

'Hi,' she drawled, leaning back, toying with her ponytail.

'Oh, er, hello?' It was a male voice she didn't recognise. She sat up straight.

'Who's that?'

'Er, is that Beth?'

'Yes, who's calling?' said Beth, tired of this game of hide and seek.

'Oh, er, my name is, um, Richard. I'm sorry, I don't usually do this...' he tailed off.

'Do what?' said Beth, baffled.

'Well, I was given your number, um, and I was wondering... if you'd like to go for coffee?' His voice sank away at the end, as though he was a balloon emptied of air, or as if someone had a gun to his head and was forcing him to get the words out against his will. She couldn't remember ever receiving such a tentative invitation.

'What? I'm sorry, who is this? Where did you get my number?'

'Oh, well, it was my, erm, cousin, Jan. I think you might be work colleagues?'

Beth thought rapidly. Jan? *Janice*. What on earth was she up to? She'd had that odd smile on her face earlier. Beth had just put it down to a surfeit of pregnancy hormones, but she'd had this up her sleeve all along. Christ, she was going to kill her. Janice'd set her up.

'Aha, yes, yes, we are indeed colleagues,' said Beth, but maybe not for all that much longer, the way she was feeling. 'So, erm, you're Janice's cousin?' It was Beth's turn to be suddenly unsure. Should she go with her first instinct and slam down the phone and give Janice a piece of her mind, or was she going to play along with this? She took a deep breath. If she ducked out with an excuse, she'd not only hurt this harmless-sounding man, who'd clearly screwed his courage to the sticking-place to make this call, but she'd also have to face Janice's inevitable wrath – more than a match for her own irritation.

'That's right. I think she thought we'd, erm, well, be good together?'

Did she now? thought Beth crossly. Surely that was for her and this Richard to determine, together, without interference. Though admittedly they might never have met, left to their own devices. And it was still quite likely that they wouldn't manage to make a sensible arrangement, unless Beth stepped up. Richard sounded even shyer and more retiring than she was.

'Um, what did you have in mind?' Beth said, trying not to sound quite as unenthusiastic as she felt.

'Well, as I said, a coffee? You probably get a break at some point, do you?'

'Oh, do you work round here?' said Beth, instantly perking up. Going for coffee in the village was one of the things she did best, though generally it was with Katie or one of her very small group of friends. Like Jen, she thought with another stab of worry. But she supposed she could also have a coffee with a member of the opposite sex without too much drama ensuing. She and York had shared enough cappuccinos in the past, for goodness' sake. This thought had its own little stab of pain, too, but for different reasons. And actually, it would serve York right if she went off and had coffee with someone else. He ought to return her calls more promptly.

'Yes, yes, er, my office is, erm, not far,' said Janice's cousin Richard, somewhat elusively. 'So, when would be good? Er, maybe next week sometime...'

Beth thought for all of a second. If she knew Janice, she'd be bursting into the room any moment now, demanding a full blow-by-blow account of their conversation. She could just imagine the tongue-lashing she'd be in for if she said they'd agreed to meet for twenty minutes in a week's time. Might as well get the whole thing over with as quickly as possible and make sure she had at least a two-line story to tell.

'How about now? Do you know Romeo Jones, in the village?'

'Oh. Er...' Richard sounded aghast. Beth immediately suspected he'd been put under huge pressure to make this call, and felt very sorry for the poor man. He probably had no real desire to meet her at all, and was just doing his own best to get out of a ticking-off from the lovely but redoubtable Janice.

Beth remembered just enough about dating in the Dark Ages to recall that it wasn't done to sound overkeen. She was willing to bet this was one thing that wouldn't have changed a bit. She'd now given Richard the impression that she was a complete desperado by biting his hand off like this, but never mind. When it came to boils, she was heartily in favour of a nice, quick lancing, and she was always going to be the type to rip the bandage off on the count of one, instead of peeling away at the corners forever. Some chores you just had to do quickly, and this date definitely fell into the 'get it over with' category.

Half an hour later, having pressed save on her slavery documents yet again, and left a Post-it on her door with wording so vague that even she wasn't quite sure what she was up to or when she'd be back, Beth was stirring a large latte at Romeo Jones, the dinky deli. This tiny place was divided into two sections: a small front shop selling blisteringly priced but wonderful foodie treasures; and a back area converted into a minuscule café, with four tables wedged into a boudoir-style décor, complete with pink flock wallpaper that Beth rather adored. If you peered with your head at an odd angle, you could see from the café into the shop, and vice versa.

Beth was wondering if she should have spent a bit more time in the loos at work, glamming up for this 'date'. As she'd brought no make-up with her, there hadn't been a lot she could realistically achieve. Even at home, she wasn't sure where her bag of tricks was lurking these days. Probably on one of the paint pots still in the hall.

She was down to a single swipe of mascara at the front door as she left in the mornings, from a tube that had definitely passed its sell-by. For those rare evenings when she went out, a bit of lip gloss had to do, and as for blusher, her sense of mild panic on social occasions sufficed to give her a hectic flush. Today, she'd just attempted to tame her hair with a brush from the bottom of her bag, had contemplated wearing it loose for two seconds, then bundled it back up into her habitual ponytail.

No point giving this man any false expectations that she hadn't the slightest intention of living up to.

As usual, she was sitting far too close to the counter, laden with all manner of delicious goodies, including the deli's famous carrot cake, which she was manfully ignoring. She was trying to concentrate on the art on the walls instead. Today it was a display from local printmaker Julia McKenzie, weaving the undistinguished flora and fauna of south London, wily scavengers like foxes and magpies and opportunistic nuisances like nettles and couch grass, into magically beautiful kaleidoscopes. Beth was also trying not to stare too hard at the time on her phone. She'd allocated ten minutes, fifteen tops, to getting this meeting done and dusted. The seconds were trickling away.

'Sorry, sorry,' said a middle-aged man with thinning blond hair, bursting through into the deli's little back-room café. He looked around him wildly, eyes alighting on Beth, then sliding rapidly away again. Apart from two teenage girls with their heads together gossiping, looking as though they might be sixth formers from the College School out on licence, the place was deserted. His gaze came back to rest on Beth, eyebrows arching, colour mounting in his already ruddy cheeks.

Not a good sign, thought Beth. He almost looked as though he'd like to plonk himself down at one of the two remaining vacant tables and wait for someone better to turn up. Beth smiled in a slightly resigned way, and he seemed to accept the inevitable, scraping back the chair opposite her with a 'May I?' and holding out his hand.

His smart striped shirt strained a little over a comfortable tummy. Altogether, he looked like Paddington Bear in a suit, maybe after a few goes at a low-marmalade diet. He definitely wasn't sex on legs, thought Beth brutally, but on the plus side he did look quite a sweetie. Then the briefcase in his other hand came down awkwardly, knocking the table and sloshing Beth's latte everywhere. She grimaced a little as the hot liquid splashed her hand and very narrowly missed her phone. Honestly, could all this be any more embarrassing?

But ten minutes later, she had to hand it to Janice. She had a lovely cousin. That wasn't to say Beth particularly wanted to extend their date, or try any more. It was just that he was an extremely nice man.

Of course, being in his early forties, he had baggage swinging everywhere. Not just his wrecking ball of a briefcase, but also three children, who now lived mostly with their mother, his ex-wife. And his feelings towards the mother of his children were, to put it mildly, still very much at the complicated stage. Beth was a bit worried he was going to break down and blub at one point, as he explained that he still had no idea quite how things had gone wrong.

'There must have been signs?' she probed gently, cursing herself for her curiosity. As usual, her love of solving a mystery was overriding the strong sense that she should not get involved in this stranger's life. If he'd gone through a whole divorce and was still really none the wiser about why things had hit the skids, then he was either terminally short-sighted, totally lacking in insight, or the only man in the country who really was married to a heartless bitch.

'Well, I suppose, with the fact that Felicity worked away from home so much, she just had a lot of opportunity to meet other men. It was part of her job, as a saleswoman,' he said, almost apologising for his ex's faithlessness. Whatever the product Felicity was involved in marketing, Beth doubted she had to throw herself into the deal to get a sale. Maybe, just maybe, Richard's abject attitude had driven her into the arms of, according to him, about eight different men in the space of as many years.

If she were Richard, Beth thought, she'd definitely want a bit of DNA-testing of the children before she forked out endless sums for their upkeep. But maybe she was missing the point.

Richard, having been responsible for the childcare while Felicity was off 'selling', was no doubt firmly bonded to the kids, whatever their provenance. God knew, Beth wasn't Magpie's mother, but she still looked on her as a wayward furry baby to be looked after along with Jake. Magpie herself, of course, remained aloof at all times, and Beth sometimes wondered if the cat would even deign to pick her out of a line-up of humans if she wasn't holding a sachet of the cat's ridiculously priced gourmet dinner.

Richard, a solicitor who worked in Lordship Lane, was a very pleasant man. But as minutes passed and the chat continued to revolve around his ex, Beth started to get restive. She was beginning to feel she knew the errant Felicity better than she knew the chap in front of her, and – worse still – the longer it went on, the more she sympathised with her. She'd like to be knocking back an elicit cocktail in a bar with a handsome stranger right now, instead of discussing how fantastic Felicity had looked in her wedding dress and how amazed Richard had been that she'd ever looked his way. Yes, it was tragic, but was this really getting either of them anywhere?

'Have you thought about being a bit less in awe of Felicity? You know, for whatever reason, she did decide you were good enough to marry and she stuck with you for long enough to have all the children,' said Beth, who'd already forgotten their names, despite Richard explaining them in huge detail. 'You seem nice. Maybe you should just stop pining over Felicity and get on with things,' she added, bracingly.

Then, to her horror, she realised Richard was looking at her like Paddington spotting an unopened jar of marmalade. Building him up a bit, then telling him he needed another woman, could definitely be misconstrued and it looked as though he was busily doing exactly that.

'I don't mean with, erm, anyone in particular, I just mean in general,' she said, rapidly trying to backtrack. But it was too late.

Before she knew it, Richard was clasping both her hands in his over-warm paws, and asking her very seriously if she'd like to come out for dinner. Tonight.

She was just starting to blush ferociously, when the door to the deli was briskly opened and cold air rushed in. Something made her crane her head, only to see a tall figure in a navy peacoat stamping around, looking at the dainty biscuits and fancy olive oils. She tried to pull her hands away, but the lawyer was surprisingly strong.

'Richard,' she remonstrated loudly, and the man in the deli popped his head round the corner into the café section, just in time to see her yanking her hands back across the table as if they were red hot. Her flustered eyes met those of DI Harry York for one second, before she looked down in consternation, then quickly looked up again.

'Afternoon, Beth,' said York in non-committal tones, raking her companion from top to toe with a quick, almost professional glance. If Beth hadn't known better, she'd have said York was running Richard the lawyer through his personal database of criminals, seeing if he could arrest him on the spot.

Coming up blank, he nodded farewell to Beth and stamped out of the shop again, just as the flustered girl on shift came out from behind the café counter to see what he wanted. The door shut behind him with a last decisive jingle, both the waitress and Beth looking at it in disappointment.

Beth was just wondering how quickly she could extract herself from the situation, and possibly even race down the street after York – though doubtless there were hundreds of self-help books out there telling her that was the last thing she should ever do – when the door jingled again. He'd come back! Beth craned over, a smile of welcome spreading on her face, only to see Belinda McKenzie's commanding form dominating the doorway, one of her acolytes behind her.

She shrank back in her seat again, before Belinda spotted

her. Damn it all. Was she coming in for coffee, or was she just going to buy something eye-wateringly expensive for her huge deluxe kitchen in Court Lane?

Beth fervently hoped it was the latter, as otherwise news of her 'date' would shoot round Dulwich faster than an infestation of nits at the Village Primary. But her luck was out. Just as she'd finally shaken off Richard's second attempt at clutching her hand in his increasingly clammy grasp, Belinda stuck her head around the divide between the two rooms.

'Ah, Beth, I thought I spotted you hiding there! I'd know all that hair anywhere,' she said with a laugh. Beth's hand instantly went defensively to her ponytail, which, when she'd last looked, had been as sleek as it ever got. 'Saved me a phone call anyway. Tutoring is going to be on Wednesday this week, OK?'

Beth nodded dumbly, although she was peeved that Belinda had agreed to this change without consulting her. But if she protested, Belinda would only stride over to argue, and then Beth would have to explain Richard. He had his back to Belinda and actually seemed to be cowering. Belinda was as unstoppable as the tides, though. She stepped forward anyway, took one look at Richard and clapped a hand on his shoulder.

'Richard! How the devil are *you*?' she said heartily.

Richard didn't quite jump, but was so sheepish as he got up to kiss Belinda on both cheeks that Beth almost looked around for a shepherd who could take charge of him.

'And how's *Felicity*?' said Belinda.

'Oh, um, well, er, we're sort of, not together, um...' poor Richard faltered.

Belinda smiled widely. 'Just kidding! Of course I know all about it, we had Felicity round with her new man last week. Well, one of them. And you must come round with Beth, very soon. I don't take sides in these things. I always say, Barty and I are like Switzerland when our friends split up,' she said, lowering her voice by one decibel, which still meant that people going about their business on the other side of the road would be picking up every nuance.

Hmm, thought Beth. Like Switzerland, in that there were cuckoos involved. But neutral? That was harder to believe. Belinda would inexorably follow the money; she couldn't help herself. If Beth and James had split up all those years ago, Belinda would have been outwardly sympathetic towards Beth, but a lot more enthusiastic about having an affluent single man available for her dinners, even if he worked in something she'd consider useful but deadly dull, like James's career in management consultancy. Media types were much more up Belinda's street, and she tended to collect them in an informal game of Top Trumps. Newspaper editors, TV presenters (on the serious channels – never cable) and the better sort of actor. *Holby City* or *Casualty* was OK, but they had to be playing a niche injury as a cameo role, *not* be a regular.

Neither Felicity nor Richard would ever be in Belinda's iPhone favourites list. But in this case, Belinda had already had Felicity round, so that meant she considered her the better social bet of the broken marriage. Either Felicity was from an established Dulwich family, or she had a very nice property that Richard had sweetly decided to leave her and her children in, or one of her new men was loaded. Even as a lawyer, Richard seemed to be coming a poor second. But maybe that was what always happened to him.

Beth decided that she'd had enough of the whole situation, just as Belinda turned her piercing blue eyes to her.

'And Beth? How's that wonderful institution of yours?' Was it Beth's imagination, or did Belinda's eyes narrow just a tad? Since she'd given up her own career, Belinda expected everyone else to follow suit. Those who didn't were considered disloyal. Belinda's friend, hovering on the fringes of the conversation, was destined never to be introduced and therefore tried to look interested in some unspeakably fancy cherries in kirsch. Named either Carol or Catherine – Beth could never quite remember which – she was amongst Belinda's chosen band precisely because she'd made exactly the same life choices, but was a comfortable notch or two less successful at everything.

Tiresome though it was to kowtow to the woman, Beth knew it didn't do to get on the wrong side of Belinda. 'I think the tutoring's going really well, don't you?' she said quickly, squashing her annoyance about this week's change of day *and* sidestepping her much-envied job at Wyatt's. The important thing, at this particular moment, was reminding Belinda that they had a joint enterprise, which had been all Belinda's idea and for which she deserved every bit of credit.

Instantly, Belinda's smile became a lot warmer. 'Oh, I'm so glad you agree. It's going to make all the difference with Jake, it will really help him turn the corner from being a reluctant reader...'

Beth's hackles instantly rocketed higher even than the price of cherries in kirsch, but she gritted her teeth. Jake had *not* been a reluctant reader; he'd just been taking a somewhat scenic route to get to his current enthusiasm for the written word. Admittedly, even now, he was more likely to be reading *Captain Underpants* than anything remotely improving, but so what? For heaven's sake, he was ten.

Though there might be the first suspicions of steam coming out of Beth's ears, it would not do to let any escape. She told herself to remain civil. She said goodbye in a friendly, though not encouraging, way to Richard, who was luckily too much in awe of Belinda to carry on with his earlier attempts at seduction. And she braced herself and dived in for the double kiss with Belinda, almost getting smothered in the woman's personal miasma of *Je Reviens* – in this case more of a threat than a promise. It was time to get back to Wyatt's.

On the way, it was York that she kept coming back to. The timing of that encounter had been terrible. At any moment, over the last eight years, York could have bumped into her anywhere around Dulwich and she would have been blamelessly knocking back coffees alone, or with a girlfriend. The one time she had allowed herself to be set up – by Janice, of all people – and York had to appear out of the blue. What was he even doing in Dulwich, anyway? It wasn't as if he lived here; he lived in Camberwell, like Jen. So why wasn't he back there, trying to find her? Why was he hanging about in the very place that Beth had subconsciously picked as too small, too chi-chi, and too darn fiddly for him ever to poke his nose into?

It was just infuriating, that was what it was, thought Beth, as she kicked a pile of stray leaves that had the temerity to have wandered into her path. Yes, they were beautiful windfalls from the blood-red acers that lined the roads here; yes, each one was a stunning explosion of crimsons and oranges, a firework in fragile organic form; but they were blimming well in her way on this most annoying day. She was so thoroughly fed up that she didn't even notice York barrelling out of the larger, less popular deli on this side of the road, with a paper bag tucked under his arm, until he'd nearly hit her.

'Oh!' she said, feeling defensive before he'd even opened his mouth.

'Beth, hi again,' he said, in measured, amused tones, taking in her high colouring, her little boots with red leaves stuck to them, and her decidedly grumpy air. 'Everything OK?'

'Why wouldn't it be?' she shot back, then cursed herself. Casual, that's what she needed to be. She tried flicking her hair to one side, but it swung back like a fire door, perhaps doing her the favour of disguising the daggers in her eyes. 'You didn't call me back.'

'Well, I did, but maybe you were busy?' he said, head on one side. 'Anyway, what can I do for you?'

Surprised, Beth realised she hadn't checked her phone. She felt as though he'd wrong-footed her. But now he was here, she might as well make the most of him. As it were. Of course, when she'd rung, she'd been thinking about Jen and what useful steps she could possibly take. But she'd also had that kiss in her mind, that gentle brushing of her cheek that had sent her to bed so tingly and discombobulated. But now, looking at York in the cold light of day, he couldn't look less affected himself, and to be perfectly honest, she didn't know what she'd been getting herself in such a tizz about. He was quite ordinary-looking really, just tall, and broad, and smiley, with that hair ruffled by the breeze, and those blue eyes smiling down at her... Oh. This wasn't going well. She burst into speech.

'How do I go about reporting a missing person? Do I have to be a family member to do it?' Her tone was abrupt, and her chin jutted out belligerently. She was acting as though she'd asked him endless times before and he'd dodged the question through laziness or sheer malevolence. But she couldn't help it. She had to build up her walls, and quickly, or he might see what she'd been feeling. And that would never do.

'Um, if you hadn't just had a coffee, I'd suggest we went and sat down somewhere while I talked you through the procedure,' said York mildly, eyeing Beth's aggressive stance. When her stare didn't waver, he ploughed on.

'You don't have to be family, you can just ring 101, that's the best way. You'll be asked for contact details for the person – address, phone and so on, and also for details on their relatives. You don't even have to wait twenty-four hours, as most people seem to think. Look, we could just pop into Jane's, if you like, and get out of this wind,' he urged.

There *was* no wind, just a light breeze shuffling the acer leaves up with the acidic yellows and caramel browns of the large plane leaves. And for once, Beth was impervious to offers of coffee.

'I've waited a lot longer than twenty-four hours,' she said, stricken, and with all the imbroglio of the kiss forgotten. 'I should have done this sooner, much sooner. But there always seemed to be other people who should be doing it, if they were worried. And I'm not sure that anyone else is worried. Apart from Jess. Jen's daughter,' Beth clarified. 'Listen, can you take all the details?'

York hesitated. 'It's best if you just ring 101. There's a whole checklist to run through, and you need to get that information on the system. If there's been no report from close family members, then perhaps there isn't really any cause for alarm. She may be visiting someone you just don't know, for instance. But once the information is in place, then I can take a look at it and start taking action on it. I have to tell you that it's not going to be the only thing on my plate, but I will look at it personally.' He said this kindly and, for a moment, Beth forgot all their troubles and complications, and just stared gratefully up at him. He smiled in return, and the moment stretched as long as Court Lane.

Just then, Beth distinctly heard the sound of the school bell. She looked at her phone quickly. Three thirty already. How could that be? It was chucking-out time at the Village Primary and she was, as usual, about to be late for Jake. There wasn't a moment to race back up to Wyatt's to sort out her office. Oh well, she had her handbag, which was all that mattered, and she could send a text to Janice asking her to make sure her door was locked.

'Got to go,' she said to York. 'And thank you,' she added with a smile.

York smiled back, and strode off, his paper bag under his arm. What on earth was in it, Beth wondered. That was a mystery she probably wasn't going to solve.

* * *

York, walking quickly up the street, was already cursing the urge that had made him buy a box of peppermint teabags. So what if Beth liked them? When would she ever be coming over to Camberwell, anyway? But he'd suddenly felt like giving them a go. And you never really knew, did you?

She'd been having a coffee with that sweaty-looking guy, who definitely wasn't good enough for her. Maybe he'd been advising her on insurance, or something? Yeah, right, he thought. But it had made his mind up about something. If he didn't want to end up alone, like poor Mrs Thingummybob in the high-rise flat, he'd have to make a move at some point. And the sooner the better.

* * *

Nipping back over the road to get Jake, Beth bumped into Katie, bouncing down the steps of her exercise studio tucked above the most expensive boutique in the village – which was a hotly contested position, of course. Katie was now running enough classes to fill several days a week, and as a result was as bendy as a young sapling in the wind and even a bit more relaxed about Charlie's precious routine. This was partly because the entrance exams were now looming so large that, as Katie had explained to Beth, it was important to take her foot off the pedal a little, so there'd be enough in Charlie's engine for the final push in January, when it came.

Beth was just hoping Jake realised he was supposed to have an engine at all, as he lolloped forward into the unknown like Bambi on ice. Well, he'd had a practice run, of sorts, with the grammar school exams – the results of those were due any day – but Beth was pretty sure he'd wiped the whole experience out of his memory banks by now, like a Nintendo handset when it ran out of charge.

As a result of Katie's new devil-may-care attitude, temporary though it might be, Beth and Jake found themselves happily accepting an invitation to supper. For Beth, this actually meant not getting fed, as she was used to eating her evening meal early with Jake. Katie, however, cooked something 'child-friendly' for Charlie, which meant it was rigorously organic, screened for toxins, and pumped with at least six of his five a day, and yet cunningly designed to appeal to his 'chips with everything' small boy palate. If that wasn't feat enough, Katie would then create a lovely grown-up dinner for Michael when he eventually found his way home from the coalface of his big job in publishing.

'Have you ever tried giving Michael the same thing to eat as Charlie?' Beth mused, as she took her place in Katie's kitchen, which featured more marble than the façade of the Santa Croce in Florence.

'Have you met Michael?' laughed Katie, fishing two mugs out of one of her innumerable cupboards and putting the kettle on. 'You know he can't stand vegetables. I have to hide everything under his meat. He'll eat cabbage if it's got a hunk of beef sitting right on top of it. I have a lot to thank *MasterChef* for. He's way more difficult to cook for than Charlie. Only trouble is that I have to make sure Charlie doesn't see his dad is eating mashed potatoes instead of sweet potato.'

'What do you do at weekends?' Beth wondered idly.

'There's a lot you can do with a burger,' said Katie, waggling her eyebrows.

'Wouldn't it just be easier to say to Michael, "You've got to eat vegetables", and say to Charlie, "You're basically going to live until you're a hundred and fifty, thanks to me"?'

'It would be easier,' said Katie. 'But it wouldn't work. I don't want to let too much light in on the miracle, do I? At the moment, Charlie thinks kale is more or less compulsory at every meal, and Michael doesn't recognise green things if they're in close enough proximity to protein. It's all working perfectly.'

'Except that you're doing twice as much as you could be?' Beth pointed out gently.

'The thing is that I don't mind. Yes, I'm a lot busier with the yoga, but that's great, and it's all timed around Charlie. In the evenings, I just cook, basically, which I love. So I'm quite happy.'

Beth, who'd despaired of finding new ways with fish fingers long ago, and had no intention of subjecting either Jake or herself to Swiss chard or whatever the latest in-vegetable was, decided to keep her own counsel. Although she technically had hours of free time every evening after Jake was in bed, she filled them very successfully with her freelance work and lots of idle internet surfing, as well as reading and enough housework to satisfy her OCD tendencies without making the house unliveable for a small, messy boy. There was no way she'd ever consider making more food after the last bit of their supper washing-up was done.

Maybe that was another reason to abandon dating? The whole business with York seemed to get nowhere, Tinder was frankly terrifying, and her little tête-à-tête with Richard today had not convinced her that she was missing a lot.

'Did I tell you I went on a date today?' she said teasingly to Katie, knowing the snippet would fall, like a grenade, on the calm waters of their afternoon.

Katie, transfixed, paused with the teabag-laden teaspoon dripping great gobs of Earl Grey onto her gleaming Travertine floor.

'You're kidding,' she said. Once she'd scraped her eyebrows off the ceiling and mopped the tiles as well, Katie sat down and demanded every detail.

Exhausted by the time she'd recounted everything, including the unfortunate sighting by York and their subsequent chat on the pavement, Beth sat back and watched Katie compute it all. For some reason, the only thing she hadn't divulged was that little kiss that she and York had shared in her hallway the other evening. Because that, well, it wasn't important, was it? Or even relevant. This story had all been about Richard.

'I'm a bit surprised you hadn't already heard every single detail from Belinda, anyway. Turns out she and this Richard guy's ex, Felicity, are big chums,' joked Beth.

'There *is* a missed call on my phone from Belinda,' admitted Katie, with a little moue of distress on behalf of her friend. 'So she was probably putting out an all-areas alert. Do you want me to play the message?' she said, glancing down at her phone.

'No! Please don't. Oh great,' said Beth, down in the dumps at the thought of being number one topic of conversation at drop-off and pick-up tomorrow, with all the flicking of sidelong glances and suddenly-shushed conversations that entailed. 'Well, I suppose my only hope is that something else might happen tonight, to knock me off the news agenda.'

'That's not very likely, is it? Actually, I think I've met this Felicity. She was at Belinda's last week. She seemed to have a man in tow, but she was very flirty,' Katie said, her expression pained.

It wasn't like Katie – normally sweetness and light – to notice such behaviour, or to comment on it so tartly. She must have been annoyed by the woman, Beth thought. Possibly, Felicity had even tried it on with Michael, not that he'd ever look at another woman. Well, Beth didn't think he would. But you could never be sure, could you? The human heart had many chambers, some hidden even from their owners until the worst was done. Beth chased away the sombre thought and got on with enjoying the evening with her friend instead, which was much easier to do when they'd got off the subject of her date and onto the doings of the rest of Dulwich instead.

There was plenty to say, as usual. Much of the speculation that wasn't temporarily beamed on her concerned the very annoying recent closure of the village post office, and the much more pleasing rumour that it was about to be replaced by a Waitrose. Beth was rightly suspicious of such talk. Every time any shop closed down, there was talk of Waitrose moving in. But all that usually happened was that another short-lived, madly priced cushion emporium blossomed, only to wither once the horrible truth that you can actually have too many cushions was proved beyond reasonable doubt to the disillusioned proprietor.

Beth wasn't immune to the lure of cushions. Like most men, James had suffered from an acute allergy to them, but since his death most of the chairs in her house had sprouted at least one, and when they got tatty they had to be replaced. She didn't go as far as the design magazines exhorted, and change her covers to match the seasons. But there were many in Dulwich who did, including people like Katie and Belinda, whose soft-furnishings budgets seemed to be as unlimited as the oceans.

A Waitrose, though? Ah, that was the dream. Both women gazed into the middle distance for a moment, contemplating the paradise on earth that would be Dulwich with a Waitrose. For Beth, it meant slightly healthier, though more expensive, fish fingers. For Katie, it was the promise of never-ending leafy green vegetables to stuff her best-beloved boy with. Which reminded them, it was time for the boys to eat.

Beth proudly watched her son chomping his way stoically through mounds of organic cavolo nero, which he understood was the price to be paid for an evening with his best friend. Then it was time to go.

Sitting at home later, with a restorative glass of wine and the remains of a peanut butter sandwich – the quickest and easiest way of filling herself up that she could think of – she realised she'd forgotten to do two things. She hadn't texted Janice and, more importantly, she still hadn't got round to reporting Jen missing.

Ah well, the first was probably not important. And so much time had already gone by on the second issue that another day's delay surely wouldn't be crucial, she thought, as she trundled off to bed, leaving Magpie on the sofa digesting a gourmet dinner which had contained far more nutrients than Beth's own.

THIRTEEN

It was the first of the late autumn days that had that miserable, grudging feel about it, thought Beth, as she tried to wipe her wet hair out of her eyes for the umpteenth time. She'd set off without an umbrella, as the fine mist had looked as though it would clear quickly. But those deceptive droplets had turned into a mean, cold drizzle, determined to seep through the cracks in her pixie boots and drip coldly down the collar of her coat. She hoped Jake would be OK all day in his light parka coat. At least his boots were sound. They'd been bought only last week from the shoe shop opposite the Village Primary, when she'd realised in horror that his back-to-school shoes, which she'd fondly imagined would last till February, had suddenly become distinctly too small. He was getting far too much cavolo nero from Katie, that was the trouble, and it was making him sprout, she thought with a grin that illuminated her grey eyes and cheered the porter at the gates of Wyatt's.

Through the mist, the green of the lawn in front of the school looked even more velvety than usual. Beth didn't linger to admire it, but hurried in past the heavy double doors and on past reception to the warren of corridors where she liked to think the real work of the school went on, far from the pupils and teachers. This was the engine room of the huge organisation, where the fees were raked in and processed, the arcane admissions magic was worked, and where – a small but important cog – her institute covered the inglorious history of the wicked old swashbuckler who'd been their founder and benefactor, Sir Thomas Wyatt. She worked her away along the corridors, passing the bursar's office quickly but lingering to say good morning to the development office team.

Then, at her own office door, she paused. It was open.

Surely she'd closed it yesterday afternoon? She hadn't locked it, that was true, which was strictly against school rules, particularly after everything that had happened at the school recently. She'd meant to get Janice to nip down and secure it for her, but it had gone right out of her head.

Her heart was hammering now, and she took a deep breath before stepping forward very carefully. Bearing in mind that she'd recently received a nasty blow to the head, and with no desire at all to repeat the trip to the hospital, Beth peeped cautiously round the door. She was almost relieved when she saw the chaos within. It looked as though someone had done a very thorough job of messing the place up, but there didn't seem to be anyone lurking anywhere in the shadows with a rounders bat. She felt her knees sag a little in relief, and she steadied herself on the doorframe, working up the courage to step over the threshold to have a proper check.

Though it was a massive upgrade on her first quarters at the school, it still wasn't a palatial office, just a generous rectangular box. There were blinds at the window, rather than curtains to hide behind. She could see under her conference table from here, and the space was intruder-free, as was the dark area under her knee-hole desk. There was still one possible hiding place, though. She tiptoed into the room as quietly as she could, and then flung open the door of the cupboard where she usually stowed her coat and bag. Any miscreant would have to be even weenier than her to get inside this, she realised. She felt rather silly, once she was looking at the tiny, dusty locker, but she'd had to check.

Now she was sure the place was definitely empty, she could stand safely in the centre of the room and have a good look at the damage, relieved on one hand but pretty dismayed on the other. There were drifts of paper all around her, and her beloved books had been shoved unceremoniously off the shelves, here, there and everywhere. She felt like crying as she contrasted the tidy, organised, efficient office she'd left in a hurry yesterday with the maelstrom of random, torn and dirty papers she was standing in now. But as a veteran of several attempts to intimidate her with spiteful burglaries, she knew this looked a lot worse than it actually was.

If she wasn't mistaken, the documents that had taken the white heat of the perpetrator's rage were the leather-bound volumes of the *Wyatt's Chronicle*, a desperately dull school newsletter that had been published with grim regularity for far, far too long in the interwar years when the place had been run by a head who was a lame donkey in comparison to the current sleek thoroughbred, Dr Grover. Beth now thanked her stars for this publication. Though it could induce irreversible coma in anyone unwise enough to dip into its foxed pages, as a vehicle to absorb the aggression of an angry burglar, it couldn't have been more useful.

She started hefting the volumes back onto their shelves, not worrying over-much that many of the pages were now ripped or creased. Nobody in their right mind would be reading them anyway. By the time she'd shoved them all back into line, the room really didn't look too bad at all.

It was just the area around her desk that needed attention now. Her drawers had been emptied, and a rich trove of tampons, headache pills, stubs of chocolate bars and retired hair scrunchies had been strewn around like a lumpy and distinctly Tracey Emin-style take on confetti. The tampons, in particular, had been stamped on so hard that some of them had burst out of their pastel-coloured packaging, and lay forlorn, like dead white mice littering up the place. What a waste, Beth thought, bending down, picking them up and dumping them unceremoniously in the now overflowing rubbish bin. She crushed everything down with her foot, then realised this was precisely the action that the horrible burglar had been carrying out all over her possessions. At once, this intrusion changed from an attack on a worker at Wyatt's, to a much more personal assault. You couldn't really get much more intimate than Tampax.

Before she had started clearing up, she'd had a moment when she wondered whether she should just yell down the corridor for Janice, or even phone York straight away and report the break-in. But it was her own fault, wasn't it? She should have locked the door. They were all under strict instructions that security was paramount. And while there was no sensitive information in Beth's office, now the slavery issue was well known after Dr Grover's many TV appearances, the last thing the school would want was marauding protesters shredding their precious documents, shortly to form the bedrock of Beth's slavery exhibition. Luckily, the now-famous ledgers prepared by Wyatt's team of clerks were already safely enshrined in glass cases in the school foyer for all to see, and would just be moved into position for whatever exhibition Beth dreamt up next.

That didn't stop Beth feeling guilty, though. She was supposed to be the custodian of this rich array of materials, and an important part of her duties was to keep it all safe. She couldn't afford for word to get out that she'd simply left the door unlocked. If the idea of this burglary was to embarrass her, it had been extremely effective. But who would be wandering around the school, feeling so malign towards her? Who had she annoyed or offended?

True, she wasn't always tactful. She sometimes got people's backs up, accidentally, with her forthright views on this or that. But would anyone seriously be annoyed enough at her take on house prices – the only subject in Dulwich which really inflamed passions – to trash her office? Or could it be connected to that nasty bash on the head outside Jen's house? Was all this tied in with her friend's strange disappearance? And if it was, surely there was only one person in the world who had a motive?

Even if she didn't want to admit to York that she'd been stupid enough to leave her office door unlocked, she needed to report Jen officially missing, and start taking action. If her suspicions were right, everything was pointing in one direction and she had to do something about it.

By the time she'd finished getting everything shipshape again, she was scarlet in the face and quite dusty. Even though the books hadn't been on these shelves long before they'd been flung around the place, they'd still managed to attract surprising quantities of south London grime. Beth supposed it was the dreaded South Circular, sprinkling liberal quantities of filth across its path, the direct opposite of fairy dust. The bin was now full of pages of the *Chronicle* which were unsalvageable, some bearing dirty, but surprisingly neat, footprints, which Beth was sure weren't hers. These were layered on top of the wreckage of her chocolate stash, tampons and other odds and ends – successfully concealing them, Beth noted.

Wiping her hands ineffectually on the back pockets of her jeans, she popped to the loo just along the corridor – after assiduously locking her own particular stable door, of course – and looked at herself in the mirror over the sink. Hmm. Hair everywhere. *Check.* Cheeks flushed. *Check.* Smudges of dust on her face, hands and clothes. *Check.* Could she get away with saying it had been an extremely hectic morning in the archives? Probably not. She did the best she could to remedy all these things, then dashed off to visit Janice.

Serenely studying her computer screen, a huge crystal bouquet of red roses dominating her desk, Janice looked edible in the light streaming from one of the big windows, showing the slice of verdant grass outside. The early drizzle had gone and mellow autumn sunlight caressed the gentle planes of her face. She looked up and smiled as Beth stuck her head around the door.

'Come in, sit down,' she said. If she thought her friend was looking unusually casual, even for her, she didn't say a word.

Beth rubbed at a dusty patch on her jeans as she got comfy in the chair, and tried to loop her hair more tidily behind her ears. She'd done her best with it just now in the mirror, but something about this morning's chaos had transmitted itself to her unruliest feature, and the calm and peace of Janice and her surroundings seemed to be pointing up the contrast in a rather cruel way.

'Having trouble with your laptop this morning, are you?' said Janice expectantly.

'Er, no, why do you ask?' said Beth, put off her stride by this unexpected start. Her laptop was about the one thing in her office that wasn't misbehaving – as far as she knew. She hadn't even turned it on yet.

'Oh, it's just that we had a major computer glitch yesterday afternoon. I popped round to your office to see if you were affected, but you weren't there,' said Janice.

'What time was this?' Beth was instantly alert.

'Oh, must have been about two-ish, two thirty. Before you left for the day, anyway. I saw your note.'

Hmm, thought Beth. Little did Janice know that the note, written in reasonably good faith – though deliberately opaque in its wording – had been over-optimistic about her return to the office.

'What was the computer problem? The intranet?' Beth asked hopefully. The intranet was the school's major information loop, almost as dull as the *Chronicle*, and harder to escape than one of the circles of hell.

'No, it was everything. For some reason, the whole lot went down. And it would happen the week when our IT guy is away on holiday. Luckily, I managed to get someone to sort it at really short notice. Someone you know, actually.'

'Oh? Who was that?' Beth was listening with half an ear now, still mulling over who could possibly have gained access to her office. Who did she know, with a grudge against her, who wanted to make her life more difficult? Was it really anyone at the school? She got on well with everybody, she thought. It was hard to imagine who disliked her enough to cause such havoc.

'Oh, that guy, Ted. I think he's married to your friend, Jen?'

Suddenly Beth had the curious feeling that everything in the office had just come much closer to her, that colours had become unmistakably sharp, and that noises, including Janice's mellifluous voice, were shriekingly loud.

'Hang on. Say that again. Ted was dealing with our IT, yesterday afternoon?'

'Yes, he was on it right away, as soon as I emailed him. Are you all right, Beth? You've gone white as a sheet.'

'I'm fine,' said Beth grimly, though there was a ringing in her ears and she was gripping the sides of her chair with both hands. 'Just tell me what happened. Please.'

'It's just like I said.' Janice seemed mystified. 'Some weird computer freeze-up affecting us all, and I just found the first emergency IT contact in the folder, which turned out to be this chap, Ted. He was great, actually.'

'I can't believe you got him to help.' Beth leant forward, aghast.

'I'd have thought you'd be pleased,' Janice remonstrated. 'He's your friend's hubby, after all. But it was a one-off; our usual guy will be back on Monday. It was a bit manic round here yesterday afternoon. They've been interviewing for a new marketing person. Well, you know what it's like. Advertise for anything, even a loo cleaner, and the place is swamped with applicants.'

It was true. Even the most mundane jobs routinely attracted sheaves of hopefuls, mostly overeager parents.

'Everyone thinks if they get a job, it'll either get money off the fees for their kids, or they'll be able to shoehorn them in here without doing the entrance exam.' Janice sniffed. 'As if!'

Beth nodded automatically, though she had harboured very much the same thoughts herself when she'd applied, and was still hoping against hope that Jake might have a better chance of wiggling his way in because of her job.

'But what did the marketing post have to do with it?'

'Oh, nothing really, except there were just so many people around in the afternoon, doing the full tour. You know how we always show people over the whole school as part of the interview process, even if they're no-hopers. I've told the bursar time and again that it's a terrible waste of time, but you know what he's like,' said Janice. Beth, no fan of the bursar either, did indeed know him only too well. 'Didn't you see all the people being taken around, they probably popped their heads round your office, didn't they? It's one of the highlights now, thanks to all your clever research.'

Normally, Beth would have taken this compliment to heart and would have been thrilled. Today, keen only to cover up her absence yesterday, and realising with a sinking feeling that there had been all too many potential room-wreckers prowling her corridor at the vital time, she tried to turn the conversation back to her main concern.

'But Ted, did he manage to sort things out? And how long did it take him?'

'Well, everything's working perfectly this morning, so I'd say he did a great job,' said Janice, seeming to pat herself on the back for finding the man.

If only she knew, thought Beth.

'You won't hire him again, though, will you?' she asked.

'That's an odd question, Beth. Is there anything going on I should know about?' said Janice. You could mistake her, easily enough, for someone who was just fluffy and gorgeous, a Persian cat of a girl. But Janice was sharp enough to run the school, and now Dr Grover, too, for good measure. It was a mistake to underestimate her.

Beth was wondering how far to take her into her confidence, when there was a rap at the door. Talk of the devil. It was the bursar, Tom Seasons, and, typically, he didn't wait for an invitation. He breezed in with all the aggression of a retired rugby player, still more at ease on a muddy pitch than in this pretty, light-filled room. He eyed Janice's bump a little askance, threw even more of a sharp look at Beth, then – without being asked – dragged one of Janice's occasional chairs up to the desk, and plonked himself down.

'Just wanted to talk about the marketing candidates. Dr Grover is tied up at the moment, so I just thought I'd go through the runners and riders with you. Power behind the throne, and all that,' he said, creasing his eyes in a genial smile.

Beth could tell that this éminence grise comment, meant to be a tremendous compliment, had not gone down well with Janice. Like many women who were influencers rather than movers and shakers in their own right, she hated to be reminded that the real power was not hers to command.

'Um, this might not be the right time, Tom,' Janice began.

'Nonsense, we can say anything in front of Beth, can't we?' said the bursar forcefully. He clearly wanted to get this off his chest and get on with other things, and wasn't planning to hang around for anyone. 'No secrets here.'

'Right,' said Janice with a set face.

Beth could see her dilemma. If she insisted on deferring the meeting, she might be inadvertently insulting Beth, and would certainly be challenging the bursar's authority. She really had little choice but to let it go ahead. Beth, meanwhile, knew she could have excused herself and saved her friend this dilemma, but as usual her curiosity was piqued. She just loved knowing stuff, even if it wasn't particularly relevant to anything. And also, she was still feeling a little light-headed after the revelation about Ted. Staying put would be good all round.

The bursar was announcing a litany of names. They seemed to be the candidates that had so far shimmied under or over the array of fiendish obstacles in their path before they would be allowed the signal honour of joining the marketing team. Wyatt's was a product that needed little introduction, and absolutely no selling, to any parent with a child the right age to go to this or any other school, so the job was little more than a sinecure with, as Janice had already pointed out, the tantalising prospect that it might offer an unfair advantage to the successful candidate's offspring. Beth wasn't surprised that all the possibles sounded like total whizzes in their fields.

She allowed the names to wash over her as she reflected on the events of the morning and the thunderous news of Ted's tinkering yesterday. She was just starting to feel a little steadier, and wondering if she shouldn't toddle back to her own office for a final tidy-round, a serious think about this morning's news – and the remote possibility that she might settle down to a bit of work of her own – when she realised the bursar and Janice kept coming back to one particular name. *Barbara Pine.*

'I thought she was a reasonably strong candidate,' said the bursar, damning with faint praise as usual. Janice said nothing more than a 'Hmm.' Beth wasn't sure that was because she was disagreeing with the man in front of her, or simply reserving judgement for her own reasons. But wait a minute. That name. She'd heard it before. But where?

It took her a few more minutes, while Janice and the bursar moved on to another woman entirely, then back to Barbara Pine again, before Beth realised why the name rang a bell. Barbara. *Babs*. It was Babs; little Jess's slightly out-of-her-depth step-mum, who'd all but blubbed over her kitchen table the other night, and seemed to be the only person in the world, apart from Beth herself and Jess, who had the slightest concern over the whereabouts of Jen.

'Is that *Babs* Pine, Tim Patterson's partner, you're talking about?' piped up Beth suddenly. Both the bursar, who'd more or less forgotten Beth was present, and Janice, who'd been so involved in wrangling with this wilful man that she'd become oblivious to her friend as well, turned to her in surprise. There was silence for a beat.

'Well, she could be a Babs. She said, "Barbara", and we called her that in the interview, but I suppose she's allowed a nickname, it's not against the law,' said Janice airily. 'No idea what her partner's called.'

'Do you think she'll get the job?' asked Beth.

'Now, well, we really can't discuss such things with anyone outside the official recruitment process, Beth. I'm sure you understand that,' said the bursar, spreading his meaty thighs and doing what he did best, patronising an underling with a small smile of pleasure.

Instantly, Janice rose to the defence of Barbara, whom she'd hitherto seemed unconvinced about. 'In fact, Dr Grover is terribly keen on Babs and, yes, he's thinking strongly that she'll be a real asset to the team. She's got tremendous skills to bring to the table, she's been taking a leading role at her current employer for quite some time, and seems ready to stretch her wings with all the opportunities for personal growth and development that we can offer here at Wyatt's,' she said, slightly breathless by the time she'd finished her spiel.

The bursar, with a tetchy look that took in both women, said a little more quietly, 'Well, I didn't realise the head's thinking was developing along those lines, but it's a very sound point of view, very sound. Well, must get on. The under-thirteens rugger lot won't coach themselves.'

With that, he hoisted himself out of his chair, clearly feeling the twinges of old injuries besetting him, as well as the current blow landed upon him with such dainty accuracy by Janice. With a nod at both women, he took himself off, his heavy tread soon receding down the corridor.

Beth looked at Janice. 'I'm surprised you were that keen on Babs. I didn't like her that much when I first met her.'

'To tell you the truth, I can't even remember which one she was. We saw so many people yesterday, coming out with the same old jargon. I'm sure they were all really good; they'd made it to the interview stage. We weeded out loads before we got to the sessions yesterday. But once you've heard one person telling you how wonderful they are at selling stuff, you've kind of heard them all. It was a bit like an endless episode of *The Apprentice*,' Janice said with a smile.

'God, it sounds a nightmare,' said Beth. There were few things she'd dislike more than being up close and personal with an *Apprentice* wannabe.

'Added to that, we had a load of prospective parents in for a whistle-stop tour. Not just potential Year 1s but all the way up the school, right to sixth form. It was a really busy afternoon. I'm surprised you didn't notice.'

Beth nodded and tried to look well aware of all the comings and goings. It was a bit absurd, really. Janice was nominally her line manager, yes, and in that capacity wouldn't have been officially amused at the idea of her bunking off all afternoon to attempt flirtation in a Dulwich café. But with her dating mentor hat on, Janice would have been screaming, 'Go for it, girl!' and punching the air. After all, the whole thing had been her idea in the first place, and poor old Richard *was* her cousin.

But the fact that Beth's office had been ransacked, due to her own negligence, had put her so much on the back foot that she decided not to burden Janice by mentioning she'd been MIA for hours yesterday.

Mind you, she was going to have to tell her about the coffee date soon, or someone else would get in first. Since she'd been spotted by Belinda McKenzie, the Dulwich grapevine would be heavy with this low-hanging, ripe and juicy bit of gossip. Beth didn't overestimate her own worth, as far as Belinda was concerned. The woman had as keen an interest in matchmaking as Noah did when preparing for embarkation, but Beth had so far flouted her generous attempts to set her up with emotionally damaged bankers. Although she had never said as much, Beth suspected Belinda had now abandoned her as a hopeless case.

Felicity – Richard's ex – was firmly on Belinda's list of approved chums, however, so the fate of her discarded other half was always going to be of interest. And the two of them getting together would be an irresistibly neat conclusion, which Belinda could easily convince herself she'd always seen coming.

So trouble was looming, but Beth was willing to chance her luck and delay mentioning her coffee with Richard until at least this afternoon, if possible. In the meantime, she wondered if there was more research she could usefully be getting on with. Nothing to do with her job, of course.

'Do you have a list of names of parents who came on the tour yesterday?' Beth said to Janice, aiming for a casual tone but sensing, from her friend's sharp glance, that she had failed.

'Of course. Why would you want to look at that?'

'Just working on some early marketing strategies for the institute,' said Beth vaguely, hoping her nose wasn't growing as she spoke.

Janice looked at her again, but said, 'Well, I don't see the harm in letting you have the list. I'll ping it over to your email.' She turned back to her screen and got busy.

Beth took the hint and got up to go. 'Will you have time for a coffee later?' she asked, her hand on the door.

'Lovely,' said Janice. 'But decaf. This little person isn't keen on coffee.' She smiled, fondly stroking her bump.

'Not keen on coffee? They'll have to move out of Dulwich when they're finally with us, then,' Beth said, laughing.

Having carefully unlocked her office, Beth was glad to see everything was, of course, just as she'd left it. She was always going to have that little pause now, she realised, just before going in; that moment when she braced herself for what she might see. It was a nasty little aftertaste of the malice that had been at play. She hoped the perpetrator, whoever it was, would lose sleep over their actions, feel guilt corroding their pleasures. But people who could do stuff like this didn't *have* remorse. Their consciences, if they possessed them, were like stainless steel, fighting off the rust of doubt and self-reproach.

In her swivel chair, and swaying gently from side to side, Beth peered down the list that Janice had sent across. The number of people turning up for a speculative tour of the school should have shocked her, but knowing Wyatt's – and Dulwich, and parents – she scrolled down name after name after name and wasn't even surprised. She probably should have gone on the tour herself just to have seen what the competition was like, even though she knew the school front to back these days. She was, she very much hoped, going to be a Year 7 parent herself, next September. She sighed.

She'd just had the results back on Jake's eleven-plus attempt. He'd done well, but, as they said, no cigar. It was a respectable effort, but he wasn't in the top echelons that were guaranteed places. That meant he'd almost certainly fall foul of catchment areas. It was disappointing, but not unexpected.

Anyway, it had been practice, more than anything. But had she missed a trick with this Wyatt's tour? She could have asked pertinent questions, made the teachers leading the tour think, 'Oh, she must have a smart kid, must look out for him.' Except that they'd recognise her as their archivist and probably think she was crazy instead.

Such musings occupied her as she waded through names, letting them go in one eye and out the other. Until she got nearly to the end. There, she found a name which really did astonish her. She sat up straighter. That was beyond bizarre. What on earth was this person doing on a Wyatt's School tour? They had no possible reason to be there.

She already knew Babs, Jen's ex's new partner, had been touring the school yesterday. Meanwhile Ted, Jen's current husband, had been merrily fixing an IT problem. And, if this register was correct, a third person with a connection to Jen, who had no business at all to be at Wyatt's, had also been floating around the school, large as life.

The mystery had deepened by yet another degree. Beth hit the desk in front of her with the flat of her hand. It was all so frustrating! If she hadn't had her office burgled, she'd be on the phone again to York, trying to prod him into investigating the whole matter. But the only reason she now knew about this strange triangulation of people in the right zone and time to be the culprit, and therefore probably – she knew she was making a leap here, but she was willing to bet she was right – the person who'd whacked her on the head as well, was because she'd left her office unlocked. So she couldn't tell York, because it was all her fault. He'd see in two seconds that her door hadn't been forced, and she'd have to admit she'd left it more or less swinging in the breeze.

But maybe that didn't matter. He could hardly arrest her for carelessness, could he? And yes, Janice and all the powers of the school would also be furious with her, but was that the end of the world?

For once, she understood Jake's reluctance to 'fess up when he'd been naughty. Knowing you were going to be punished, and realising you deserved it, was worse than being told off out of the blue. Miles worse.

She decided to mull it over for a while. In the meantime, there was one thing she could usefully do. Apart from her actual job, of course. She could finally get round to reporting Jen missing. First of all, though, she'd try giving her a quick ring. She could imagine the way her friend's freckled nose would wrinkle, and how she'd shake her head, when she picked up the phone and told Beth not to be such a fusspot.

Beth dialled, and the little icon with Jen's familiar face popped up on the screen. It rang once, twice, three times... and clicked. Beth sat up straighter, said, 'Hello?' then felt her hopes plummet as the answering machine came on. The same old phrase: '*Leave a message after the tone.*' Oh Jen, Jen, thought Beth. I've left so many messages after that damned tone. Have you heard them? She hesitated to leave yet another, but after a second, just said quickly, 'Hope you're OK, Jen. Please ring me.'

Right, she had no choice now but to get busy with all the admin necessary to report someone missing in a big city like London. Should she ring 101, as York had suggested, or would doing it online be quicker? She'd certainly feel less of an idiot tapping in the details from behind a nice safe screen, but would it be as effective? Would her form ever meet a human? Well, she could sort that out by asking York to do as he'd promised and look into the matter for her. No need to mention the office ransacking if she didn't want to.

A quick Google search brought up a form, and immediately she faced a choice. *What would you like to report: a missing person, a sighting of a missing person, or a person you haven't seen or heard from in days, weeks or months?*

Jen fitted both the first and the third options. The wording of the third box was a little odd. Were the police trying to screen out people who'd just had spats with each other; those who weren't missing, but just sulking or moving on? Fair enough, she supposed. If the police wanted to concentrate on solving major crimes, they certainly couldn't get involved in he said/she said tussles. And from what Beth remembered about Sam and Lily's strictures on Tinder, half the men on there could easily fall into that category.

She clicked box three, though. She didn't really know if Jen was missing, as such. All she knew was that she hadn't seen her. The next screen asked whether Jen was in immediate danger. This was impossible to know. If Beth hadn't seen her for weeks, she couldn't possibly judge her current circumstances. So that, she supposed, had to be a no.

In this situation, we'd always advise you to take the usual steps, said the site, telling her to check with friends, family and neighbours. All perfectly sensible, but she felt as though she'd been fobbed off.

Beth went back to the beginning, and this time firmly declared Jen as a missing person. Now she was told to ring 101, with a list of details about her last sighting of her friend, a description, down to the clothes she'd been wearing, and details about her car and even whether she had an Oyster card to get around the city. It was very sobering.

Where was Jen? She had to be somewhere. Was she just lying low in Camberwell, not getting in touch for reasons of her own? Or had she taken off in her car? One of the last times Beth had seen her, Jen had been coming back from a trip, with a bag weighing down her shoulder and the general demeanour of someone who'd tangled with public transport all too recently. Camberwell was a hub for buses; they drifted up and down Camberwell Church Street restlessly like whales looking for plankton. Jen could have gone anywhere. But, for some reason, Beth was sure the answer lay nearer to home.

It was time. She'd prevaricated long enough. She had to ring 101, give all the details to the police, then she'd call York and get him to make good on his promise, set the wheels in motion. They'd find Jen, they would. They had to, for Jess's sake.

Half an hour later, Beth felt as though she'd got a load off her mind. It had taken forever, but the report was now in the system. At last.

Which meant that Beth could now get on with some of her legitimate work, like the slavery exhibition. Judging by the portrait displayed with great pomp in the School Hall, Sir Thomas's outfits had been almost as spectacular as Queen Elizabeth I's. The painted ruff he wore was so vast he would have had to go sideways through most doors, but his motto with his slaves might as well have been *no frills*. Life on the Wyatt plantations had been nasty, brutish and short.

She hoped the exhibition would make the overprivileged, shortly to be overfed denizens of Dulwich think for a moment about how delightfully cushy their own little world was. You never knew, possibly even some of the sniping among the more brattish kids about who'd got the best presents would be silenced, when they saw how children their age, a few centuries ago, would have been allocated a meagre extra half-scoop of breadfruit on Christmas Day. That had been the carbohydrate-heavy staple diet of the Caribbean at the time, thanks to Captain Bligh, who'd brought it to the islands from Tahiti.

Beth's ledgers showed there was a temporary Christmas Day armistice throughout Wyatt's holdings on the usual public floggings, designed to spread fear through the ranks and ensure iron discipline. But there would certainly have been no visit from Santa, no mince pies, and definitely not one single Brussel sprout to show for the Lord's birthday.

Though she worked away diligently enough, at the back of her mind Beth had a little plan forming. She couldn't execute it until tomorrow morning, but she was sure it was going to work. Well, pretty sure. OK, put it this way – it was worth a try. And she'd be in a public place, so there was very little risk. What could possibly go wrong?

FOURTEEN

Next morning, in order to put her scheme into operation, Beth had set her phone alarm ten minutes early, but for some reason Jake's own personal clock was going in reverse. He couldn't find any clean socks, though his drawers were exploding with them. Then he'd lost a crucial comic that he'd promised to discuss in depth with Charlie at breaktime. Once they'd turned the house upside down and found it at last, under Magpie's fluffy behind, Beth was in despair. She was pretty sure she'd missed her chance.

But as they ran towards the school gates, trailing scarves, gloves, Jake's PE kit and the all-important comic, Beth caught sight of her quarry just about to cross the road. She kissed the top of Jake's head, much to his evident disgust, and pushed him through into the playground, turning round and running for the zebra crossing. Too late, the lights had changed, and she wasn't brave enough to play chicken with the school-run traffic.

She pressed the button on the crossing without much hope in her heart, but to her surprise the lights changed to amber almost immediately. She could almost hear the cursing of the mothers in their people-carriers as they screeched to a halt on either side of the black and white markings in the road, and then remained poised with their tiptoes resting on the accelerator pedals, like sumo wrestlers gearing up for their first bout. In moments, all the expensive schools in the area would be ringing their bells for the first lesson. For the stay-at-home mums, getting their children in on time was much more important than avoiding pedestrians who should know better.

Nipping over the road with a cowardly wave of her hand to each mother, just in case she knew them and would have to face them later, she realised she'd managed to corner her quarry, as they'd just gone into the chemist's.

The door jingled when she opened it, and Tim Patterson looked round automatically then smiled vaguely as he recognised her. There was no one else in the shop, apart from the white-coated assistant, trying to look like a proper pharmacist after two days in the job. The real pharmacist was in the back somewhere, steeling herself for another full day allaying the fears of mothers too lazy or busy to organise a doctor's appointment.

Beth stepped briskly towards Tim. He'd been lingering near the men's hair loss solutions, but sidled away to the nit shampoos as she approached, before realising that was little better and coming to an awkward halt near family planning.

'Oh, hi Bess, how are you?' he said ingratiatingly, no doubt thinking a bit more free childcare might be handy at some point.

'*Beth*. I'm fine. I just thought I ought to tell you, I've reported Jen missing. Officially. To the police.'

'Really?' he said, the wind clearly taken out of his sails. 'Is that necessary, do you think?'

'Well, have you seen her recently?'

'Um, no, but well, she's been working very hard...'

'On some amazing project, yes, I've heard the story. The thing is, she wasn't working on any such thing when I last saw her, and she certainly didn't mention it to me.'

'Well, why would she? She doesn't have to report to you, Bess, er, Beth, does she?' said Tim, with a slightly baffled smile.

'Aren't you worried about her? Don't you think it's odd, the way she's disappeared?' Beth persisted, infuriated by his attitude.

Tim seemed to think for a moment. 'Nah. She's always been a bit like that.'

'She never has, not while I've known her, and that's been years now,' said Beth. They'd only become close recently, but Beth had always respected Jen. They had stood shoulder to shoulder in the playground as working women, against the yummy mummies of Dulwich. Well, not exactly against, but with a joint solidarity which had been a really important bond for Beth.

'Look, the thing is, Tim, I'm really worried about her. As far as I can tell, she hasn't been around for weeks now, and it's having quite an effect on Jessica.'

'Is it?' Tim looked surprised.

Beth sighed. It always astonished her how oblivious even the best fathers could be to the ebbs and flows of life with their children. And she wasn't including Tim in that category.

'She's been getting into trouble at school, she's a bit of a handful at home... you must have noticed? She was always good as gold before. She's missing her mum.'

'Oh, she's just going through a stage, that's what Babs says,' said Tim airily.

'What would Babs know? Jess isn't her child, and she's told me she's got no experience of bringing up kids. Look, Tim, take it from me, Jess is not enjoying this long absence of Jen's. And anyway, as I say, I've reported it to the police. But if you and Babs want to discuss it, why don't you meet me at Jen and Ted's in Camberwell, this afternoon? I've got to take Jake somewhere anyway, so I thought I'd arrange a meeting between all of us who care about Jen.'

'Have you got hold of Ted, then? I've tried a couple of times but it just goes to voicemail,' said Tim.

'And doesn't that make you think? When did you last even speak to him, or Jen for that matter?' Beth knew she shouldn't let her frustration show, but she couldn't help letting her voice rise in irritation. The pharmacy assistant had abandoned all pretence at tidying the shelves of Nurofen, and openly hanging on every word.

Tim just shrugged. 'You don't know what it's like after a divorce. Not speaking to Jen all the time has been great, really. No hassle, just letting me and Babs get on with things our own way. We're both busy working people, you know.'

Beth looked at him in astonishment. His selfishness was extraordinary. Yes, he had a full-time job, and so did Babs, but he also had a daughter who needed his time and attention.

The sooner they found her other parent, the better for everyone.

'Jessica needs her mum. It's as simple as that. So, can you come this afternoon? Round about four thirty? It's really important, Tim. You need to be there,' said Beth.

Tim twitched and shifted from foot to foot. Reluctance was written all over his weaselly face. What on earth was he trying to hide now, wondered Beth. Another assignation, maybe? They did say that when a man like Tim marries his mistress, he creates a vacancy.

'Oh, all right,' he said eventually. 'Though I don't see why I have to be there, or what good it's going to do.'

Beth thanked him and decided to leave the shop before he changed his mind. She did have a degree of sympathy with him; she, too, was unsure what effect the meeting was going to have. Would it, could it, get them any further on? Maybe the police route really was better. She knew York would say so. But it was bound to be much, much slower, and this situation had been dragging on long enough already.

Besides, Beth was a firm believer in direct action. No one seemed to care as much about Jen's whereabouts as she and Jess did. And Jess, bless her, was only a child and could do nothing on her own. No, Beth had to try and take charge of this business, get the grown-ups to take some responsibility. And she had a feeling that gathering all the interested parties together was going to shake some secrets out and into the light, and finally drive them towards some sort of resolution.

But as the morning and the afternoon trickled on, Beth realised she was dreading the rendezvous in Camberwell. Though she had left copious messages for Ted, he hadn't returned a single one, yet he'd definitely been around the day before yesterday, sorting out Janice's IT distress call.

So there was no guarantee he would show up. As for Tim, if anyone could slither out of a commitment, it was him. And Babs? She might well appear, but what on earth could she do to shed any light on the matter? No, this was another of Beth's hare-brained ideas, and if York knew about it, he would doubtless insist she cancel it and just plod through the orthodox missing persons circuit, probably getting nowhere but at least reaching this destination in an orderly fashion.

Just the thought of sitting back and letting the creaking police bureaucracy take on her burden was enough to show Beth that she had to go ahead, much though she hated the idea. And she had to be in Camberwell anyway as, thanks to Belinda's high-handed action in switching days, it was tutoring night. Like all good multi-tasking mothers, she was killing two birds with one stone.

By the time she finally set off, Beth's stomach was as full of knots as Jake's shoelaces. As a precaution, she texted York before she got in the car, just giving him the bare bones of her plan, then set off to join the snail of red brake lights that marked the route to Camberwell. Eventually, she pulled up in Camberwell Grove, just round the corner from Jen's.

The little house, she could see from here, was in darkness. Either she was the first to arrive, or the others had simply wimped out. She wasn't sure if she'd even be sad if it was the latter. The sky was pitch black already, and there was a cold wind blowing, ruffling the few leaves still in the gutters, strong enough to make the tall street lights sway a little in its wake. Pale yellow light and big dark shadows chased each other over the façades of the white houses. She reluctantly got out of the cosy little Fiat and wrapped her scarf tightly around her neck, trying to minimise any gaps that the wind could worm its way into.

Her boots rang out on the pavement, still shiny from drizzle earlier in the day – probably when she'd been cooped up in her office, she thought. God, it was freezing. She wished she'd put on her gloves. They were somewhere in the car. She decided she'd go back, then saw a dark shadow walking towards her from the other end of Jen's little road. Uh-oh. Too late now.

She walked forward a little reluctantly, then realised by the size of the shadow that the figure was Babs. She speeded up and met her outside Jen's house.

'Hi, thanks for coming. I just thought we all needed to talk, see if we can make sense of what's going on,' she said.

'Hi Beth,' said Babs, leaning in for the obligatory Dulwich kiss. 'Good to see you. Yes, I agree, it's worrying. Tim told me you wanted to meet and I think it's a great idea. Did you manage to get hold of Ted?'

'I left him loads of messages. Well, I've been leaving them for weeks now. No response. I don't know whether he's getting them or not.'

'It's so hard to say, isn't it? Have you seen him around at all?'

'I haven't, but then I only come to Camberwell once a week, and he hasn't been going to the school since you've had Jess. I know he was doing a job for Wyatt's on Monday, but I suppose he could have been doing that remotely from anywhere. Have you seen him around?'

'Nope, not for ages. I don't know whether Tim's been in touch with him, though. They might have discussed arrangements for Jess, I have no idea.'

'Wouldn't Tim normally just talk to Jen about stuff like that?'

'Well, yes, Beth, he would. But of course, she hasn't been around.'

'Is that what you think? That she's gone away? Tim still seems convinced she's doing some sort of work project...'

'Oh, you know Tim. He'll think anything that's convenient for him.'

'But it's not really convenient, is it? Not for you two to be taking all the childcare on?'

'It's certainly not convenient for *me*, that's for sure. But as you've probably noticed, Tim isn't doing a lot, is he? All right, he walks her to school in the mornings. But that's not a big detour for him really, he's got to get the train from somewhere. Other than that, he's pretty much on the same schedule as usual.'

'That's so unfair on you, Babs,' said Beth, before she could stop herself. She really shouldn't criticise someone else's partner. Whatever the resentments playing out in a relationship, a direct snipe at someone's other half rarely went down well. But Babs seemed to take it very lightly.

'Oh, he is what he is, you know. I lost my illusions about him some time ago,' she said flatly. 'Listen, I don't feel that comfortable discussing all this in the middle of the street. Shall we maybe go round the back?'

'The back of Jen's house?' said Beth, startled. There was no one else in sight, the street was deserted, and so was the much larger Camberwell Grove. But their voices did carry, and she supposed it wasn't the best place to have a frank chat. And the wind was still blowing up a storm.

They could adjourn to the high street, see if there was anywhere at all they could pop into for a coffee, but Beth knew the options were limited. And they were still waiting for the others. Perhaps Jen's garden made sense. But her memories of being attacked there, not so long ago, were a very powerful disincentive. She hesitated.

'Oh, I'm sorry, Beth, that's where you had that awful accident, didn't you? Of course you don't want to go round there,' said Babs in concerned tones. She'd accidentally lit on exactly Beth's dilemma.

'Oh, well, it's not that,' said Beth heartily, though of course it was. 'It's just that the others won't see us…'

'I'll just text Tim and tell him where we'll be,' said Babs brightly, fishing out her phone and tapping away quickly. 'There. All done.'

'It's trespassing…' said Beth, a little reluctantly.

'That didn't stop you before,' said Babs, pushing with her shoulder at the side door, which gave with a creak straight out of a horror film. 'Here we go,' she said, smiling over her shoulder.

Feeling a bit foolish left on the pavement alone, Beth looked up and down the street, wondering where on earth the men had got to. She pulled out her phone, but there was no winking icon from a text, WhatsApp or voicemail. Reluctantly, she followed Babs and shoved at the door, smelling again the musty, disused odour of the pathway where she had lain unconscious for hours.

* * *

York, looking up and down the very similar, though slightly less grand, Grove Lane, running parallel to Camberwell Grove, was fed up. His feet were really feeling the cold, right through the ridiculously thick socks his mother had given him last Christmas, which at the time he thought he'd never need to wear outside the Arctic Circle. But Camberwell could do a pretty sterling impression of a frozen waste when it wanted to. He'd been out and about all day, trudging streets which, even if they weren't quite mean in the Raymond Chandler sense, certainly seemed full of spite on days like this.

First, it had been a credit card fraud down at the Morrisons. It had turned out to be just a rather confused old gentleman, who seemed to be in the first stages of Alzheimer's, trying to buy his shopping with his late wife's Visa and insisting, when questioned, that his name really was Violet Ferguson. Well, it took all sorts, but if the man was a late-stage transitioner, he really needed to make a bit more of an effort with his outfits. An ancient tweedy jacket and trousers hitched up to his armpits were not the sort of thing that would ever pass muster as women's clothing, even on a decidedly dress-down day. It had all taken an age to sort out, and was distinctly below his pay grade, but when he'd seen the unsympathetic reception the poor old geezer was getting – particularly, he was ashamed to say, from the PCs who'd been called to the supermarket – he'd felt he had little choice but to stay on.

Then there'd been another G5. He could hardly believe it when the call came in. He hadn't had one for months, until the case of the little old lady and her ghoulishly overfed cat. This time it was even sadder, in a way. A young man, only in his mid-twenties, who'd overdosed alone in his flat. What a terrible waste of life. The lad seemed to have been doing quite well for himself, with a really good job at a local accountancy firm. A small company, but they'd seemed to genuinely value him and, luckily for York and the team at the scene, they'd noticed his absence first thing on Monday morning, when he hadn't shown up for client meetings. That meant, when York authorised the stoving-in of the lad's front door today with the 'big key', as the red metal ram was known, there was nothing like the dreadful scene that had confronted them at the old lady's house. The boy was relatively fresh.

York hated himself for thinking of a fellow human being in those terms, especially one who until so recently had been enjoying what appeared to be a purposeful and reasonably fulfilled life. But there it was. A long delay between demise and discovery was not only a human tragedy, but also often resulted in a very unpleasant mess for those who had to deal with a literally sticky end.

Toxicology would confirm the cause of death, but York was reasonably certain that the syringe still hanging out of the boy's cold, dead arm was to blame. The flat had been furnished in a trendy but, to his eyes, unimaginatively macho style – heavy on shiny black leather, and with a telly so massive it took up almost one entire wall of the small living room. Looking around, York wondered what devil had possessed the lad. From the looks of the works on the chrome coffee table, the boy had been a regular user, but he'd been doing OK. He was high-functioning, holding down a job, paying his rent and, to all intents and purposes, making his way in life. He wasn't whacking every penny into his arm. Probably just a weekend user, a hangover from uni days. Maybe he was just sad and lonely, and the drug eased the pain. His death would probably come as the most horrible shock to his family. Maybe not so much to his friends.

There were so many stories like this in the city. York, going outside and handing over to the SOCO team, peeled off his latex gloves, wishing he could slough off some parts of his job as easily.

He fished his phone out of his coat pocket – to distract himself, as much as anything – hunching against the wind as he keyed in his code. To his surprise, a text flashed up. Must have come in when they were battering down the door. It was from Beth. He peered at it in consternation. No! She couldn't mean what he thought she meant. *Not again!*

He set off at a run, pushing past the SOCOs and the paramedic team who'd just arrived to certify death and cart the lad off to an even bleaker and more masculine bit of interior design than the one he'd lived in – the refrigerated, stainless steel drawer of the mortuary in King's College Hospital.

* * *

'Babs! Where are you, Babs?' Beth called, emerging cautiously from the dank passageway and peering round into the garden. It all seemed deserted. The wind was less bitter now, but it was still dark and freezing, with the sort of late autumn chill that crept into your very bones. There might be a frost by morning, leaving what passed for a lawn crunchy and white, but now it was wet and lumpy, pockmarked with piles of decaying leaves.

It was plain, even in this gloom, that Ted's plans to revamp the garden had still not got off the ground. Had they left Camberwell? Set up somewhere else? Was that the secret? Had they decided to start a new life somewhere else? But Jen would never leave Jessica behind. There were so many questions, Beth thought, but the most pressing, at the moment, was suddenly something entirely new – where on earth had Babs disappeared to? Drat the woman. Beth had only hesitated for a couple of minutes in front of the house, when Babs had hared off into the garden, but she seemed to have had enough time to vanish off the face of the earth.

'Babs! This isn't funny! Where are you?' Beth shouted. Her voice, to her own ears, sounded thin and strained. Well, no point standing here like an idiot. She'd have a quick look around, then she'd just get going. Babs could play hide and seek if she wanted to, but Beth didn't have time to join in. She still had to pick up Jake. The men hadn't turned up anyway, so she couldn't have the confrontation she'd planned. Well, never mind. She'd reschedule, preferably for a day when Camberwell wasn't doing a very good impression of *Wuthering Heights*.

Beth straightened her spine and edged forward into the looming shadows of the house. All was dark inside, again. She didn't want to press her nose up against the glass, as she hadn't exactly had the best results doing that last time. She'd just call out once more for Babs, then she'd be off.

But before she had a chance to yell, she heard something that made her blood freeze in her veins. It was a scream, coming from the far end of the garden, over by the railway tracks. She squinted into the distance. She could just see the boundary fence in the darkness, its blacker shape standing out against the dark grey masses of the trees and overgrown shrubs.

Reluctantly, she stepped forward, off the patio and onto the wet, uneven grass. 'Babs? Is that you?' she called, as strongly as she could.

There was another muted sound from the end of the garden. Not a shriek, more of a muffled cry. It seemed to be coming from the centre of the darkest patch of tangled trees. She edged forward uncertainly, feeling the wetness creeping into her little boots and start to leach into the fabric of her jeans. Yuck. This was the last thing she needed. She was going to be soaking and she'd have to drive home like this. Blast Babs.

'Babs, where are you?' she yelled, and this time she was exasperated rather than scared. Bugger. There was nothing for it now. She was already wet and cold, so she might as well get this over with. She marched as best she could across what had once been a nice lawn, but was now a flourishing collection of weeds and potholes. A couple of times, she nearly lost her footing.

As she reached the tangle of undergrowth, and what looked like a huge pile of mouldering cuttings, she slowed. There was still no sign at all of Babs. It was weird. Could the stupid woman really be hiding? And why, on God's earth, would she want to do that?

All of a sudden, she remembered Jen's fear. The hole. The old Anderson shelter. Had Babs fallen down it?

'Babs! Are you OK? There's an old air raid shelter round here somewhere, you need to be careful. If you don't watch your step, you could get stuck down it,' she shouted out.

'I know,' said someone very quietly in the inky dark.

Beth was suddenly frozen to the spot, rooted in fear. The voice was right behind her.

FIFTEEN

York was cursing commuters, mothers with heavily laden buggies, people walking their dogs, even the elderly, all littering his route as he hurtled down Mary Boast Walk as though the hounds of hell were at his heels. But most of all, he was cursing Beth Haldane. Why couldn't she leave well alone? Why couldn't she steer clear of trouble? Why couldn't she... just stop being Beth Haldane?

By the time he reached Jen's house, he was panting and feeling chronically out of shape, cursing all those times he'd meant to go to the gym and had settled instead for rereading a Ngaio Marsh *Inspector Alleyn* mystery with a bag of crisps on the side. He'd called for back-up – or rather, wheezed for it – as he'd done his sprint, so he wasn't surprised to hear the faint wail of sirens already, though he hoped they weren't heading to another incident. Blues and twos were part of the background noise of this area, so close to the centre and so teeming with life. Holding his aching side, he saw the garden gate was swinging open in the gusts of wind. He turned his phone to torch mode.

As he advanced, a woman came running out at him. For a glorious second, he thought it was Beth, but this woman was much taller and wearing a smart camel coat, smeared with mud. 'Thank goodness, I don't know who you are, but something terrible's happened,' the woman gabbled.

York looked at her swiftly. 'Show me,' he said, wasting no time.

She led him across a surprisingly long stretch of unkempt lawn into a tangle of trees. 'Look! There,' she said, pointing downwards.

With horror in his heart, York could just make out what looked like two small boots and maybe legs, lying crumpled at an odd angle at the bottom of what looked like a tunnel, divided from the lawn by a ragged line of shrubs. Pushed to the side was a sheet of rusted corrugated iron, which he guessed usually covered the drop, plunging at least five feet down into the darkness. The wavering beam of his phone picked out jeans past the boots, but the rest was hidden from sight. There was definitely someone down there, and by the size of those little boots, it could only be one person. Beth.

York swallowed, then flicked into official mode. 'Wait here. Police officers are on their way,' he said to the woman, who appeared to be in shock, still and trembling, hunched in her dirty posh coat.

He clambered down into the narrow tunnel, feeling for secure footholds and bracing his hands on anything sturdy. The tunnel, once he was in it, seemed to be the entrance to a larger space. One of those old war-time shelters, he was willing to bet. Death traps, and why everyone hadn't got rid of them, he couldn't begin to imagine. But that wasn't the most pressing matter now. He shuffled forward in the cramped space, his back brushing up against the roof of the shelter when he tried to stand. He suddenly realised how precarious the whole structure was. It could easily come down on top of them. The sooner he got them both out, the better.

Inching forward, he knelt down. A thick mass of hair was all over the woman's head and neck. He smoothed it away carefully and was looking at Beth's pale oval of a face; with her hair off her forehead, for once, she looked absurdly young and like Jake, only prettier. He shook his head to keep his thoughts clear, and pressed two fingers into her neck, just below her ear.

The warmth of her skin would have reassured him, even if he hadn't felt the steady beat of a pulse. She was alive. She was going to be fine. He breathed, and then took stock of her situation. From the way her leg was bent beneath her, it looked as though it was broken. And there was a nasty gash over one eye. But that seemed to be it. He wasn't going to risk moving her.

'Is she...?' came a voice from up above.

'No, she's alive! She's going to be fine,' said York triumphantly.

In the gloom, only just relieved by the eerie glow of the phone torch, and talking very gently to the unconscious Beth, York became aware of the smell around them. It wasn't just the loamy, damp reek of the earth walls pressing around them. There was something worse, overlying the natural scents of a garden busily composting, ready for spring. A heavy, unmistakably unpleasant pungency, redolent of reeking, rotting fish, that meant only one thing. Death.

He looked around, while keeping a hand on Beth's arm, stroking it reassuringly. In the depths of the far corner, only a couple of feet away, there was a pile of cardboard. Odd. It showed someone had been down here, and quite recently. Though looking sodden, the brown mass was still intact, despite the pervading damp down here.

York edged over, and pulled at one soggy corner.

Instantly, the smell was stronger. He waved his phone into the space, conscious his battery would be running low. What was that? A bundle of clothes? He pointed the torch. At once, the shape assumed more definition. And much though he didn't want it to be, he could see it looked like a figure, curled in a foetal position. Preternaturally still. In the cold beam of light, he could see it was wearing a stripy top.

SIXTEEN

'What do you call it when you've had déjà vu twice? Déjà vu-vu? Or déjà-déjà vu?' said Beth drowsily.

York, holding her hand across the now familiar over-washed blue coverlet, smiled at her. It was either the look in his eyes, or the strong painkillers they'd given her after resetting her arm, that were making her head swim, and whatever the provenance, she was actually enjoying the feeling very much, thank you. Well, it took the edge off her situation. Back in hospital again, for the second time in a term, having been brutally attacked twice by the same person. When she thought about it like that, she felt like a total idiot.

It had been Babs all along. Babs, whose bitterness at being lumbered with someone else's child had spilled over into the most corrosive human emotion of all: jealous hatred. And it was something the woman had been unable to vent. It was the worst possible situation – she'd made her bed, now she was having to lie in it. She had spent years winkling Tim away from his wife, only to find that when she got sole ownership of this great prize, it hadn't been worth the effort after all. And she'd got an unwanted stepdaughter thrown in. Initially, she'd tried to win

Jessica over, but had been rebuffed so many times that she had forgotten to be philosophical and play the long game. Babs's anger and frustration had her well on the way to losing her marbles. Even then, probably she would just have settled down and developed sour lines down the sides of her mouth, like most discontented women.

But, York had told Beth, one day Babs had driven over to confront Jen and ask her to take more of the childcare burden. For reasons she didn't understand, Jen had been dumping Jess on them more and more, even though the girl obviously hated spending time with her.

Sitting in the dreary interview room at the Camberwell Green police station, Babs could have remained silent. But she'd wanted to talk, as though what she had to say could possibly ever justify her actions.

Jen, she'd explained, had been stubbornly unyielding, not willing to explain herself, generally unhelpful and, as ever, had had the moral high ground. She'd been the injured party, the victim in the break-up, while Babs had been the evil temptress. Everything had soured now for Babs, and that made the fact that Jen was still shining with virtue doubly infuriating.

They'd been in the garden, where Jen was attempting to get things into some sort of order. It looked as though someone had recently hacked back some of the most overgrown shrubs in a fit of wild enthusiasm, but had run out of steam. It didn't take a genius to guess that would probably have been Ted, Babs decided. Now Jen was shoving the cuttings into a wheelbarrow and dumping them in one corner of the plot. The perfect wife as usual, Babs thought sourly, clearing up after another man just as she had clung to Tim for all those years. Years when Babs could have been having babies. Busily trundling back and forth, Jen had stonewalled Babs, politely but firmly. All her work seemed to be making no difference, as far as Babs could see. The garden was still a wreck. But the fact that Jen seemed to be putting her heart and soul into tidying up after her husband had goaded Babs that little bit too far.

'Can't you leave that for a second? I'm trying to talk to you,' she'd said, exasperated.

'I've got a lot to do out here, as you can see. And the house is a mess as well. Today isn't the best day for all this, Babs, I really do have to get on,' Jen had said with a very brief, distracted half-smile.

'Look, Jen, I'm begging you. Tim and I want to start a family of our own, and it's so hard with Jess around the whole time, you've got to understand,' Babs had said, trying to appeal to Jen's better nature.

That seemed to have got through to Jen at last. She'd stopped the gardening, straightened up, and looked Babs right in the eye. 'Don't you know, Babs? Tim's had a vasectomy. I'm sorry, but you won't be having any kids.' She'd turned away, and she'd laughed. That had been her big mistake.

Babs, pushed too far by circumstances, was goaded into shoving in real life. The news that Tim had been lying to her, yet again, and that her dearest dream was never coming true, had proved too much. Like Tigranes the Great, she took out her rage on the messenger. She put her hand between Jen's shoulder blades and gave her a mighty push. Before she knew it, Jen had missed her footing, whacking her head on the tip of a spade that Ted had left lying around, and fallen headlong down the tunnel into the Anderson shelter.

Babs, though wary of scuffing her office shoes, had ventured down but had been certain that Jen was dead. In a mad panic, she'd dragged the body into the corner, and covered it up with flattened-out cardboard boxes from her victim's own recycling bin. Jen's middle-class determination to do what she could for the planet had unwittingly provided her killer with a handy shroud to cover her body.

But the pathologist's report made grim reading. Jen, it

seemed, had not died instantly, but had been unconscious, bleeding very slowly into her brain from a fractured skull. The injury was incapacitating, but would not necessarily have been fatal, if she'd only had treatment in time.

Unhinged now by her crime, Babs sometimes managed to convince herself that Jen was fine, and just lying low to spite her. Other times, she was sure that she'd killed Jen and would face life in jail. Sometimes she just didn't know. She had taken to lurking outside Jen's house on the only night she could, during Jessica's football practice on Tuesdays. That's how she'd seen Beth sneaking round into the garden.

She'd been desperate to stop Beth finding Jen, but Beth had had no idea of the horrible secret lurking in the Anderson shelter. Picking up the rounders bat and thwacking the smaller woman with all her might had been another of Babs's insane impulses. Despite missing the gym, thanks to Jessica, the woman was still strong and wiry, and packed quite a punch, as Beth could attest.

Trying to do away with Beth a second time, having told Tim not to come and trusting in Ted's continued avoidance, was Babs's way of trying, finally, to clear up the mess she'd made.

Tim, meanwhile, self-absorbed and self-satisfied though he transparently was, had started to worry about Babs's mental state, not least because she spent a lot of time in sole charge of his daughter. Whether he loved Jessica only because she carried his genes, or whether he was truly fond of her for her own sake, was something that even the most sophisticated lie detector test could probably never get to the bottom of. The consequence of his doubts had been that he'd noticed Babs was behaving oddly, and had decided to keep a bit of a closer eye on what she was up to. That was why he'd turned up at Wyatt's on the day that Beth's office was trashed, giving rise to Beth's suspicions and engendering her almost-fatal plot to induce him to turn up at Jen's.

While Ted had been fixing the IT glitch, Babs had also had a legitimate reason for being in the school, trying to land the marketing job. But what about Tim?

One thing was for sure. He was not, and never could have been, a prospective Year 7 parent. For, unless the centuries-old policy of Wyatt's had changed in the short time that Beth had stepped out to play hooky in Romeo Jones with Richard the lame lawyer, Wyatt's was boys only from Year 7 to Year 13. And Tim's child was a ten-year-old girl. He was there to spy on Babs, knowing about her interview, but he hadn't realised how thorough the Wyatt's tour guides were. He'd been no use at all, spending the afternoon being dragged round the boys' changing rooms at the distant playing fields, while Babs did her worst.

It was the first time that Beth had been a little bit out in her suspicions. She'd been close, zeroing in on Tim, realising how peculiar his appearance on the parents' list was. But not close enough. It had actually been Babs who'd rampaged through her office.

Now that Beth thought about it, the vicious attack on her tampons should have shown her it had been a woman at work. A man would either have shied away in terror from women's doings, or simply not known what the little cache was. Only a woman would have trashed sanitary products with such malicious glee.

Beth shook her head slightly, wincing as the gash over her forehead ached. She'd have another reason to keep her long fringe now. After five stitches performed in double-quick time in A&E with York sitting over the emergency team, she'd be left with a permanent reminder of a night she'd rather forget.

That brought her back to Babs's first attack. 'You thought it must have been a man who'd hit me, that time?'

'I did,' said York. 'But at that point, I hadn't seen Babs's biceps. She's got some pretty impressive guns there. I'd be willing to bet she was rounders champion at school.'

Beth nodded, thinking grimly of the time when she and Babs had sat round her kitchen table, and Babs had calmly displayed the muscles that she'd used to clout her only a couple of days before. She couldn't believe the nerve of the woman. It definitely should be a point of Dulwich etiquette, that you weren't allowed to attack someone you'd been formally introduced to in the playground, and you certainly then weren't allowed to mooch cups of Earl Grey tea off them.

But Babs had been a desperate woman by that stage. Jen's death had been a horrible accident, but failing to get her medical attention, not reporting the death, and then covering everything up, had pitched her into a different, deliberate category – that of murderer by default. Stressed by the constant war of attrition with Jess, and knowing that she'd shot herself catastrophically in the foot by killing her only other reliable childcare alternative, Babs had been forced to go to any lengths to cover up her crime.

Beth had been in the wrong place, looking in the wrong direction, at the wrong time. She was very lucky to be alive. If Babs had decided to cart her across the lawn to the pit where Jen already lay, or succeeded in dragging her down the passageway to her car, or if Jen's neighbour hadn't been putting his bins out, then two children might have been left motherless, instead of one. Thank goodness the woman had lost a bit of muscle tone when her gym trips were suddenly curtailed by killing Jen.

Lucky escapes made Beth remember something from her last stay in hospital. 'There was a doctor who was kind of lurking around before, in the dead of night, when I got knocked out. Who on earth was that?'

'Probably just a lost medical student. You know what hospitals are like,' York said with a smile.

Beth thought back to the little flock of baby medics who'd followed their mother goose consultant on ward rounds. If one of those had got lost, she could well imagine them drifting aimlessly round the hospital, until they caught up with her twelve hours later.

That reminded her of another puzzle. 'What happened to Ted? Did you ever find him?'

'We've just run him to ground. In Corfu, of all places. Seems his ex-wife is there.'

Beth frowned painfully. 'But wasn't he at Wyatt's the other day? He was fixing the computers, Janice said. Why would he go straight to Corfu? From what I heard, he hated his ex.'

'He's been in Corfu a little while, still freelancing. I suppose he did the Wyatt's job remotely. Easy enough, if you know the system. From what his ex-wife has told us, Jen had thrown him out. Maybe he had nowhere else to go.'

'Wait, what? Jen threw him out? Seriously? She never said a thing to me. And they'd only just got married.'

'Well, we've had a long chat with the ex, who isn't pleased that he's lurking around her again. She said it was all over between him and Jen. Something about Tinder?'

Oh, thought Beth. 'I saw that Ted was active on Tinder. Erm, the girls at the office were showing it to me,' she said, scampering quickly over her own interest. 'I meant to tell Jen about it but, well, I could never find the moment. Maybe she found out for herself. I wonder why she didn't say.'

'Maybe it was too humiliating? Or maybe she didn't have time. From the state of the house, Jen and Ted had had one almighty row just before she died, or maybe he just messed things up out of spite when she made him take his stuff. Either that or Babs trashed it. We'll be talking to her about it.'

Beth thought silently. Babs was certainly efficient at turning places over, if her own office was anything to go by. She still felt guilty about not having locked up that day. But Harry was still talking.

'If Babs hadn't admitted to the whole thing, Ted would be in a pretty difficult position. We'll never know what went down with Jen, but it certainly seems that he used to hit his ex. She's got a strapping new partner who looks like he'd knock Ted's block off himself if he got too close. The Greek police are keeping an eye on the situation.'

'I'm glad Jen kicked him out,' said Beth. 'That must have taken a lot of courage.'

'Yes. If she threatened him with the police, maybe he decided it was easier to leave the country. The Camberwell house was in Jen's name, and she left it to her daughter, so there was nothing for him to hang around for.' York paused, and looked at Beth. 'When we searched the house, Jen's phone was still plugged into the charger. All your messages were there. And, in case you were worrying, the neighbour's looking after the cat.'

Beth closed her eyes. She'd never even given little Meow, Jen's beloved moggy, a second's thought. Her friend's ghastly fate blotted out everything else. 'I don't want to think of all the time that passed, with Jen lying down that awful hole, before I finally got my act together.'

'Look, though she didn't die instantly, it wouldn't have taken long, and she never regained consciousness. She didn't suffer,' said York, seeing the quick glitter of tears.

Beth sighed, and turned her mind from her friend's terrible death to the disturbing thought that Jen's last months had been plagued with unhappiness too.

'I can't believe that Jen wouldn't have told me things had gone wrong with Ted, if he was violent.'

'Can't you? It's difficult to admit you've made a bad choice,' said York thoughtfully.

Beth pondered. That had been the trouble, for both Jen and

Babs, then. One had worked for years to get her hands on a man who'd turned out to be a terrible disappointment, and a liar as well; the other had thought she was making a fresh start, only, it seemed, to face a whole new set of problems. York was right. It would have been hard, after the lovely wedding at the Horni-man, and all the promise of happiness that seemed to be rolling out in front of Jen, for her to admit she'd picked another wrong'un.

Beth thought back to the last times she'd seen Jen and Ted together. There had been a tension there, it was true. The odd thing about Jen wanting to distance herself from Dr Grover's all-encompassing Dulwich fan club. Ted's jibe of 'butterfingers'. Even the whole doomed idea of the garden makeover. Had she misinterpreted all those scenes as the jokey interplay of a happy couple when the truth had been horribly different?

This dating game. Why was it never as easy as it seemed? Jen and Ted had given the impression of being genuinely mad about each other. Maybe mad was the right word, but only for Ted. And now, as a result, her lovely friend Jen was dead and gone. Beth still couldn't quite believe she'd never see that freckled face again, hear Jen's clear voice, see her bright Breton tops across the playground and know there was a kindred spirit there to chat to.

And Jessica. Without a mother now, and without a step-mother, either. Beth was willing to bet that it wouldn't be long before Tim was auditioning new candidates for that role, though. She had no idea what his appeal was, aside from being a single man in possession of a reasonable income. At least she wouldn't be standing around at the Village Primary for much longer, watching that spectacle and aching for Jen. Jake would soon be moving on, to secondary school, and Beth was finally glad of it.

She still had Jen's wedding present tucked away somewhere in her car. That would have to go straight into the rubbish.

Should all her own hopes of a happy-ever-after be shoved in there, too? And if they were, there was instantly a very Dulwich dilemma to solve. Should they go in the brown bin, to rot away as compost; were they destined for the slightly more hopeful recycling bin; or should they simply be consigned to landfill in a black plastic shroud?

She raised her fingers, shaking very slightly, to brush her hair away from her stitches, then laid her hand down on the cover again. York's hand came down instantly on top of hers to squeeze gently. It was warm, steady, comforting. Beth looked up at him with a faltering smile. She really must delete that Tinder app from her phone again. As soon as she had the strength. And a free hand.

In the midst of this bleakness, there had to be hope, didn't there, that someone, somewhere, really would have a happy ending?

And this time, why shouldn't it be her?

A LETTER FROM ALICE

Thank you so much for choosing to read my book. I love writing about Beth Haldane and I hope you've enjoyed finding out what she got up to this time. If you'd like to know what happens to Beth next, please sign up at the email link below. Your email address will never be shared and you can unsubscribe at any time.

www.bookouture.com/alice-castle

If you enjoyed the story, I would be very grateful if you could write a review. I'd love to hear what you think. I always read reviews and I take careful account of what people say. My aim is always to make the books a better read! Leaving a review also helps new readers to discover my books for the first time.

I'm also on Twitter, Facebook and Goodreads, often sharing pictures of cats that look like Magpie. Do get in touch if that's your sort of thing. Thanks so much again, and I really hope to see you soon for Beth's next adventure. Happy reading!

Alice Castle

Alicecastleauthor.com

Printed in Great Britain
by Amazon